WIZARDOMS LEGENDS: TEMPLE OF THE UKNOWN
TOR THE DUNGEON CRAWLER
BOOK ONE

JEFFREY L. KOHANEK

© 2023 by Jeffrey L. Kohanek

All rights reserved. No part of this book may be reproduced, stored in a retrieval system or transmitted in any form or by any means without the prior written permission of the publishers, except by a reviewer who may quote brief passages in a review to be printed in a newspaper, magazine or journal.

The final approval for this literary material is granted by the author.

First Edition

This is a work of fiction. Names, characters, businesses, places, events and incidents are either the products of the author's imagination or used in a fictitious manner. Any resemblance to actual persons, living or dead, or actual events is purely coincidental.

PUBLISHED BY JEFFREY L. KOHANEK and FALLBRANDT PRESS

www.JeffreyLKohanek.com

ALSO BY JEFFREY L. KOHANEK

Fate of Wizardoms

Eye of Obscurance

Balance of Magic

Temple of the Oracle

Objects of Power

Rise of a Wizard Queen

A Contest of Gods

* * *

Fate of Wizardoms Boxed Set: Books 1-3

Fate of Wizardoms Box Set: Books 4-6

Fall of Wizardoms

God King Rising

Legend of the Sky Sword

Curse of the Elf Queen

Shadow of a Dragon Priest

Advent of the Drow

A Sundered Realm

Fall of Wizardoms Boxed Set: Books 1-3

Fall of Wizardoms Box Set: Books 4-6

Wizardom Legends

The Outrageous Exploits of Jerrell Landish

Thief for Hire

Trickster for Hire

Charlatan for Hire

Tor the Dungeon Crawler

Temple of the Unknown

Castles of Legend

Shrine of the Undead

Runes of Issalia

The Buried Symbol

The Emblem Throne

An Empire in Runes

* * *

Runes of Issalia Bonus Box

Wardens of Issalia

A Warden's Purpose

The Arcane Ward:

An Imperial Gambit

A Kingdom Under Siege

* * *

Wardens of Issalia Boxed Set

JOURNAL ENTRY

While I always considered myself a professional salvager, committed to reclaiming lost artifacts and returning them to the world of the living, others often chose to label me otherwise – Ranseur the Adventurer, the Great Relic Hunter, the Filthy Grave Robber...Tor the Dungeon Crawler. Some of those monikers I found flattering, others irritated me like a burr stuck in my smallclothes. Such is the price one pays for fame.

Looking back on my days as a relic hunter, I now realize that my actions had a far greater impact than I could have ever imagined. Items of power – artifacts imbued with magical abilities – have forever altered our world. Almost every one of the most powerful artifacts has been in my possession at one time or another. Had I left them hidden in the tombs, temples, and ruins where I found them...I can only guess at the future that might have resulted. Since it is impossible to change the past, I choose not to dwell on such things.

My success and fame led me down a road untraveled by any apart from those in my crew. Honestly, they deserve as much credit as me, even though their names rarely touched the tongues of those who have regaled my exploits. How did I come to meet my companions? Well, it is a long story and *one involving two of the most powerful and impactful enchanted artifacts in recorded history.*

The tale begins with my dearest and oldest friend, one who has been by my side since my first day in the Murguard, all those years ago. While you may find elements of the tale difficult to swallow, I assure you that every word is true. This is the story of how the greatest adventuring team in history was formed. Enjoy.

-*Tor Ranseur*

CHAPTER 1
IN THE DARKNESS

The crunch of boots on loose rock echoed in the narrow tunnel confines. Tor Ranseur, adventurer extraordinaire, held a brass rod before him, the glass section in the center glowing blue. The azure aura from the rod caressed the surrounding rock and pushed shadows into recesses while darkness loomed ahead.

He climbed a small rise. The shaft opened into a spacious cavern, the ceiling too high for his meager light to reach. A few strides in, Tor stopped and slowly rotated while eying his surroundings.

Smooth walls bore evidence of tool work. Rubble lay in the middle of the chamber, surrounding a broken, dilapidated cart. Thick shadows clung to every crevice, masking whatever might lurk within.

Tor approached the mine cart wreckage, squatted, and lifted a chunk of rock. The reddish tint appeared purple in the blue light, making the rock type easy to identify.

"Ore. This was a mining chamber, just like the others."

He lifted his gaze as a hulking man emerged from the path he had just vacated. The man's vest left his muscular dark-skinned arms bare from the shoulders down. A shiny, black-tinted gauntlet bordered by runes covered the man's left arm from his elbow to his fingertips. His right-hand wiped beads of sweat off his bald head.

"Just how far do these warrens extend? We've been down here for two days."

Tor tossed the chunk of ore to the ground. "You've visited Maker-built capital cities of numerous wizardoms, Koji. Each is large enough to house a hundred thousand people. I suspect the Makers' own cities might approach that scale, even those found underground."

Kojinko grimaced. "I miss the warmth of the sun, the blue sky, the tree-covered mountains turned to the reds and yellows of autumn..."

"They will be there waiting for you when we are done here. If we ration our food, we can survive down here for few more days. If we don't find the city by tonight, we will turn back."

Arching a brow, Koji said, "The great Tor Ranseur would actually consider turning back from an adventure?"

Tor ignored the jibe. It took more than a comment to throw him off balance. "Only because you are my dearest companion, I will consider it."

Koji grunted. "Since we lost Navarre, I am your *only* companion."

A shadow crossed over Tor at the mention of his departed friend. Navarre had not been the first companion he had mourned, but he was the most recent. The sting of his death had yet to numb.

Tor pushed such thoughts aside and continued across the cavern, heading for another opening. "I am not ready to give up quite yet, so let's keep moving."

The path widened, the walls now far enough apart that Tor could not touch both at the same time. It left him with conflicting emotions – one part of him relished the less confining quarters while another part worried about what might be lurking in the shadows of the boundaries. Koji, on the other hand, stood seven feet tall and no longer had to duck below a low ceiling, so he undoubtedly enjoyed the added space.

They came to an intersection with a cart blocking the route, which forced Tor to circle around it. When Koji attempted the same but did not fit, he pushed the cart aside with one hand, tipping it up until he was past it. The cart tipped back down, its metal wheels crashing with a heavy thud that echoed through the underground warrens.

"What's wrong with you?" Tor snapped.

"What did *I* do?"

"You know not to make noise when we are working."

"We haven't seen signs of anyone in days."

"It doesn't mean we are alone."

Koji pulled on his chin while frowning. "I'm sorry, Tor. I guess I'm just tired of poking around in the dark."

While Koji was a mountain of a man, he was as softhearted as anyone Tor had ever met...until it came time to fight. The mere thought of facing Koji in battle was likely to drive an icicle of frozen fear through the heart of the most stalwart of warriors. The reality of fighting him...well, most would do anything to avoid it.

Tor sighed and closed his eyes for a beat while his anger quelled. "Just try to be more careful. You never know who or what might lurk around the corner."

The duo resumed their journey through the underground warrens, one that had already covered dozens of miles over the previous two days. Although he refused to voice it, Tor worried that they had only visited a small portion of the subterranean maze and was concerned that the directions he had found in an ancient text had been misinterpreted. *It might take weeks to find the legendary city...if it even exists.* He sighed inwardly. *If only we had some clue that indicated we were heading in the right direction or some marker that proved it was real...* As the thought crossed his mind, something changed.

Stopping, Tor stared down the tunnel while covering the light rod with his hand.

Warm light faintly illuminated the rock walls ahead of him.

"Do you see that?" he asked.

"Looks sort of like firelight," Koji observed.

"Good. I was hoping I was not going crazy."

Koji grunted. "While I see it too, it does not mean you haven't lost your mind."

The comment stirred a grunt from Tor. "Thanks for that."

"You are welcome."

Tor slid his pack down his arm, stuffed the light rod inside it, and shouldered the bag again before reaching over his other shoulder to lift his weapon from the harness on his back. The weapon slid out, flipped over in his hands, then settled in his grip. Claw was the name Tor had given the ranseur – a rare weapon type that had made Tor memorable and had, somehow, sparked the names others told stories about… names Tor had learned to accept, even the names he detested.

His ranseur was a notable weapon with a pair of pointed tines at one end and a bent claw ideal for prying on the other end. Four feet long and made of thick black iron, the weapon weighed nearly as much as Tor himself. Upon further inspection, one would note the silver scrawl of enchantment on the metal shaft while a black ring with similar scrawl adorned Tor's third finger on his right hand. The bearer of the ring benefited from the weapon's enchantment – a spell that made the heavy weapon feel as if it weighed little more than a feather. To anyone else, it felt like a heavy lump of hard iron.

Koji stepped up to Tor's side, gripping his razor-sharp, massive machete while his gauntlet-covered hand clenched into a fist. "I am ready to battle evil!"

Tor sighed inwardly. He had grown used to Koji over their years together, yet his melodramatic declarations and serious demeanor… often misplaced…sometimes wore on him. Still, he had never met a warrior he would rather have at his side when facing a daunting enemy force.

The two of them advanced warily while rounding a gentle bend. A tunnel mouth came into view, the orange-tinted light coming from the chamber beyond. The tunnel widened into a massive chamber where the two of them stopped to stare in wonder.

Before them was a city built inside a mountain, its overall design long and narrow with the buildings built along opposing walls of a steep, underground canyon. Half of the structures were carved from rock marked by metallic striations. The other buildings were crafted of metal sheets held together by silver rivets, which reminded Tor of heavy plate armor.

Tor and Koji stood at the edge of a broad street that ran through the city. Straight across from them was an arching bridge made of stone. The bridge spanned a daunting crevice that ran down the middle of the street. From the depths of the fissure came a reddish orange glow that filtered throughout the cavern and illuminated the city. Hundreds of feet above it all, shadows clung to the recesses in a ceiling of rock.

"We found it, Koji," Tor said in a hushed tone.

"Oren'Tahal. The steel city," the big man muttered in awe.

"And you thought it was just a myth."

Koji snorted. "I've seen enough to know most myths are founded in reality. I never said I didn't think it existed. I simply doubted that the map would lead us here."

"Even after we found the tunnel entrance?"

"Not then. My doubt came later, after two days of nothing but darkness."

"Well, don't doubt..."

A cry echoed in the city.

"What was that?" asked Koji.

Another cry rang out. It was a male voice and in obvious distress.

Tor pointed toward the bridge. "It came from the other side. Let's go."

He ran across the street and up the slope of the bridge. The air temperature immediately grew hotter.

Koji stopped at the foot of the bridge and warily eyed the crevice. "What if the bridge collapses from our weight?"

Tor glanced over the stone railing. Red hot lava bubbled two hundred feet below. "Hurry, so you won't be on it if it does fall."

The two men raced over the peak and down the backside of the arch, heading toward a plaza occupied by what seemed to be an oversized well and the largest anvil Tor had ever seen. He rushed down a short run of stairs and across the plaza before realizing that what he had thought was a well was actually a strange forge. Beyond it, he came to a building carved into the rock and slowed.

Atop a short staircase, thick square pillars stood along the facade, the open doorway thrice the height of a man. Tiers of column-supported balconies loomed above them, each smaller than the one below, immediately giving Tor the impression of a temple dedicated to some unknown deity.

Again, the voice called out, this time far closer and the words audible. "I will kill you!"

Tor signaled to Koji and climbed the stairs. He snuck past the columns and approached the open doorway, which was too tall for him to reach without the extension of his weapon. He stepped into the darkness beyond the doorway and paused to survey a chamber covered with painted murals, each depicting the same faceless god with a halo of golden light and outstretched arms. Below the god knelt thousands of brawny dwarves and willowy elves. The dwarves wore metal armor or fabrics of blue, purple, or red. In contrast, green, tan, and brown hued clothing covered the elves.

The duo crossed the room and came to an open doorway leading to a much larger chamber. Notably, it was occupied by a scene from a nightmare.

CHAPTER 2
RESCUE

The temple was a cavernous room, its ceiling so high that it disappeared into shadows. The path split to the left and right with a broad center aisle leading straight ahead. The middle path overlooked recessed seating to each side. Those seats were made of stone, the rear row the same height as the center catwalk while each forward row was two feet lower than the one behind it.

An amber glow came from an opening at the far end of the center walkway. Beyond the glow was a dais upon which stood a massive, faceless statue carved out from the wall of rock. In the warm light stood dozens of wiry, gray-skinned humanoids dressed in ragged loincloths. Some of the creatures were armed with rusty swords or shoddy spears. Every one of the monsters possessed overly large eyes filled with a blood lust that was all too familiar to Tor.

"Goblins," he whispered in the shadows of the doorway.

"Darkspawn," Koji echoed in his ear.

A short stocky male with a long red beard stood among the circle of goblins. Ropes bound his wrists together while others wrapped around his torso held him tight against a stone column.

A goblin with a necklace of bones descended from the dais and approached the captive.

"Oh, no. A shaman," Tor muttered.

The goblin magic user chittered and yapped in its incomprehensible language while gesturing toward the prisoner. Other goblins hooted and rushed in with splintered parts of a broken door, which they piled around the captive's feet. He kicked at the kindling and sent it spraying across the floor. The goblins hooted and yelped with a fury. The shaman's eyes bulged in anger as it drew close to the captive and poked a finger in his bulging stomach.

"Don't touch me, damn dirty darkspawn!" the captive growled.

As the goblins gathered the scattered kindling, Tor pulled back into the temple and turned to Koji. "We need to save him, and we have to do it before the goblins light that fire."

"There are dozens of darkspawn and two of us." Koji's tone was even, lacking emotion.

"It's not the first time."

"I know. I wanted to ensure you comprehend the risk."

"Noted. Are you ready?"

Koji made his gauntlet into a fist. "Let's play."

"Right." Tor spun around and burst into the room.

He rushed down the aisle, toward the circle of goblins, and wound back. The eyes of the monsters on the far side of the circle widened, while those with their backs to him remained completely unaware. Hoots echoed throughout the chamber, and the nearest goblins spun around just as he reached them. Tor swung Claw in a broad arc. The shaft and tines smashed through three goblins, the full weight of the weapon taking them off their feet and launching them past the prisoner and into fellow monsters.

A nearby goblin raised a sword and chopped down at Tor, who raised his ranseur. The blade slid between the two tines of Tor's weapon and stopped with a clang. He twisted Claw, and the tines snapped the sword blade off, leaving only a stump sticking out from the hilt. Another creature thrust at him with a spear, but the attack never reached him. The creature's eyes bulged as Koji's gauntleted hand clamped around its neck. The Kyranni warrior lifted the goblin off its feet and then tossed him like a ragdoll directly into a crowd of onrushing monsters.

"Free me!" the captive urged. "Let me fight!"

Tor raised his weapon to block another attack, the monster's blade deflecting off Claw's shaft before he twisted his torso and smashed the monster in the face. "I'm a little busy."

Left and right, Tor spun, jabbing and striking at the monsters that came at him in a relentless rush. At his side, Koji used his machete to lop off arms and heads while his fist crushed faces, chests, and necks as if they were made of paper. The big man then spun and slashed at the prisoner. His blade struck the column, severing several sections of rope. Freed, the captor roared and charged a pair of goblins with his head down and arms out. He grabbed each by the waist, lifted them up, and slammed them into the ground.

Tor thrust, driving a goblin backward and over the rim of the pit. The creature plummeted toward the bubbling lava at the bottom. He then lifted his gaze to find the goblin shaman on the dais, waving its arms and hopping about while chanting. The creature's eyes glowed red with the magic it was summoning. Desperate, Tor snatched the bola hanging from his belt, swung it in two rapid loops, and released. The four-foot-long bola cord wrapped around the shaman's neck and the two weighted discs at the ends of the weapon twirled around until one smacked against the shaman's cheek. Upon contact, the enchantment in the bola triggered. The shaman stiffened, toppled over, and began to shake violently. Tor raced up the dais stairs and drove the forked end of his weapon into the shaman, ending the threat of the monster's nefarious magic. He then spun around, wary of the next attack. None came, for the others were cleaning up the last of the mess.

Koji's gauntlet-covered fist smashed into a monster's face, breaking bones and sending the creature into three others. The former prisoner rushed in and squatted beside the downed monsters. Incredibly, he dug his hand into the stone floor and came away with a chunk of stone half the size of a man's head. He used the rock as a weapon, cracking goblin skulls until the last ceased moving. The chamber fell quiet.

The freed captive stood and spit on the corpses at his feet. "Bloody-arse darkspawn."

"Greetings," Koji said. "I am Kojinko Maulo. My friend is Tor Ranseur."

The stout warrior thumbed his chest. "I am Borgli of the Handshaw Clan."

"Well met, Borgli." Tor, standing on the dais, turned and got his first good look at the statue towering over him. A muscular body carved out of the rock wall stood above him, the face blurred and featureless, the body unremarkable other than an odd star-shaped pattern hidden in the shadows of the navel. He knelt and unwound his bola from the neck of the dead shaman. "You are lucky we happened upon you. A few more minutes and you'd have been burned alive."

"Aye." Borgli nodded in agreement. "Your timing was fortunate. For that, I owe you a ludicol."

What ludicol was, Tor had no idea. *This one is strange. There is something about him...*

"What are you doing down here?" Koji asked.

"Down where?"

"You are in an underground city thought to have been abandoned for a thousand years. We expected to find it empty."

Again, Borgli nodded. "Empty it was when I arrived. At least, that is what I thought as well"—Borgli grimaced— "until the stinking darkspawn caught me by surprise."

Recalling how Borgli had dug into the stone floor, Tor asked, "How'd you do that?"

"Do what?"

"Your hand. It slid into the stone like it was as soft as butter."

"Oh. That." Borgli waved it off. "I am a stone-shaper."

In response to Tor's questioning glance, Koji shrugged. "Is that some sort of magic?"

"We dwarves are creatures of magic. While others possess different skills, some of us can shape stone." Borgli's barrel chest puffed up. "I happen to be the greatest of my generation."

Koji narrowed his eyes, his gaze sweeping Borgli from head to foot. "Dwarves? You expect us to believe you are a dwarf?"

Borgli grimaced. "You humans think you know everything. Just because you haven't met a dwarf does not mean we don't exist. After all, who do you think built your great cities?"

Tor crossed his arms. "If dwarves exist, how come I haven't seen one before?"

"Easy. Because we live beneath a mountain in the distant south."

"A mountain?"

"Aye. With the Seers."

"The Seers of Kelmar?"

The dwarf grunted. "At least you've heard of them."

Koji said, "Yet, we find you *here*."

The dwarf's face darkened. "I came to Oren'Tahal seeking something my family lost long ago."

Tor secured his bola back on his belt and then examined his ranseur. The tines were wet with darkspawn blood, so he wiped them clean on a dead monster's loincloth. "Did you find what you were seeking?"

Borgli shook his head. "I have searched the city but have yet to find it."

"Could you tell us more? Perhaps we could help you," Koji suggested.

The dwarf stepped up to Koji and glared up at him menacingly. With Koji standing two feet taller than Borgli, the sight was comical… especially when Koji stepped back.

"Do you think me a fool?" Borgli growled.

"Um. No."

"First, you must tell me why you are here."

Tor said, "We are salvagers who specialize in retrieving legendary artifacts."

The dwarf narrowed his eyes. "What sort of artifacts?"

"Amulets, swords, gems, jewelry, hammers…"

The dwarf snapped. "Hammers?!"

"Yes. We came seeking a hammer of legend mentioned in an ancient tome we recovered during our last quest."

"This hammer…does it have a name?"

"The text was in the old language, so the interpretation is not exact. The name translated to 'shake' or 'vibrate.'"

"Or 'Tremor'?" Borgli asked.

"Tremor? Yeah. That sounds about right."

The dwarf stomped over to Tor, who was average height for a man, yet the top of Borgli's head barely reached Tor's chin.

A storm brewed in the dwarf's purple-tinted eyes. "Tremor is more than a mere relic. It was the first weapon ever forged in Vis Fornax… forged for my ancestor, Arangoli the Fierce, the greatest warrior of his age. It is connected to the blood that runs through my veins."

Tor glanced at Koji, who shrugged. "We have traveled far and discovered this lost city the same as you. Let's say we find this hammer and allow you to claim it…then what? Would you have us leave with nothing to show for our efforts?"

Borgli furrowed his bushy red eyebrows. "I…don't know."

"What do you plan to do with this hammer?"

"Claim it as my own."

"And go where?"

"Hmm." The dwarf tugged at his beard. "I suppose I could try to return to Kelmar..."

Tor noted the doubt in Borgli's tone. "Or you could join us."

"Join you?"

Koji blurted, "Join us?"

Tor ignored him. "Tell me, Borgli, this stone-shaping magic you possess, what can you do with it?"

The dwarf walked over to a wall beside the dais, pressed his fingers against it, and slid them inside. With rapid shaking movements, he ran his hand up, turned a corner, and continued until he had carved a square into the wall. The square came out with a pop, the dwarf lifting it with a grunt. It was a perfect cube, half a foot square.

"Impressive," Tor nodded.

"Watch."

Borgli slid the cube back into the cavity he had created. When he pressed his palms against the seams, the stone around the gaps liquified and melded together. In moments, there was no trace of the cube ever existing.

Tor gave his partner a glance. "What do you think, Koji?"

The big man nodded. "There have been many times we could have used such a skill."

"That was my thought as well." He turned to Borgli. "If we help you recover this hammer, will you join us?"

Borgli frowned, his glare heavy and intense. "It would be a life of adventure?"

"That, I can promise."

A smile bloomed in the dwarf's thick beard. "I accept your offer." His smile faded. "However, I have been here for two days and have searched the city but have been unable to locate my ancestor's legendary hammer."

"Why are you in this building then?"

"I only revisited the temple to pray to Vandasal for guidance."

"Vandasal?" Koji asked.

Borgli stared up at the statue atop the dais. "This is Vandasal. The temple, a dedication to his might."

"Yes." Unlike most men, Tor had studied ancient histories and recognized the name. "He is among the two elder gods. The other is…"

Borgli interrupted before Tor could voice the other god, "Don't even say his name. We do not wish to draw the Dark Lord's attention." He gestured toward the dead goblins. "His minions already soil this sacred place."

Although Tor did not believe in such superstitions, he held his comment back.

Koji proposed, "Let us rid ourselves of these darkspawn by tossing them into the pit."

Borgli grinned. "Aye. We will feed them to the liquid fire. Then we can put our efforts toward recovering my ancestor's hammer."

Tor found himself nodding, for that was the purpose of his quest.

CHAPTER 3
ENTOMBED

Borgli Handshaw watched the two men closely, attempting to gauge their trustworthiness. One was a towering giant with dark skin, a bald head, and a heavy gauntlet covering one hand and forearm. The other man had piercing hazel eyes, light skin, and a neatly trimmed brown beard. Although he was significantly shorter than the dark-skinned man, he stood nearly a full head taller than Borgli, and he carried a weapon unlike any Borgli had ever seen. The two men had freed him and helped him defeat the goblins holding him captive, but he worried about their motives.

Cleaning up from the battle, Borgli and the two men dragged the goblin corpses and severed limbs, tossing them down into the pit at the foot of the dais stairs. Each time something landed in the lava, a burst of flames shot up into the temple and the air grew hotter. By the time they were finished, Borgli was covered in sweat and had to back far from the pit to cool himself.

Standing to the side of the dais, he wiped his brow. "It is hot in here."

Beads of perspiration coated Koji's bald pate. "Yes. Far hotter than when we first arrived."

The statue above the dais represented Borgli's god. The temple had been built to honor him. Even after the darkspawn remains had been consumed by the lava, he felt compelled to say a prayer.

Dropping to one knee, his head down while facing the statue on the dais, Borgli said, "Oh, Vandasal, we have cleansed your sacred temple of the filth that once desecrated it. I ask you now to guide us in our quest." He then rose and turned toward Tor. "I am now ready.

The two men led him back toward the temple entrance, where they retrieved their packs before heading outside. In the warm light coming from the fissure splitting the city, Tor stopped and removed a leather wallet from his pack. From it, he withdrew folded parchment, the paper yellowed with age.

"What do you have there?" Borgli asked.

With care, Tor unfolded it. "This is the map that brought us here."

The man squatted and spread the parchment out on the street, allowing Borgli to examine the map. The topography and natural landmarks of the southeastern wizardoms covered most of the document. In the corner was a box with text above it. It was immediately apparent that the illustration in the box was a top-down view of Oren'Tahal.

"While the larger portion of the map led us to this system of tunnels, this section in the corner is focused on the city itself." Tapping his finger on the northwestern corner of the illustration, Tor said, "This is the forge."

Borgli glanced over his shoulder, toward the well and anvil that stood only a couple hundred feet away. "Vis Fornax. It is legendary among my people – where the most talented metal shapers crafted weapons of power designed for use in the battle against darkness. The forge stands right behind you."

Tor glanced at Borgli. "I know. I mentioned it as a point of reference for this map." He ran his finger along the diagram, stopping at a tunnel at the far end of the city. Beside the entrance was a circle and some ancient foreign text. "According to the text, this is the location of a key of some sort. How to use it or what it even opens, I cannot say. All I know is it is tied to a hammer of legend."

"Tremor." As Borgli spoke the weapon's name, an eagerness welled up inside of him. For decades, he had longed to obtain the hammer of his forefathers, but duty had held such ambitions at bay. With his duty now relieved...

Tor said, "I could be interpreting it incorrectly, but it is the one clue we have, and it is where I believe we must go next if we wish to locate the hammer."

Borgli peered closely at the map and then raised his head to gaze toward the far end of the city. A lump of dread caught in his throat. "The map indicates the one building I avoided inspecting."

"Why did you avoid it?"

"It is a crypt. The dead sleep there, and I was reluctant to disturb their slumber." A shiver racked his stout frame. "Besides, it is a creepy place."

After carefully folding the brittle map, Tor inserted it back into the wallet and then stuffed it into his pack. "It is time to pay that crypt a visit. I just hope we don't run into more darkspawn."

As they walked, Koji rubbed his chin. "We are hundreds of miles from the Fractured Lands. How did the goblins get this far south? Why were they here in the first place?"

Borgli knew much about darkspawn. The creatures originated in the Murlands in the distant east, and their only known path to the west was through the Fractured Lands. For them to be in Oren'Tahal seemed too unlikely to be a coincidence.

Tor said, "Those are good questions to ask but difficult to answer. Perhaps they are here at the Dark Lord's bidding. Perhaps they are lost. Or maybe they found these tunnels as refuge. After all, we know how much the monsters despise daylight."

"Daylight," Borgli grunted. Adapting to it had been among the more difficult things he'd experienced since leaving his former home. As such, when he located an entrance leading to Oren'Tahal, it had elicited both relief and excitement. "After I departed from Kelmar, It took me weeks to get used to the sky. Having all that open space above seems…unnatural. The sun, well, it is even worse."

Koji's brow arched. "You had never seen the sky before?"

He shook his head. "Not in over fifty years." As a child, he had once ventured outside of Kelmar, only to be scared into returning. *The sky is so vast…no wonder I was so afraid.*

"You are how old?"

"Sixty-six."

Tor stopped and stared at him. "I thought you were in your thirties."

"Aye." Borgli understood. Humans, both Seers and Thrall, lived in Kelmar as well, their lives passing at twice the rate of his own kind. "We Makers age slower than you humans. It is why we live longer lives…but not as long as elves."

Tor blurted, "You've seen elves?"

"No," Borgli confessed, "but I know of them. In fact, the Sylvan live to be four or five hundred years old before they pass."

Koji stared into space. "I would like to meet an elf."

Borgli grunted. "Be careful what you wish for."

"Why do you say that?"

"Long, long ago, my people and the Sylvan were close, but the elves sought to rise above other races, which created a division between us. This division grew worse and worse, until we became enemies. With our two races focused on each other, we did not notice the true threat."

"Which was?"

"The Dark Lord, of course. I don't know how it happened, but he nearly erased our peoples from the world and forced us into hiding to survive. The elves fled to some distant forest, while we dwarves took shelter deep underground. Thus, it has been for two thousand years."

Koji whistled. "Two thousand years is a long time."

"It is...even for us dwarves."

Tor said, "You never explained why we would not wish to meet elves."

"Oh. Yes." Borgli shrugged. "It is because they are aloof, arrogant, and absolutely no fun."

Tor arched a brow. "As compared to dwarves?"

"Yes." Borgli grinned broadly. "Especially compared to dwarves."

Their laughter echoed in the otherwise silent underground city, and when the sound faded, it was replaced by the tapping of their boot heels on stone as their conversation ended. A heavy sorrow overwhelmed whatever mirth Borgli had momentarily felt. *This city...it should be thriving with life and the prosperity of my people. Instead, it lies dead and empty.* As he passed closed doors of empty shops and homes, Borgli imagined them opening and one of his people stepping out with open arms, ready to welcome him home. The present offered a different reality.

A ten-minute walk took them to the far end of Oren'Tahal. The fissure that had split the city continued into the rock wall, the crevice glowing with an angry heat that left beads of perspiration on Borgli's brow. Pillars and the facade of a structure carved into the cavern wall stood a dozen strides from the fissure. Centered on the structure was a closed door standing twice Borgli's height. Embossed runes and debossed bones bordered the image of a skull on the arch above the door. Inset in the skull's eye sockets were amber gems half the size of his fist. Although he could not read the runes, the skull and bones indicated the type of ominous warning that made him wary.

"You were correct," Tor said from Borgli's right.

"About what?"

"This appears to lead to a crypt."

Koji, towering to Borgli's other side, added, "And it is a creepy place."

"That as well," Tor agreed, "even though we have yet to go inside."

The statement caused Borgli to draw in a breath of courage. He walked past Tor. "Entering is something we can no longer avoid."

He approached the closed door, rested his hand on the bronze-colored plate beside it, and applied his will. The metal in the plate responded, causing the magnetics to alter. A rumble arose, the ground shook, and the door swung open to reveal an interior too dark for the cavern light to penetrate. Immediately, Borgli was reminded of the circular stone door he had found in the dark cavern three days prior. Dwarf engineers often implemented tried and true designs in their constructs, creating a recognizable pattern for all who were familiar with such concepts, yet bewildering to the untrained, such as darkspawn. *What were they doing down here?*

Tor said, "This is similar to the doorway we used to reach Oren'Tahal."

My exact thoughts. Borgli knew the ways of his people and suspected that neither Tor nor Koji would be wise to the subtle nature of dwarven design. "When we go inside," Borgli said. "Do not touch anything unless necessary. I do not wish to disturb the slumber of my ancestors."

"Should we be wary of traps?" Koji asked in a hushed tone.

Over his shoulder, Tor replied, "You saw the skull above the door. If nothing else, it was a warning, and we had best be wary."

"Aye," Borgli agreed. "We Makers are known for the cleverness of our traps."

Traps often protected the treasures Tor pursued. Even if the dwarf had not accompanied them, he would have assumed something dangerous loomed in the crypt.

He said, "We proceed with caution. If either of you sees anything that might cause alarm, say so."

"Agreed," said Borgli. "But dwarven traps are unique and often nigh impossible to identify. Since I am aware of their nature, I should go first."

While Tor was used to leading, especially when it came to dungeon exploration, in this case, he was happy to defer to Borgli.

After a glance at Koji, whose face reflected resolve, Tor followed the dwarf inside.

The air smelled stale, aged, and tinted with must. Three strides in, the gloom enveloped them, the light of the underground city forgotten. Tor dug into his pack, removed his light rod, and activated it by twisting the brass cap at one end of the rod. Pale light bloomed, revealing a corridor five strides across and stretching off into shadow.

Standing at the edge of the light, Borgli spoke over his shoulder. "I appreciate the light. It was getting dark...even for me."

The dwarf continued, passing beneath another rune-covered arch. Beyond the arch, the corridor widened with alcoves to either side. Within each of those recesses were stone caskets, one lying on the floor and another on a shelf the height of Tor's chest. Carved into the side of each casket was a complex crest; Borgli paused to examine each before moving along. As they advanced deeper into the crypt and came upon similar caskets occupying alcoves, the dwarf slowed to examine the carving before continuing forward.

Although used to exploring tombs, this one was different. It felt as if the dead might wake from their slumber at any moment, which caused the hair on Tor's arms to stand on end. Attempting to focus on the practical aspects of his quest, he asked, "What exactly are you looking for?"

Borgli replied, "I am seeking my ancestor's crest. Among other things, it contains a heart gripped by an iron fist."

The information gave Tor reason to pay closer attention. He spied an eagle with a stone in its talons, a snake coiled around a diamond, an axe and a tree, a hammer and an anvil, and a dozen other designs marking the sides of the coffins they passed.

Suddenly, the dwarf stopped. "There it is."

Before them was a side tunnel. A heart in the grip of a gauntlet graced the keystone above the arched opening. Beyond the arch, darkness loomed.

Tor said, "The gauntlet reminds me of you, Koji."

"Heh." Koji grunted while flexing his metal fingers. "I've yet to squeeze a man's heart like that."

"True, but you've made plenty piss themselves."

All three of them chuckled, the sound accompanied by a nervous edge. Moments later, the laughter settled, and silence crashed in.

Tor indicated the archway. "Your ancestor lies inside. It only seems right if you were the one to lead us."

The dwarf entered the tunnel. While holding the rod up before him, Tor warily followed.

CHAPTER 4
WHERE THE DEAD SLEEP

In a narrow tunnel made of perfectly smoothed stone, Tor held his light high while following Borgli. The dwarf stopped when he came upon a spiderweb blocking the way. Light shimmered off the pale gossamer strands running from the floor to the ceiling and from wall to wall. Tentatively, Tor leaned past Borgli and blew a puff of air at the web, causing it to waver. A black and yellow spider larger than Tor's hand skittered out of a dark recess in the tunnel ceiling and scurried toward the heart of the web. The dwarf backed into Tor, causing them both to stumble.

"Woah," Borgli said. "That is a huge spider."

"A golden torvat." Tor had seen them before. He had seen men die from their bite as well. "They are seldom found outside of the Kyranni jungles."

"Is it poisonous?"

"Oh, yes...and quite deadly."

Tor reached over his shoulder, gripped Claw, and pulled the weapon free. He took aim and thrust, driving a tine into the spider's exoskeleton before pinning the creature to the ceiling. The web tore, strands snapping and pulling back into corners. Green ichor dripped from the spider to the floor. With a flick, Tor sent the dead arachnid flipping down the corridor.

Rather than holstering his weapon Tor used it to clear away the remainder of the web and ducked past it with his light rod held before him. A dozen strides later, he came to an abrupt halt.

Up to this point, the walls had been perfectly smooth, bare rock. A pattern of diamonds surrounded by angular lines graced the walls ahead of him.

Over his shoulder, Tor asked the dwarf, "What do you think?"

Borgli indicated the nearest diamond, which was at the height of Tor's chest. "I sense a cavity behind this one." He motioned toward the opposite wall, at a diamond the height of Tor's knees. "There as well."

"You sense?" Koji asked.

"Aye," Borgli nodded. "I can sense the solidness of the surrounding rock and a lack of solidness when there is a cavity. It is related to my stone-shaping ability."

Tor nodded in satisfaction. "That is another useful skill for someone in my profession. Now, don't move. Give me a moment to think."

With narrowed eyes, he examined the two indicated diamonds. Both were outlined by a deep groove while those beside and across from them lacked such detail. Reaching out, he used his weapon to tap a diamond lacking the groove. Nothing happened.

Frowning in thought, Tor bent forward, extended his weapon, and dropped the end to the floor. A rushing sound filled the corridor. The nearest diamond-shaped section of stone thrust out, shot across the corridor, and stopped just shy of striking the opposing wall. A metal pole attached to the diamond then slowly eased back into the wall until it appeared as it had from the beginning.

"It behaves like a piston that strikes when you touch the floor," Tor noted.

Koji said, "That would have hurt."

"It was chest-high for me," Tor said over his shoulder. "I'd have been crushed between the piston and the wall."

Borgli slipped past Tor, squatted, and ran his fingers across the floor. "I sense a seam. It is nearly imperceptible, but it is there." A smile bloomed on his face. "You must admire dwarf craftsmanship."

Tor snorted. "It's difficult to admire something if you are dead."

The dwarf stood up. "Step where I step, and you will survive to admire its beauty."

Without waiting, Borgli shifted to the side of the tunnel and took a step. He then spread his other leg out wide and placed his foot far on the other side. Tor wondered if that would have even been possible if Borgli's legs were any shorter. In this position, with his boots planted far apart, he rocked from foot to foot and advanced, all the while staring intently on the floor.

"You heard him," Tor took his first step, taking care to place his foot where Borgli had tread.

Down the trap-laden corridor, Tor and Koji followed in Borgli's footsteps, rocking from side to side in odd, staggering steps, some strides covering no more than a foot, others stretching as far as four feet. For those, Borgli's short legs forced him to hop. After two dozen carefully placed footsteps, the carved walls faded behind them, and only smooth ones waited ahead.

Tor sighed in relief. "I swear I age a year every time we are forced to endure something like that."

Koji grunted. "Wouldn't that make you something like eighty years old?"

"I am only thirty-seven," Tor snapped. "Besides, you are a year older than I am."

"True, but I age gracefully while you only become increasingly more ornery."

"I do not," Tor growled.

"My point is proven." The big man folded his arms over his chest, a smirk curling his lips up at the corners.

With his lips pressed together, Tor glared back at his friend. A dozen retorts passed through his mind, but he kept them bottled up, unable to think of one that would not reinforce Koji's accusation.

Finally, he spun around. "Let's find this crypt."

Advancing with caution, Tor led them down the corridor while his light rod ate away at the darkness. Another arch waited ahead. The keystone at the top was again graced by a heart in the grip of a gauntlet. Unlike the last, a door filled this arch. Rather than rock, the door was made of a semi-transparent substance with no handle or knob visible.

Tor eased up to the door and held a palm against it, the smooth surface cold to the touch. "Is this glass?"

"Crystal," Borgli said.

"Should I break it?"

"You can try."

Tor wound back and thrust Claw at the door. It bounced off and sent vibrations into Tor's hand and arm, nearly causing him to drop the weapon.

Borgli chuckled.

Tor turned on him. "What is so funny?"

"That door is crafted of adaunton quartz, hardened by stoneshaper hands and unbreakable."

"Then why'd you let me strike it?"

"For the humor."

Koji chuckled until Tor shot him a seething glare.

"How do we get past it?" Tor growled.

"You cannot. I, however, have the ability required to advance."

Tor stepped aside, his patience worn thin. "In that case, get to it."

The dwarf stepped forward and pressed his palms against the quartz. He closed his eyes and fell silent. Moments passed before a low hum arose, gradually growing louder. Borgli's hands vibrated rapidly as the quartz panel shook within the arch frame. Cracks began to form around his hand before branching and spreading outward. A massive pop resounded in the tunnel as the door shattered, causing both Tor and Koji to lurch with a start. Chunks of three-inch thick quartz sprayed into the room beyond the arch and tumbled across the crypt floor.

Borgli dusted his hands off. "It is a shame to destroy such beautiful work, but it had to be done. I'm just glad it was not a larger piece, or I'd have never been able to shatter it on my own."

Tor leaned past the dwarf, held his light rod up, and peered into a hexagon-shaped chamber ten strides across. A single stone coffin stood in a recess along each of the over five walls. A gauntlet gripping a heart marked the stone surface of each of the coffins.

Tor asked, "Should we open them all?"

"And disturb the dead for no reason?" Koji's face twisted in revulsion.

"They are dead. I doubt they will mind."

"There is no need." Borgli slipped past Tor and approached an alcove while pointing up at the strange symbols in the arch above it. "Those runes tell me Arangoli the Fierce lies here." A sense of awe lingered in his voice. "This is the resting place of my ancestor, the greatest warrior of his time."

Tor flipped his weapon around as he approached the casket. "Let's see if Arangoli rests with his legendary hammer."

He wedged the clawed edge of his weapon into the narrow gap beneath the coffin lid, which was four inches thick and made of ornately carved stone. The lid moved slightly. Again, Tor shoved and lifted, the stone panel rising two inches. Koji gripped the lid with his gauntlet-covered fingers and lifted while Tor used his weapon as a lever. The coffin lid rose, and then slid aside.

Anticipation raged in Tor's stomach, causing it to flutter. He lowered his weapon and stepped up to the coffin with his light held over the opening. Koji stood to one side and Borgli to the other, as the trio peered into a stone box that had been closed for two thousand years.

CHAPTER 5
THE TWISTED KEY

Dust swirled in the light, obscuring the interior of the coffin. Tor coughed and waved at the airborne ash, hoping to shoo it away. The dust soon settled to reveal the bones of a ribcage impressively full for the short stature of the skeleton. Sections of armor – shoulder plates, breastplates, bracers, and a strange helmet with wings and a star-shaped disk at the front – adorned the bony corpse. Whatever cloth had once held the pieces together had long since disintegrated and joined the pile of ash at the bottom of the coffin.

Koji was the first to say what all three were thinking. "I don't see a hammer."

Tor added, "Or any other sort of weapon."

Borgli sighed, his disappointment obvious. "I thought it would be here."

"Perhaps someone else got here before us," Koji offered. It was like him to try and cheer up others, even someone he had just met.

"No." The dwarf shook his head. "The seal to this chamber would have been destroyed and only a dwarf with stone-shaping magic could have done so."

Tor frowned in thought while staring at Borgli's ancient ancestor. A three-dimensional star-shaped sapphire graced the bronze disk on the front of the helmet. The disk and the design of the gem tickled his memory, waiting for recognition to connect him to where he had seen something similar.

A moment later, Tor remembered. "The statue. That's where I have seen this."

Koji grunted. "I don't follow you, Tor. What statue and what have you seen?"

Pointing at the disk, Tor explained, "This same design was carved into the abdomen of the statue in the temple."

"The sculpture of Vandasal?" Borgli scratched his bearded chin. "Now that you mention it, I recall seeing the same thing."

Tor added, "It is also similar to the point drawn on the map that led us here."

"You believe they are connected?"

"There must be a connection." Tor's intuition seldom led him astray. "Let's take the helmet and return to the temple."

He reached for the helmet but stopped when Borgli gripped his wrist.

"No!" The dwarf pulled Tor's hand back. "Removing the helmet would be wrong." He reached into the coffin, gripped the disk, and twisted his wrist. The disk spun a half turn and popped free in his hand. When pulled away, it revealed a recess in the front of the helmet and a small post in the center of the recess. "We can go, now." Borgli stepped back with the disk in his hand.

Unsatisfied, Tor shuffled into the spot vacated by Borgli and leaned over the corpse, staring into its empty eye sockets. He carefully gripped the skull, gently turning it to the side to reveal a twisted metal cord secured to the back of the helmet.

"What is this?"

Tor dug into the dusty coffin bottom and followed the cord, which ran past the skeleton's feet and through the end of the coffin. He moved his light rod, squatted, and peered between the coffin and the wall. The cord was visible, spanning the gap before fading into a hole in the wall.

"A trap." He stood and turned toward his two companions. "Had we attempted to remove the helmet, we would have triggered something nasty."

Borgli nodded. "It only makes sense. No respectable dwarf would steal the helmet off one of our slumbering ancestors. The trap was put in place so no other race, be it men or monster, would escape this chamber."

"In that case," Tor turned toward the corridor. "Let us be away before we stumble into any other nefarious surprises."

∼

Kojinko Maulo was a quiet man by nature. He preferred to avoid attention, which was difficult due to his stature. As far back as he could recall, he had always been taller than his peers and often outweighed them as well. Such a stature, among a people of warriors, had made his path clear from a young age. He always knew he would fight darkspawn. It was his duty. Thirteen years in the Murguard had cured him of such idealism. He eventually realized that even if he had remained in the Fractured Lands and fought for another thirty years, the darkspawn would keep coming.

From the moment Koji met Tor, he knew the man was much more than a typical soldier. It did not take long for Tor to rise to the position of squad leader, and once in that role, he became renowned for his ingenuity and ability to keep his soldiers alive. Koji often told himself he followed Tor after retiring from the Murguard because the man was his friend. In truth, Koji had not known what else to do after a lifetime of assuming there was nothing ahead of him other than soldiering. So, here he was, stuck in an underground city that had died centuries ago.

The journey back to the temple was quiet, the empty doorways and vacant windows they passed no less creepy than before. It felt as if ghosts occupied the city, and even though Koji now made a living exploring places long abandoned, an air of melancholy clung to Oren'-Tahal as if the city itself mourned for days long past. When they finally returned to the temple, Borgli took the lead. Koji and Tor followed the dwarf up a half-dozen steps, past thick pillars, and into the dark entrance.

The temple looked exactly as they had left it, but much of the heat had dissipated, leaving the room warm rather than hot. Still gripping the disk retrieved from his ancestor's crypt, Borgli crossed the room, climbed the dais, and stared up at the massive man-shaped sculpture.

The statue towered over Borgli, the statue's arms extended and its palms turned up in supplication. Lean and muscular, it was the image of a perfect man...other than the featureless face and lack of genitals.

"I can't reach it," Borgli said.

Tor climbed the dais and stood at the dwarf's side. The star-pattern that matched that of the disk was located where the statue's navel might exist, which was more than ten feet up. "I can't reach it either. Luckily, we have Koji."

At the mention of his name, Koji flinched. "Reach what?"

Pointing up, Tor said, "The recess."

Even with his height and reach, Koji considered the recess high. The star pattern in the statue's navel was an oddity, one he had not noticed during the earlier visit to the temple. Noticing such things was Tor's job. Koji's skills lay elsewhere.

"Why would you want to reach it?" he asked.

"To press the disk to it."

The dwarf held out the disk. Koji opened his palm, and Borgli handed it to him.

Koji stared down at the object, his stomach twisting with an undefinable unease. "What will happen?"

"I have no idea," Tor turned to the dwarf. "Borgli?"

"Perhaps nothing will happen...or maybe it'll trigger a deadly trap." Borgli shrugged. "Or it could be something in between. Who knows?"

Koji furrowed his brow and raised his gaze to the statue. "What lies in between nothing and a trap?"

Borgli rolled his eyes. "Just put the disk into the hole and find out."

"And be ready to run," Tor added.

"Huh," Koji grunted. While he'd rather not perform the task, it had to be him. The others lacked his reach, one of the reasons Tor valued him as part of the crew. "You two are not reassuring."

Stepping forward, Koji raised his arm and held the disk high, so the star-shaped ruby faced the recess. He slowly moved it closer while Tor and Borgli backed to the edge of the dais. The disk slid in with a click, leaving the gear-tooth edges still exposed. Koji hurriedly backed away until he stood beside Tor and Borgli. All three stared up in anticipation.

Nothing happened.

"Maybe we got it wrong," Koji ventured.

Tor considered the situation and how perfectly the disk fit in the recess. "No. This is right. I can feel it."

"I agree," said the dwarf.

"Do I try it again?" Koji asked.

Recalling how Borgli removed the disk from the helmet, Tor suggested, "Try gripping it and turning it."

"Turn it? Which way?"

Both Tor and Koji looked at the dwarf with an arched brow.

Again, Borgli stroked his bushy red beard. "I rotated it left to remove it. I say you do the same here."

"Why?"

"Because that is what I would do."

Koji approached the statue and raised his arm to reach for the brass disk, the unease returning, this time causing his stomach to roil.

"However," Borgli added, "if it were me designing this, I'd also have set a deadly trap to foil anyone who turned it the wrong direction."

Koji froze with his hand on the disk and spoke over his shoulder, "That is not reassuring."

Borgli grinned. "I am happy to help. Just be ready to run."

Flashing the dwarf a grimace, Koji turned back to the statue, his fingers gripping the disk. Tension filled the air, and they held their breaths. As the disk turned, a clicking sound emitted from the statue, as if the gears engaged some unseen mechanism. The disk stopped after a quarter-turn. Koji released his grip and backed away.

Nothing happened.

"Huh," Borgli grunted.

"Did you turn it all the way?" Tor asked.

"Yeah. It stopped hard, so I backed away."

A hum arose, and the dais beneath their feet began to shake.

Borgli's eyes grew round. "Run!"

Koji spun around as Tor leapt from the dais, dropping four feet by the time he landed on the floor. When he reached the stairs, Koji jumped at the same time as Borgli. An explosion shook the temple, thrusting him forward as shards of rock pelted him from behind.

∼

Tor raced around the deep lava pit with Borgli and Koji chasing after him. Just after he passed the far end of the pit, an explosion shook the temple and sent him rolling across the tiles. Tiny shards of stone skittered past and forced him to cover his head. When the building settled, silence rushed in. He lifted his head and looked back to see if his companions were injured.

Both Borgli and Koji lay on the floor just shy of the pit. They lifted their heads, their eyes meeting Tor's before all three turned their attention to the sculpture.

Dust and debris swirled in the air, The upper portion of the statue appeared as it had before, but the lower half had been destroyed with everything from the waist on down now gone. The remaining portion, carved out of the stone wall itself, gave the appearance of a floating statue since there was nothing beneath to support it. Chunks of rubble covered the dais and the floor below them.

Tor stood, dusted himself off, and approached Koji. "Are you injured?"

The Kyranni warrior staggered to his feet. Blood appeared from small cuts on the back of his bald head and his bare arms. "I am well enough."

Turning to the dwarf, Tor asked, "How about you, Borgli?"

The dwarf removed a shard of rock from his beard. "It'll take more than an exploding statue to cause me harm. We dwarves are made of tougher stuff than that." He strode toward the dais. "Especially when my ancestral prize awaits."

Then, Tor saw it – a three-foot-long shaft hanging down from what remained of the statue. *It was hiding inside the sculpture the entire time.* Borgli climbed onto the dais and stopped below the statue. With his arm raised above his head, he gripped the end of the shaft, turned it a quarter turn, and pulled it free. Spinning around, the dwarf triumphantly held his prize high above his head, giving Tor his first clear view of the weapon.

The war hammer's head was made of platinum-tinted metal, its ends flat, the body ornately carved with tiers and ridges, the center embossed with runes. Gold rings graced the bottom of the shaft. As Borgli held his prize up, the warm light from the lava pit reflected off the hammerhead edges.

Tor climbed the dais and stopped beside Borgli, who cradled the hammer to his chest like a newborn babe. "You have acquired your prize and could not have done so without our help. Remember our arrangement."

A broad grin split Borgli's beard. "Aye. With you, I am...if this is, indeed, the weapon of legend."

The dwarf roared, his eyes going round with fury. He wound back with the hammer and swung it over his head. Tor dodged to the side to avoid the killing blow. When the hammerhead struck the dais, a thump reverberated throughout the temple, the ground shaking as if rattled by an earthquake.

A rolled sheet of parchment fell from the hole in the broken statue. The scroll bounced off the rubble and settled at Tor's feet.

Tor turned to Borgli. "What was that about? Were you trying to kill me?"

"Nothing of the sort." The dwarf caressed the hammer. "Before I committed to join you, I had to test the weapon to ensure it was indeed Tremor, the hammer of legend."

"Are you satisfied?"

"Aye," the dwarf crooned.

"Good." Tor squatted, picked up the scroll, and unrolled it.

A map was drawn on the inside, but Tor did not recognize the landmarks and could not read the notes. Still, it was a prize he could claim from his quest, although it wasn't the only prize.

Again, he squatted, this time tipping a chunk of stone over to reveal the disk still embedded in it. A quarter turn to the right released the disk. Rising, he turned it over and eyed the sparkling star-shaped sapphire. "We will return these two items to our benefactor. I don't yet know where the map will lead us, but it must be important if it was hidden away with the hammer. As for the disk, while not a legendary weapon, the sapphire's worth is significant and will easily fund our next expedition even if it holds no other value."

"Expedition?"

"Tombs, temples, castles, and ruins await our discovery."

Koji added, "Along with monsters, traps, and other unknown dangers."

The dwarf's grin faded. "What in the blazes have I gotten myself into?"

CHAPTER 6
GRAKAL

Tor stopped and waited as Borgli pressed his hand against a metal panel in the cavern wall. A circular stone door rumbled open to reveal another chamber. Chilly air drifted through the opening, much colder than the tunnels of Oren'Tahal. Tor inhaled the fresh air and felt a cool breeze, soothing after four days of meandering through the twisting underground tunnels.

Following the dwarf, Tor passed through the doorway and into a natural cave no more than twenty strides deep and half the width. Dim light emanated from the entrance, and he had to fight against the urge to run toward it.

Thank the gods.

"I told you this route would take us north." Borgli pressed his palm against the wall. A seemingly innocuous rock sunk in slightly, and the stone door rotated closed.

"I didn't doubt you," Tor replied. "I simply noted that it was not the way we had taken to reach the lost city where we found you."

The dwarf grunted. "I see." He turned to Koji. "Tor doesn't like to admit when he is wrong, does he?"

The big man chuckled. "He behaves as if it causes him physical pain to do so."

Unwilling to be drawn into a trap, Tor chose to ignore the comment. "Let's see what waits outside."

He crossed the cavern and ducked his head at the low entrance, crouching until he was in the open air, the bite of the wind seeping down his neck. He stood upright and gazed upon the surface world for the first time in days, his breath swirling in the twilight.

The western sky was purple, while in the sky to the east, the glow of the rising sun highlighted incredibly tall mountain peaks. A white-capped mountain loomed over them, the snow turning to gray rock just a few hundred feet above where they stood. Below their position, the rock led to pines encircling a vast lake, the far shore barely visible despite their elevation above it.

Tor breathed deeply, enjoying the bite of the fresh air as he took in the view. The sun slowly edged over the eastern peaks, gifting the valley with the first moments of dawn. It was peaceful and spectacular.

Breaking the silence, Borgli proclaimed, "It is the sea!"

Koji snorted. "There is no sea in sight."

Tor pointed at the body of water, its shore a mile away. "That is Lake Grakal. While large for a lake, it is still just a lake. The sea is far more expansive, so vast that you cannot see land on the other side."

The dwarf's eyes widened. "Truly?"

Koji patted Borgli on the head. "Tor tells the truth."

Borgli swatted Koji's hand. "Do I look like a dog for you to pat?"

"Well, other than your scalp, you are quite hairy..."

"Pat my head again, and I'll bite your hand."

Koji's face darkened. "You wouldn't."

Borgli thrust his chest out and glared up at Koji. With the two-foot difference in height, Tor was forced to cover his mouth to hide his smile.

After a moment, Tor recovered enough to say, "The city of Grakal lies on the north bank. Let's hike down to the shoreline and see if we can find a boat. The lake is twenty miles across, and I'd rather not walk all the way around it."

Without waiting for a reply, he began his trek down the mountainside and into the forest. The going was slow as he forged a path through the underbrush. Soon, a gurgling sound arose, drawing his attention. He angled toward it to find a rivulet trickling down the hillside. They refilled their waterskins and continued their descent.

The sun was well into the sky when they reached the lake where waves crashed against the shore, driven by a stiff mountain breeze. In the distance, white sails dotted the water's surface.

"Those must be fishing boats," Koji said.

"Let's follow the shoreline." Tor headed west. "Perhaps one will be close enough to flag down."

The wind coming across the water was cold, but not bitterly so, which was unsurprising. With the air warmed by the Novecai Sea to the west, it was often warmer north of the mountain range than it was on the southern side.

In some spots, the forest ran right up against the water's edge, but for the most part, the shore was clear of anything but small shrubs and yellowed grass. On five separate occasions, they crossed water running down to the lake. Four were rivulets, easy to navigate by hopping from rock to rock. The fifth was a rushing creek, the water much too deep to cross without getting wet. A quarter mile upstream, they found a fallen tree and crossed while balancing carefully.

It was midday when they came upon a boat near the shore, tucked in a sheltered bay near the southwest corner of the lake. Tor led the party out to a small peninsula, stood upon a rock jutting up from the water, and began to shout. He called out numerous times before someone on the boat reacted. The fishermen called back, their words unintelligible. When Tor waved his arm, a man on the boat waved back. Moments later, the crew hauled in a net filled with fish and raised the sail. Tor breathed a sigh of relief when the ship turned and drifted toward them.

∼

A LARGE MAN named Blake sat at the tiller, guiding the small fishing boat. Although a fisherman and standing well over six feet tall, he was surprisingly well-kempt, his dark hair and beard neatly trimmed and his vest and collared tunic quite stylish.

The other two in the crew were noticeably less refined – one a tall, thin man named Hemet, the other an overweight young man named Griner. Those two sat in the middle of the boat, adjusting lines and tying them off according to Blake's commands. In between them was Borgli, seated on the floor while gripping the seat beside him with white knuckles, his eyes wild and full of fear. In the stern, Koji chatted with Blake, a conversation Tor could barely hear since he sat at the bow, his cloak cinched tight, and his hood raised to block the spray from waves striking the hull.

After sailing out into the middle of the lake, Blake set a course toward the northwest. Since the boat could not sail directly into the wind, he sailed at an angle to it for a short time, then changed course in a zigzag pattern as he worked his way across the lake. That indirect route caused the trip back to Grakal to consume three hours, leaving the sun low in the sky by the time the boat drifted into the bay beside the city.

Far from any sea and with little risk of foreign armies attacking, no wall surrounded Grakal. The bay also lacked any sort of pier. Instead, the city's shore was lined with a slew of short wooden docks. The buildings were all made of wood; many were two stories tall, some three. Peaked roofs capped each home, and dark smoke rose from many of the chimneys. The houses and shops were colorful, painted with reds, blues, yellows, and greens, making the city itself strikingly distinctive amid the dark green pines surrounding the lake.

When the boat drifted near the shoreline, the sails were lowered and tied off. Hemet and Griner each dug an oar from the hull and set the pin into a mount. They then began to row, the craft lurching forward as Blake steered toward an empty dock. Reaching it, Hemet discarded his oar, grabbed a rope, and hopped onto the dock. In moments, the boat was secured.

Tor climbed out of the boat and waited while Borgli and Koji followed.

Reaching from the dock back to the boat, Tor extended a hand toward the boat captain. "Thank you, Blake. You saved us from many hours of walking."

Blake chuckled as he shook it. "I'd not wish to walk from the south end of the lake." The man cocked his head. "Did you truly come through the mountains?"

Koji, still seated beside Blake, shrugged. "Why else would we be out there in the middle of nowhere?"

Blake rubbed his jaw. "Honestly, I can't think of *any* reason to be out there. I've been fishing this lake since I was a teen. I've never seen anyone on the south shore."

"There is a first for everything," Tor said.

Blake eyed Koji as he stood. "You are a giant, aren't you? I don't often meet others who stand taller than I do."

With sadness in his voice, Koji said, "Oftentimes, it feels like I am too big to fit in with other men."

"I know what you mean." Blake continued appraising Koji as he climbed out of the boat.

Once on the dock, Koji spoke again. "You live here, Blake. We need food and a place to sleep. Do you have any suggestions?"

The grin stretched across Blake's face. "I certainly do. When you clear the docks, take the main road toward the heart of the city. Look for an inn called the Randy Bull. Tell Maisy I sent you, and you will be treated well."

With a nod, Tor again offered, "Are you sure we can't pay you something for your trouble?"

Blake shrugged. "No trouble. However, if you end up at the Bull, I'll find you there, and you can buy me a drink."

"Fair enough." Tor turned toward his companions. "Let's go find this inn. I'm starved. If I feel this hungry, Koji must be ready to eat rocks about now."

Borgli's brow furrowed. "How can someone eat rocks? You'd break your teeth, and I can't imagine how they would feel coming out the other end."

The statement aroused a round of laughter as the three adventurers stepped on shore.

They walked down an alley between two houses, crossed a quiet street, and continued down the alley. It brought them to a busy avenue, far wider than the previous one with wagons coming from one direction and people on foot approaching from the other.

Tor began down the street. "Blake said we would find the Randy Bull in the middle of town, so we should go that way."

They passed shops of various types – a tailor, a butcher, a furniture maker, a weapon shop, and a baker, each with a covered porch in the front. Then they saw a red building with a sign over the door, depicting a red steer sporting a broad grin.

"This must be it," Tor said as he opened the door.

Stepping inside, Tor surveyed the room and took a moment to appraise the patrons, quickly counting twenty people, more than half of them men, a few visibly armed. All were well-dressed for such a small city. None appeared to be wizards.

Tables filled the spacious dining room, a third of which were occupied. Positioned near the center and nestled between two thick posts was the bar. Enchanted lanterns on the posts provided pale blue light that illuminated a vaulted ceiling supported by exposed beams. A hallway ran between the near end of the bar and an open stairwell rising to the second story. While the hum of conversation was a welcome sound after the quiet tunnels of Oren'Tahal, the smell was the main attraction; the scent of cooking food left Tor's mouth watering.

He crossed the room, removed his cloak, and attempted to draw the attention of the barkeep. Koji loomed over one shoulder, impossible to miss. Borgli stood with arms crossed over his barrel chest, facing the room, his grimace a challenge for someone to try to cross him. Tor sighed, fearing the dwarf might start trouble.

The woman behind the bar sauntered over with narrow hips swaying overtly. She had long dark hair and far too much makeup, painted up like some street performer. Her blue dress was tight at the waist and accentuated a full bust. When the woman approached, Tor noted she was taller than him, which was uncommon although he was only average height for a man. More so, the woman had broad shoulders and large hands.

Borgli leaned toward Tor and whispered, "Wow. What a woman."

"How can I help you?" The barkeep's voice was artificially high and obviously unnatural.

Tor's eyes widened in realization, but he quickly recovered. "You must be Maisy."

The barkeep nodded. "I am."

The dwarf thumped his chest. "I am Borgli Handshaw, a vaunted warrior among my people."

The barkeep blinked. "A warrior?"

"Aye, and proud of it."

Maisy frowned. "I hope you don't intend on starting any trouble in my taproom."

"Trouble?" The dwarf sounded confused.

"We won't cause any trouble," Tor said. "In fact, we came because Blake recommended this place."

The worried look transformed into a smile that spread across Maisy's face. "Blake is such a good boy to send you men my way. What can I do for you?"

"We are seeking hot meals, cold drinks, and soft beds. Can you help us out?"

Maisy put a hand on her hip and began teasing her hair. "Depends. Do you have coin? A meal and beds for the lot of you will set you back a silver piece."

"Drinks included?" Borgli asked.

"Two rounds of ale."

"Ale?" Borgli frowned. "What is ale?"

"You don't know about ale?" Koji asked.

"Is it like ludicol?"

Tor interjected. "I don't know what ludicol is, but I suggest you give ale a try. Consider it a reward after a long day of travel." He dug out two silver pieces and planted them on the bar.

Arching a brow, Maisy said, "I only require one silver for the food and drink."

"The second coin is for additional tankards. Two each won't be near enough."

She swept the coin up with a smile. "I'll tap a new barrel right now."

A grin stretched across Borgli's face as he watched Maisy sashay through the doorway and into the kitchen. "I have a good feeling about this place."

Koji arched a brow at Tor. "What do you think?"

"I think we are about to get drunk with a dwarf. What could go wrong?"

CHAPTER 7
THE RANDY BULL

Tor ate with fervor, his mouth and stomach begging for more. He cleaned his entire plate – the fish, potatoes, greens, and two fresh-baked dinner rolls, chasing it all down with ale. By the time they finished dinner, he was on his third mug and Borgli was on his fourth.

The dwarf took a deep pull of ale, wiped the foam from his lips, and released a satisfied sigh. "I must admit, this thing you call ale is a revelation."

Tor took his own swig. "I thought you might enjoy it. Just be careful. If you keep at your pace, you'll find yourself passed out before the evening is over."

"Pfft." Borgli waved it off. "We dwarves are a hardy folk. Ale is a tickle compared to the bite of ludicol."

Tor furrowed a brow. "Ludicrous?"

"No. Ludicol. It is a heated drink. It warms your insides in more ways than one. Drink enough of it and you'll crawl home."

"I'll admit that sounds interesting," Koji said. "Where can we find this ludicol?"

"In Kelmar, of course."

Tor leaned back in his chair. "You claim to have come from Kelmar. While it is a place whispered in stories, I've never met anyone who knows where to find it."

The dwarf took a long drink and slammed his empty tankard on the table. "I can't tell you where to find Kelmar exactly, only that it is located underground, beneath a mountain surrounded by trees made of ice."

"The Frost Forest?"

"I suppose."

Tor rubbed his jaw in thought. The Frost Forest was in the distant southeast – a region few ever traveled. He had examined maps indicating the fabled wood but none depicting a city in the area or giving a hint at what lay beyond the forest.

Rising to his feet, Borgli said, "I'll fetch another round...assuming you two are finally finished nursing those mugs."

"Another ale sounds good," Koji said with a smile.

"Wonderful. Besides, it gives me another opportunity to talk to Maisy."

When Borgli turned away, Koji leaned across the table. "Does he not realize the truth about Maisy?"

Tor smiled while watching Borgli speak to the barkeep. "He either doesn't know or he enjoys that sort of thing. After all, what do we know of dwarves and their preferences?"

"True." Koji nodded, his expression serious.

As the evening advanced, the tables of the Randy Bull filled, and the male patrons outnumbered the females four to one. Many patrons stood against the walls once all of the tables were occupied. Tor noted how the men dressed in a dashing flair, many in brightly colored doublets or vests, all well-groomed. It seemed odd for such a remote city. Dismissing the issue, he turned back toward Borgli, who was regaling him and Koji with the tale of how he arrived in Oren'Tahal.

"...and that is when the darkspawn found me. The bloody monsters knocked me out before I was ready to fight. When I woke, I found myself tied to a column with my wrists bound to my chest. Of course, I screamed that I would kill them, but the bastards were too stupid to understand the threat."

Koji nodded gravely. "You were lucky we heard you shouting at the darkspawn. Had we been a minute later, you would have been burned alive."

"Nonsense," the dwarf scoffed. "I would have escaped, somehow. I am a Handshaw. My ancestors were known across the land as the fiercest of dwarven warriors."

Tor chuckled. While Borgli was brash and boisterous, he found him likeable all the same.

Maisy emerged from behind the bar and sashayed across the room. Borgli noticed and turned to watch with a smile as Maisy climbed up on the stage, which was only one table over.

The barkeep clapped loudly, drawing everyone's attention. The room quieted. "Welcome, everyone," Maisy said loudly.

Scrutinizing the barkeep's physique – narrow hips, broad shoulders, a visible lump in the throat – Tor wondered how he had ever believed Maisy was a woman.

The barkeep continued, "For tonight's entertainment, we have the return of a local favorite."

"Entertainment?" Koji mumbled.

Maisy continued. "Taggert, Jed, prepare the music. The rest of you, please welcome the Gemini Sisters!"

The barkeep climbed down while gesturing toward the two men at the end of the platform, one holding a lute, the other with a drum on his lap. The duo began to play a lively tune, the crowd clapping in time with the beat. A door at the end of the room opened and two figures emerged. One wore a red dress, a white corset, and skirts made of white and red ruffles. A green and white dress covered the body of the other performer. They wore garish headdresses made of feathers and beads and held up fans that covered their faces, leaving only their eyes exposed. One stood just over six feet, the other a few inches taller. Both had broad shoulders and were a bit overweight.

The performers wove past the tables, climbed onto the stage, and began to dance in unison. They turned to face the wall, bent forward, and wiggled their backsides. The crowd clapped and cheered. The dancers spun again, stood back-to-back, lowered their fans, and began to sing. Their voices were deep, their faces bearded.

"What is this?" Borgli asked, his eyes gaping.

"Apparently, this act is two men dressed as women," Tor noted.

Borgli took a deep drink and sat forward in his chair, his eyes affixed to the performers. Tor found himself watching Borgli to gauge his reaction but saw no indication as to whether the dwarf was enthralled or appalled...until the song finished.

The crowd clapped and cheered, but Borgli took it a step further by standing and bellowing. He then plopped back in the chair and slapped the table. "That is the greatest thing I have ever seen!"

"I, too, am impressed," Koji added. "Those men sing well and managed to create a tremendous harmony. More impressively, their dance was in step with one another the entire time."

The music began again, this tune slightly slower than the first. Tor leaned back with his ale and watched the show.

∽

After the performance concluded, the two men removed their headdresses and joined the patrons who offered them drinks. Tor bought the performers a round as well after urging from Borgli. The dwarf asked the two men numerous questions before they moved along. By then, Tor's vision had begun to blur, and the room tilted slightly when he moved.

Koji, who was significantly larger than Tor, hardly ever displayed the effects of alcohol. Borgli, on the other hand, stood ten inches shorter than Tor, his stout build making them roughly the same weight. The dwarf had tackled the ale like it was an enemy force and he a hero of the ages, felling foe after foe at a near unmatchable rate. Yet, he seemed no more intoxicated than Koji.

Borgli planted his tankard on the table and stood. "Pardon me. I've something to tend to."

Expecting the dwarf had to relieve himself...finally, Tor nodded. "We'll be here."

Borgli walked off and Koji shook his head. "For a little guy, the dwarf sure can drink"

"And his bladder must extend down both legs. I've gone six times, and this is his first trip to the privy."

Koji chuckled. "He sure seems to enjoy ale as well."

"I thought the extra silver would cover us for the evening. I wasn't even close." Tor frowned. "Perhaps I was wrong to recruit him. His consumption might cost me more than he is worth."

Koji laughed, his deep voice like an intermittent rumble. "He is likeable, though."

"That, he is."

A roar came from across the taproom. "What is this?!"

Tor turned to find Borgli seated on a chair with Maisy on his lap. The barkeep's towering height over the head of the dwarf looked odd, but it wasn't the most alarming aspect of the scene.

Borgli had his hand up Maisy's skirts while the barkeep kissed his face. The dwarf's eyes bulged as he bellowed, "You are a man!"

Maisy kissed Borgli again, pulled back, and smiled. "Why, of course I am, honey. However, I am flattered if you thought otherwise."

Borgli yanked his hand from beneath the skirts and shoved Maisy off his lap. The barkeep fell to the floor, landed on one hip, and released a yip.

Rising to his feet, Borgli rubbed his hands down his torso. "I am not attracted to...I didn't mean to..." He shook his head. "Sorry. I made a mistake." He turned and bolted out the front door.

Maisy stood, approached the bar, and poured a drink.

Koji shook his head. "Every time I think I can see nothing unexpected, I am proven wrong." He finished his beer and stood. "I am off to the privy and then bed."

While Koji headed out the back door, Tor staggered to an upright position, walked to the bar, and patted Maisy on the back. "I am sorry about our friend. While he clearly found you attractive, I suspect what you hide beneath your dress came as a shock to him."

"Based on his reaction, he was certainly surprised. Although I enjoy the way I dress, I do see myself in the mirror each day and wonder how he could not have known."

Tor sighed. "He is rather...naïve about the ways of the world."

The barkeep arched a brow. "Where has he been hiding all this time? A cave?"

"Actually, yes." Stumbling past Maisy, Tor headed toward the stairs. "If he happens to come back, be sure to direct him to our room. We leave early in the morning."

CHAPTER 8
LAMOR

An albatross slowly circled in the clear morning sky. Below it, swells rolled across the Novecai Sea, the cerulean waters becoming a spray of white each time the ship's bow sliced through a wave. In the week since they had exited the tunnels of Oren'-Tahal, Tor found himself growing increasingly anxious to return to his home in Lamor. He leaned against the starboard rail and stared toward the distant, familiar shoreline.

The wizardom of Balmoria formed the northern border of the inner sea. It formed an arc from a river in the east to a western tip of the wizardom, where a fifty-mile-wide channel connected the Novecai Sea to the larger Ceruleos Sea. To the south, only open waters were visible, the island wizardom of Cor Cordium, home of the enchanters, now beyond his view.

The ship angled toward a natural harbor with a city looming over it. The city walls stood four stories tall along the shoreline and half that height on the inland side. The crenulations of a seaside castle thrust up above the wall, its design all angles and straight lines and flat rooftops in true Balmorian fashion. Green and brown mountains formed a backdrop for the castle and added to the striking view.

Koji appeared at Tor's side and bent to lean his elbows on the rail. "I figured you would be out here."

"I have spent enough time huddled in a cramped ship's cabin to last a while"—Tor scrunched his nose— "besides, Borgli's snoring is outpaced only by his flatulence."

The big man chuckled. "His squat body does pack a punch." He peered toward the approaching landmass. "How long have you been out here?"

"The sun had yet to crest the horizon when I emerged on deck." Tor noticed a trio of dolphins in the water, swimming before the ship. "However, I haven't eaten yet, and my stomach yearns for sustenance."

Koji peered toward the city. "It looks like we will be docked within the hour. I'd prefer to eat at home anyway. I miss Goren's cooking."

"That is my thought as well."

A gravelly, shaky voice came from behind them. "Is that where we are going?"

Tor turned to find Borgli standing in the middle of the ship and gripping a rope secured to the foremast. "You actually left the cabin."

The dwarf's eyes appeared wild and his face pale. "Your knack for observation is impressive."

"Other than you peeking out now and then, I haven't seen you on deck since we reached the sea."

"That was different."

"Why?"

"We weren't this close to shore."

It was clear Borgli had a fear of being on the water. The four-day barge trip from Grakal carried them down a river never wider than a mile across. The dwarf had spent the entire first day hiding in their cabin and only appeared on deck once on the second day. After they transferred to a new barge in Tiamalyn, the Orenthian capital city, he emerged from their cabin for short periods that grew longer until reaching Shear, where they boarded a ship bound for Lamor. A day of sailing down a narrow channel then brought them to the sea. The mere fact that Borgli could not see land on the far side of the open water rattled him. During each of the following three days, he would poke his head out of the hatch, look for land, and then retreat to the cabin for the rest of the day.

"Well," Tor said, "we will soon land, so you can put your fears to rest."

The dwarf snapped. "I'll stop worrying when I step foot on solid ground and not a moment before."

Koji chuckled, and Tor shot him a frown. "Don't encourage him," he said in a hushed tone before raising his voice. "I was serious when I told you we often travel by ship to reach distant places. You had better get used to it if you wish to honor your commitment."

A frown darkened Borgli's face. "Are you suggesting I lack honor?"

"Not at all. I am simply setting your expectations."

"Well, you can expect me to participate in your little adventures until you die or retire."

"What if you die first?"

Borgli laughed. "Ha! We dwarves are made of hardier stuff than you soft humans."

Tor rolled his eyes as the ship's captain called out for his crew to furl the sails. A sailor scrambled up each mast, including the one Borgli clung to. Others manned lines secured to the deck but were forced to circle around Borgli, who steadfastly refused to move or release the line in his grip.

"Stay here," Tor said as he walked past the dwarf. "Koji and I will return to the cabin to get our things."

"Don't forget my hammer," Borgli called out from behind Tor.

"How in the blazes would we forget his hammer?" Koji whispered. "It was the reason for our trip in the first place."

Tor spoke over his shoulder. "I am surprised Borgli came on deck without it. He sleeps with it cradled in his arm like a nursing babe." He reached the staircase and descended into the shadows.

⁓

A PAIR of sailors dropped a plank connecting the ship to the pier. Tor thanked the ship's captain and crossed with Koji in his wake. The two of them paused on the pier and turned back toward the ship.

Tor sighed. "Come along, Borgli. Just focus on the plank, not the water below."

The dwarf's knuckles were white as he gripped the rail and eyed the plank. A large hammerhead poked up over his shoulder, the hammer now resting in the leather harness they had purchased in Tiamalyn.

"Fine!" Borgli growled. His face exhibited determination as he stepped forward. With his arms extended to each side as if he were walking a tightrope, the dwarf descended the three-foot-wide plank. Upon reaching the pier, he backed from the edge and wiped his brow. "I am thankful *that* is over."

Koji bent toward Tor, his voice low. "What are we going to do next time we need to sail?"

"I don't know yet, but we have to get him comfortable with ships, or every voyage will be an ordeal." Raising his voice, Tor waved. "Come along, Borgli. We need a hot meal and should find one waiting at home." He headed up the pier with Koji at his side.

The dwarf rushed to catch up. "Did you say home?"

"Yes. This is where we live...when we are not away on some quest."

"When you mentioned Lamor, you said it was where you needed to meet your patron. You never said anything about a home."

Tor cast his memory back; the dwarf was correct. "I suppose I haven't." He climbed the uphill drive leading to the open city gate. "I also realize that you have little experience dealing with the human world. It would be best if you remained quiet, paid attention, and followed my lead."

Eight guards stood at the city gate, all dressed in standard Balmorian army garb: chainmail beneath a yellow and gray tabard. A guard in his thirties and another in his twenties, both unshaven with dark stubble on their faces and steel helms on their heads, stepped forward to block Tor's path.

The elder guard waved his arms flamboyantly, his tone sarcastic. "Oh, my, the great Tor Ranseur has returned to grace us with his presence." He leaned in, looking Tor up and down before tilting his head. "I don't see any treasure chests or prized relics. Have you come away empty-handed?"

The four guards manning the top of the wall laughed, joined by those loitering by the gate.

"Hello, Merrick." Tor didn't attempt to hide his disdain. "I considered bringing a boatload of roses in hope of improving the odor around you, but there aren't enough flowers in the world to do the job."

The guards laughed again while Merrick's face darkened. "It is Sergeant Merrick, you..."

The guard standing beside Merrick interjected, cutting the retort short, "What kind of treasure did you find this time, Tor?"

"Greetings, Clausen. I am happy to present the rarest treasure of all. You've heard the legends and thought them only myth. For the first time in millennia, a dwarf walks among men."

"A dwarf?"

"Yes." Tor patted Borgli on the shoulder. "Please meet Borgli Handshaw, a dwarf from the legendary city of Kelmar."

The guards stared at Borgli for a long, silent moment before they burst into laughter yet again. This time, even Merrick laughed.

"Good one, Tor," Clausen slapped Tor on the shoulder. "You almost had me there."

After a glance at Koji, who shrugged, Tor walked past the guards. "In that case, I am heading home. You know where to find me, Merrick, if you wish to attempt any additional sparring."

Once inside the city gate, the street ran parallel to the wall separating the castle from the city until it reached a square occupied by a bubbling fountain. A sculpture consisting of a swarm of cat-sized bees in a twisted spiral rose up from the heart of the fountain. Inside the closed castle gate, stairs climbed a steep hillside until reaching the castle entrance, three stories above. Tor had been inside that castle on only one occasion – one he preferred not to repeat.

He turned from the castle and crossed the busy square, bypassing carts and wagons where farmers and vendors offered goods for sale, some of whom were still setting up his or her display. He wove his way through clusters of citizens eager to purchase food for the day. When across the square, he climbed a staircase bridging the narrow gap between buildings made of stone. Every twenty steps, the ground leveled at a street before resuming a hillside ascent when the path met the next row of buildings.

After a dozen staircases, Borgli stopped and wiped his brow. "How much higher do we need to go?"

Tor smirked. "I thought you dwarves were made of tougher stuff than we humans."

The dwarf puffed up his chest. "Of course, we are. I was merely wondering."

"We are nearly there."

Tor climbed one last run of stairs before turning down a street that followed the gentle curve of the hillside, the buildings lining it hiding behind ten-foot-tall walls until those fell behind and only trees surrounded them. The street came to a dead-end where a lone massive building waited. There, Tor stopped before a man-sized iron gate.

"This is it." Tor lifted the latch and swung the gate open, the iron hinges eliciting a squeak in protest. He stepped inside and peered up at the building he and Koji had called home for the past six years.

The building stood four stories tall with balconies and terraces at every level. Like the other structures in the city, the lines were straight, the towers square, and the rooftops flat. Ivy covered much of a brick facade, interrupted by barred windows at every level.

"You live here?" Borgli asked in shock. "It is akin to a castle."

"Not quite. However, Koji and I live in only a corner of the complex. The rest is owned by our benefactor."

"You mentioned this benefactor before."

"And you will meet him soon...assuming he is in the city at the moment."

A brick path led them past sculpted shrubs and dark Cypress trees, thrusting upward like fingers pointing toward the sky. After passing beneath a sculpted arch made of ivy, they came to an entrance bordered by a pair of thick square columns. The front door, made of solid oak with riveted metal panels, was stained black. A circular bronze plate occupied a bronze panel the height of Tor's chest. A ring of tiny rubies encrusted the edges of the plate while a raised eight-pointed star surrounded by strange symbols occupied its center. Making a fist, Tor pressed his ring to the star; a crimson glow flared from the ring of rubies. A click followed, and the door swung open.

Borgli grunted. "Magic is used to unlock the door?"

"Yes. Don't ever attempt to open it from the outside without my assistance."

"What would happen?"

"You don't want to know." Tor stepped inside and held the door open.

Koji walked past Tor, followed by Borgli, who stopped dead with gaping eyes as his jaw dropped.

CHAPTER 9
THE SORCERER

Borgli stepped inside and got his first view of the manor's interior. Startled, his muscles tensed, and his brows climbed his forehead.

They stood at the mouth of a spacious chamber with a dark corridor straight ahead, opening to a pair of sitting rooms on one side and a parlor with bookshelves, a window seat, and a table surrounded by chairs on the other. Tapestries, paintings, and an array of interesting artifacts covered every part of the parlor walls other than the four recessed alcoves, which were each occupied by a human skeleton mounted to a post. At varying heights, human skulls dangled from the ceiling, giving the impression that the dead were raining down on them. In the center of the room stood a round table, a ball of milky-white crystal resting atop it.

"What sort of man lives in a place like this?" Borgli asked.

Tor replied in a wistful tone. "A man of means. A man of secrets. A man of magic."

"A wizard?"

"No." Tor shook his head. "You stand in the home of Lazio Vanda, the greatest sorcerer in the world."

"Sorcery?" Borgli had studied enough of human histories to know what was accepted…and what was not. "Isn't blood magic frowned upon?"

Tor nodded. "Wizards find it repulsive enough to warrant execution should you be caught practicing it."

Yet, this man practices the forbidden magic anyway. "And you trust this sorcerer?"

"In six years, he has yet to give us any reason to distrust him."

A male voice came from the darkness. "I am glad to hear you say that."

Borgli turned as a man with gray hair and a neatly trimmed beard emerged from the gloom. The man was dressed in all black – trousers, shoes, tunic, coat, and cloak. When his gray eyes met Borgli's, it felt as though they peered right into his soul.

Although the man's presence was disconcerting, Tor and Koji appeared used to it. Tor dipped his head. "Hello, Master Vanda."

The sorcerer turned his attention on Borgli. "I see you brought a guest."

Borgli swallowed hard, unsure if he should speak. He did not understand the magic of humans, be it wizardry or sorcery. A fear connected to that ignorance stirred concerns unfamiliar to him. *Can this sorcerer read my thoughts? Can he place a curse on me if I say something wrong?* Disturbing questions sped through his thoughts in a moment of silence…until Tor saved him.

"This is Borgli Handshaw." Tor clamped a friendly hand on Borgli's shoulder. "He has agreed to join my crew."

The sorcerer's intense gaze remained fixed on Borgli. "Now I am curious. Where did you find a dwarf?"

He knows what I am. Borgli swallowed the lump in his throat. *What else does he know?*

Tor blinked. "How did you know he was a dwarf?"

"Just look at him. Isn't it obvious?"

You are a fierce warrior, Borgli told himself. *Show this man you will not be intimidated.* He thumped his chest to reinforce his resolve. "I hail from Kelmar. Tor and Koji happened upon me in the halls of Oren'-Tahal while I was in a bit of trouble."

Tor nodded. "He was tied to a pillar in the Temple of Vandasal and surrounded by goblins. A shaman led the darkspawn and was intent on sacrificing him. Once we freed him, Borgli agreed to join us if we could help him retrieve his ancestor's weapon."

The sorcerer nodded, his gaze still affixed on Borgli. "The ancient war hammer. I noticed it the moment you entered."

Borgli reached over his shoulder, his hand gripping the hammer's head as he scowled. "I will fight you to my last breath before I allow you to have it."

Vanda laughed. "Such ferocity!" He shook his head while still grinning. "I do miss dealing with you dwarves. Your people are rarely dull."

"You mean dull like the elves?"

The sorcerer gave a slight nod. "It is true. Your cousins can be a bit stuffy." He gave the hammer a brief visual inspection, nodding as if it were familiar to him. "Do not fear. I have no intention of claiming your prize." His smirk slid away, his eyes flaring with a frightening fire. "However, if I wanted it, the hammer would be mine, and you would be sleeping with your ancestors."

Rather than flinch at the threat, Borgli grew angry. His face darkened, and his fist clenched until Koji clapped a hand on his shoulder. When he looked up, he found a friendly smile on the tall man's face, and his anger quelled.

Clearing his throat to draw everyone's attention, Tor opened his pack. "Koji and I did not return empty-handed." He removed an item wrapped in cloth, holding it before him as he unwrapped it.

The cloth opened to reveal the bronze disk with gear teeth on the outer edge and a star-shaped sapphire on its face.

The sorcerer accepted the object and stepped to the window to view it in better light. "Ah, I recall this badge. It once adorned the helmet of Arangoli the Fierce."

This time, Borgli flinched. "You know of my ancestor?"

"I know much, young dwarf. Your people are not the only ones who study history, nor are you the only ones who have impacted it. The only way to avoid repeating the mistakes of the past is to learn from them, not allow them to pass unheeded."

What kind of man is this? Borgli turned to Tor to gauge his reaction.

∼

Tor and Koji shared a knowing look. Both had frequently expressed curiosity at the sorcerer's extensive knowledge on ancient history. When asked, Vanda would explain that he was well read. Tor often researched histories, but his knowledge of past civilizations was nowhere close to that of the sorcerer.

Vanda spun toward Tor with the disk in hand. "This is excellent. While not a hammer of legend, I am happy to have such a unique relic among my collection."

"I thought you might appreciate the nature of the artifact." Tor again dug into his pack. "It was not the only item of curiosity we discovered." He removed the scroll and extended it to Vanda. "This is a map, but the land it depicts is unfamiliar to me. I hoped you might shed some light on it."

The sorcerer unrolled the scroll, glanced at it for a moment, and rolled it back up. "I will examine this further in my library."

Tor had hoped Vanda might recognize something that would reveal the map's intent or the location it depicted, but if he did, the mysterious sorcerer did not appear ready to share that information.

"I suspect you three are hungry." Vanda slid the scroll under one arm while gripping the disk in the same hand. "Go find Ivanka. She will see that you are fed. I suspect you will then wish to rest and wash up. Be prepared to dine with me this evening, so we can discuss what comes next."

The sorcerer turned, entered the hallway, and faded into the shadows.

When his footsteps faded, Borgli said, "He is a strange man."

Koji nodded knowingly. "You have no idea."

"Yes," Tor agreed. "But he gave a trio of former Murguard soldiers a purpose and a place to live. For that, I am thankful."

"A trio?" Borgli asked. "But there are only two of you."

Just for a moment, Tor had forgotten that Navarre was dead. "Yes. Well...Our quests are often dangerous. We lost a man earlier this year. It sometimes feels as if he is still with us."

Koji patted Tor on the shoulder. "I miss Navarre as well."

Clearing the tightness of sorrow from his throat, Tor coughed into his hand and turned away. "Let's find Ivanka. I am starved."

A female voice came from the corridor. "I am right here, you glory-seeking blowhard." From the shadows emerged a woman who stood Tor's height but carried nearly twice his weight. With coppery skin and raven hair tied back in a bun, she was instantly recognizable as Hassakani. Her angled brows and tight lips gave her a severe expression, as if prepared to berate anyone who dared challenge her.

Tor smiled. "I am glad to see you as well."

She stopped a stride away and put a hand on her rather significant hip, her gaze landing on the dwarf. "I notice that you brought home a pet."

"Yes. This is Borgli. I should warn you, he eats and drinks more than you might anticipate from his size."

"Wonderful," she said in a flat tone. "I supposed I had better order more food and barrels of ale when Vern arrives with the next delivery."

Borgli's face lit up. "You have ale?"

She frowned. "Isn't it a bit early to drink?"

"If you ask me, I am currently a week late."

Tor laughed. "As you can tell, he is rather enthusiastic about ale."

Ivanka rolled her eyes. "I can't believe I am saddled with another one of you." She returned her attention to Tor. "When I saw you walk through the front gate, I immediately made a trip to the kitchen. Goren should have your meal ready soon. He and I will bring it to your apartment."

"Splendid," Koji said. "You are so considerate, Ivanka. We appreciate you."

The woman glared up at Koji for a silent beat before replying. "Don't knock anything over on your way through the house…you overgrown, walking meat pie." She turned and headed down the corridor.

Borgli looked up at Koji. "Meat pie?"

Koji grinned. "She likes me."

Tor chuckled and clapped the dwarf on the back. "That is simply Ivanka being Ivanka. It's the way she is. I am only surprised she hasn't yet given you a name, such as 'red-bearded toad.'"

"Toad? What is a toad?"

"Don't worry about it. Come. Let's head to the guest house." Tor walked down the corridor, passed three closed doors, and paused. "Oh. When inside the manor, do not *ever* open a closed door."

Borgli furrowed his brow. "Why not?"

"Let's just say that it would be the last thing you'll ever do."

The corridor continued past a circular room with a high ceiling. Daylight emitted from a window fifteen feet up, revealing a curved stairwell that ran along the wall and ascended to a point beyond view. A black door, similar to the manor's front door, loomed at the bottom of the stairwell. That door led to the basement, the one area Tor avoided whenever possible.

He entered another dark corridor, passed a pair of open doors – one leading to the kitchen, the other to the dining room – and headed down a curved corridor darkened by shadows, forcing Tor to extend one hand in front of him. His palm found the smooth wooden surface of a closed door. Despite the lack of light, Tor imagined the door's appearance – made of oak with recessed panels, the wood stained to give it a reddish hue.

"Koji, we are home." He opened the door, and the light beckoned him forward.

CHAPTER 10
HOME

The guest house was a sprawling open space with intermittent columns supporting a ten-foot ceiling. In one corner sat a table, four chairs, and walls of shelves filled with sacks, jars, plates, cups and other supplies. Another corner was occupied by Tor's desk, chair, and his prized possessions – books, maps, and scrolls that spanned thousands of years of history, often containing information from civilizations long past.

Windows covered the two walls opposite the office, providing light for the entire level. A sitting area with a sofa, loveseat, and two lounge chairs occupied a corner near the windows. A marble fireplace split the windows in front of the sitting area. In the last corner, one staircase climbed to an upper level while another descended. Pedestals and racks around the room displayed some of the weapons and relics the crew had collected during their adventures.

Tor gestured toward the stairwell. "You'll find the bedrooms below us. There are four, so do not worry, you will have your own place to sleep."

"And snore," Koji said.

"And pass gas," Tor added with a grin.

Borgli grunted. "As if you two never snore."

Koji nodded. "Oh, I'll admit Tor snores, but not with such gusto."

Not to be outdone, Tor said, "And Koji can create a choking fog when he eats the wrong thing, but you are far more consistent."

Borgli chuckled and clapped both men on the back. "It appears I have found the right company!"

Tor crossed the room and set his pack on the table, happy to be relieved of the weight. A knock came from the door, but it opened before he could reply. Ivanka and Goren, a portly man with a balding head, entered. She held a platter of steaming food: scrambled eggs piled on one side, a stack of sliced ham on the other, and diced potatoes in the middle. The man carried a basket of rolls. The smell of freshly baked bread caused Tor's mouth to water and his stomach to roar. In the man's other hand was a carafe filled with pale red liquid. Knowing that Goren was an excellent cook, Tor expected even a simple meal like this would be made to perfection.

Ivanka led the man over to the table and set down the platter. "Here is your food. Feed yourselves."

The man set down the bowl and carafe.

"Is that wine?" Koji asked.

Goren arched a brow. "A bit early for wine, isn't it?"

"It's never too early for wine."

"It is cranberry juice."

"No ale?" Borgli asked.

Goren shook his head and gave Ivanka a flat look. "Another one?"

She nodded. "The new one is as bad as the other two." Walking toward the door, she spoke over her shoulder. "The master has invited you to dine with him tonight directly after Devotion. If you aren't there on time, you may go hungry."

Following her out, Goren pulled the door closed, leaving the three adventurers alone.

Koji walked over to the shelves and dug out plates, forks, and knives for the three of them. Tor grabbed a pair of glasses and a tankard, the last of which he handed to Borgli.

"What is this?"

"It is a mug. I thought you would know that by now, considering how many you emptied back in Grakal."

"No. I mean, why give this to me while you both have glasses?"

Tor poured cranberry juice into his glass. "Because I am going to wait until tonight before I drown myself in ale. You, however, seem eager and appear able to drink more than a mere man like myself."

The dwarf grinned. "Ready, I am."

Gesturing toward the wall, Tor said, "See that spigot between the two shelves?"

"Yes."

"It is attached to a barrel located in the closet on the other side of the wall – a closet carved right out of the mountain itself, so it always remains cool. Pull the handle forward and ale will pour out."

Borgli chortled in glee while approaching the tap. "We have our own ale barrels right in our home?"

"That we do."

The dwarf held the mug beneath the tap, pulled the lever, and golden liquid spilled out. His laughter echoed throughout the room.

~

HIGH UPON A HILLSIDE, seated on his rooftop patio, Tor leaned back in his chair and gazed out over the city of Lamor and the sea beyond. It was a pleasant day, the warmth of the sun balanced by the constant sea breeze. Among the places Tor had visited, few equaled the weather in Lamor, and none surpassed it. Other than evening storms and the occasional summer hurricane, the temperature was constant, never the cold that required people to wear cloaks and never the stifling heat that forced people indoors.

Koji and Borgli occupied the other chairs, the latter sipping on his third ale of the day. Empty plates and drained glasses rested on the table, indicating that they had finished their mid-morning meal, and their hunger was sated.

Borgli rubbed his full belly. "I must say, you two know how to live. The food was excellent, and the ale"—he took another drink, swallowed, and smiled— "is wonderful."

"What of the view?" Koji asked.

The dwarf frowned. "What do you mean?"

"Do you see the beauty before you?" The towering warrior extended his arm, his gauntlet-covered arm pointing toward the sea. "The aqua blue waters, the azure sky dotted with clouds of white, the city and harbor, teeming with people...it is akin to poetry so moving it draws a tear."

The dwarf turned to Tor. "Is he for real?"

Tor chuckled. "While Koji's immense stature and fierceness as a warrior are intimidating, he often oozes emotion that would make one think he might be a woman."

"A woman?" Koji crossed his arms over his thick chest. "I am only expressing my passion for beauty."

Borgli said, "Can you express it downwind from me? From here, the odor is a bit ripe."

Again, Tor chuckled, his reaction echoed by Borgli's chortling. Despite being the butt of the jibe, Koji grinned.

I didn't realize how much I missed Navarre's camaraderie, Tor said to himself. *Borgli is fitting in quite well and helps to fill the gap left by his loss.* Aloud, he said, "Enjoy the food, ale, and view while you can. Who knows how long we will be here before we embark on another quest."

"Enjoy it, I will." The dwarf swept an arm toward the open rooftop patio. "What do you do with all this space?"

Tor explained, "This is where we spar and exercise whenever we are at home. Training is critical in our business. We must never lose our edge, whether in wielding our weapons, maintaining balance, or climbing a cliffside." With his last words, he gestured toward the steep, rocky slope looming above them. "If we grow soft or slow, even slightly, it could be the difference between life and death."

"That I can understand." Borgli downed the rest of his tankard and slammed it on the table, following it with a roaring belch.

Koji arched a brow. "Is that necessary?"

"It makes me feel better, so yes." The dwarf nodded toward Koji's left hand. "Is that necessary?"

"What?" Koji lifted his gauntlet. "This?"

"I removed my chainmail and left my hammer downstairs. Why do you continue to wear that chunky piece of armor?"

Koji's eyes dropped to his lap. "I cannot remove it."

Rather than forcing Koji to explain, Tor spoke. "He cannot remove it." Borgli turned toward Tor, and he continued, "Without it, he has no hand."

"No hand?"

"It was lost in a darkspawn battle during our last year in the Murguard."

"You mentioned this Murguard before. What is it?"

"Murguard soldiers protect the Fractured Lands, the narrow canyons connecting the Murlands, where darkspawn roam, and the world of mankind. Koji and I somehow survived years fighting monsters, often while the soldiers beside us were cut down, eaten, or abducted."

Borgli stared at Tor with narrowed eyes. "You fought the Dark Lord's minions?"

"Nearly every day for ten years."

"That is honorable."

"Some say so. Others dismiss it as a lark or a waste of time. Most want nothing to do with us."

"How come?"

Tor gazed off into the distance. "Ex-Murguard soldiers struggle to find our place when we return to society. Life as a soldier is structured and your purpose is well defined. Out in the real world, such boundaries and guidance do not exist. In addition, the ghosts of our past haunt us, sometimes with injuries like Koji's, other times in nightmares that return night after night."

"A warrior's life is a hard one," Borgli agreed. "When a dwarf chooses the path of a warrior, it is for life, so I know nothing of what life is like beyond that path."

"Yet, here you sit, no longer a warrior among your people."

Borgli crossed his arms, his face clouded over. "I'd rather not discuss that."

The rustle of the wind and distant rush of the sea filled the silence.

After an uncomfortable moment, Borgli relaxed and asked, "How did you come to live here?"

"After leaving the Murguard, Koji, Navarre, and I traveled for some time and eventually found employment as bodyguards for a traveling merchant. That ended one night, just twenty miles east of Lamor."

As Tor continued his tale, the memory replayed in his head. Sometimes it felt as if it happened just days ago, other times like an entire lifetime had passed.

CHAPTER 11
SIX YEARS AGO

Tor held the reins in one hand while the other balanced a spear across his lap. His horse rode at an easy walk along a gravel road, Tor's upper body swaying in time with its strides. Shadows thickened in the surrounding trees as the sky overhead darkened. The sun, now below the western horizon, left the clouds pink and gradually turning purple.

Koji rode at Tor's right, Navarre to his left. The latter held his bow ready while scanning the surrounding trees. Behind them, a two-horse wagon was being driven by Tor's employer, Jorum. To the man's side sat his wife, Hiranya. Behind them, a faded green tarp covered the goods in the wagon bed – hand-woven Pallanese rugs and Orenthian pottery.

They rounded a bend and Navarre pointed. "There."

Following the motion, Tor spied a clearing nestled among a copse of ancient oaks. "That looks promising. I want you and Koji to ride in and scout it while I talk to Jorum."

Tor raised his spear, turned his horse, and waited on the side of the road while the wagon approached. When the driver drew even with him, Tor urged his horse to walk parallel with it, just a stride from the wagon seat.

"A clearing awaits on the left just ahead. Navarre and Koji are inspecting it," Tor said while peering into the trees. "Unless they find something alarming, we should stop there for the evening. Nightfall is nearly upon us, and we are unlikely to find another place to camp before it arrives in full." His gaze turned back on Jorum. "With the cloudbank to the east masking the moon tonight, it will soon be too dark to see."

When the wagon driver nodded, Tor nudged his steed into a trot, passing the wagon before turning off the road. He slowed in the long grass as he approached his fellow ex-soldiers.

Navarre dismounted. "This will do. Let's tie our horses to this oak and make camp.

∼

Gripping his spear, Tor paced around the wagon and stopped to stare at the road. Bereft of moonlight, the gloom was thick. His vision barely extended past the tree branches. Quiet dominated the night, the lone exception being the wind that stirred the leaves overhead. Not seeing or hearing anything of note was a good thing. Satisfied, he continued around the wagon and approached his sleeping comrades.

Orange embers glowed amid the dying fire, providing a meager halo of light in the camp. Beneath gray blankets, Navarre's long, lean form lay beside Koji's immense body. Jorum and his wife slept on a mat beneath the wagon, appearing like nothing more than lumpy silhouettes. Just outside the firelight, the horses stood in the shadow of a large oak, their heads down and sleeping. All seemed as it should be.

Until it didn't.

A twig snapped in the darkness, causing Tor to spin around. The click of a trigger was followed by the zip of a crossbow bolt sailing past him.

"Wake up!" Tor bellowed. He tossed a log into the fire, sending sparks swirling up toward the night sky. He then spun and dropped to a crouch with the firelight at his back. "We are under attack!"

The bellow of male voices came from all directions, joined by the rush of charging footsteps. Flames bloomed from the campfire behind Tor, causing flickering light to illuminate his surroundings.

A pair of bandits emerged from the darkness, raced past the wagon, and charged toward Tor. One held a sword, the other an axe. Tor stood still until the bandits were just strides away. The one with the sword raised his weapon. Tor reacted. He stepped toward the man and thrust, his spear plunging into the attacker's stomach before the sword could drop. Tor then dodged away from the bandit with the axe, using the man with the spear through his belly as a barrier. The swordsman slid off the spear and fell to the ground between Tor and the other attacker. The bandit leapt over his fallen comrade while swinging a wild horizontal strike. Tor ducked beneath the axe and thrust his spear into the man's groin. The bandit howled and fell away. Tor spun around, seeking another opponent.

A dozen strides away, Koji hacked the arm off an attacker with his machete. Navarre stood at Koji's back, loosing arrows toward rushing bandits. Pain suddenly flared through Tor's leg, causing him to stagger to one knee and look down to find what had injured him. A crossbow bolt stuck out from his thigh.

Steeling himself, Tor clenched his teeth and yanked the bolt free. Tossing the bloody bolt aside, he looked up to find a bearded man charging in with sword held high. As the sword came down, Tor rolled, the blade narrowly missing him before striking the dirt. Tor jabbed out with the butt of his spear, tripping the bandit. The man landed on his hands and knees before his momentum sent him into a roll. By the time he righted himself, Tor was there, his spear point tearing through the bandit's throat.

Panting, Tor turned from the dying bandit as Koji dispatched the last enemy.

A dozen bodies lay strewn about the camp. Three others were visible at the edge of the firelight.

Tor drew his knife, knelt beside a dead bandit, and used the blade to cut at the man's tunic. "Is anyone hurt?" He then tore the man's sleeve off and wrapped it around his wounded thigh.

"My shoulder." Koji pulled a crossbow bolt from it with a grunt. "I'll bandage it."

"What about you, Navarre?" Tor asked.

"I got lucky and was able to pick off a man with a crossbow leveled at me." He grinned. "The shot missed and struck Koji instead."

"Thanks for that," Koji grumbled while tending to his wound.

Tor finished tying the sleeve around his thigh and turned toward the wagon. "Jorum, you two can come out now."

Silence.

Tor squatted beside the wagon. A mat and blankets lay beneath it, but the driver and his wife were gone.

A scream echoed in the night.

"Oh, no."

Navarre ran toward the road while drawing an arrow from his quiver. "It came from this direction."

Tor started after the archer, but a stab of agony in his thigh caused him to stumble on his first step. He continued forward with a limp as Koji ran past.

The darkness thickened as the fire grew distant. Footsteps, grunts, and gasps filled the otherwise silent night. When Tor reached the road, he turned and limped down it. Shouts rang out, followed by a cry of agony. His mind raced at what might have occurred, while his body felt as though he were running through knee-high muck.

Silhouettes coalesced in the night – two men, one of them a towering giant. Tor slowed when he realized it was Koji and Navarre. Both stood at the side of the road, looking down at something. When Tor drew even with them, he stopped, and a lump of lead settled in his gut.

Three bandits lay dead, one with arrows jutting from his torso, another with an arrow in the eye, and the last with a gaping gash across his throat.

Among them was a woman, her dress and her throat torn open.

"Hiranya," Tor croaked.

"She is dead," Navarre said. "Two bandits escaped on horseback."

"What of Jorum?"

"Dead as well. Over there." Navarre nodded toward a nearby oak.

Tor limped over to it and squatted beside the man leaning against the trunk. Jorum's head rested on his shoulder, his eyes staring into oblivion. With little hope to hang on to, Tor put his fingers to the man's neck but felt no pulse.

His chin dropped to his chest and remained there for a few breaths before he raised it. "Let's bring them back to the camp. In the morning, we will dig a grave and bury the bandits."

"What of Jorum and Hiranya?"

"They are from Lamor, which is not far. We will bring them there and give them a proper funeral."

~

TOR SAT on the wagon seat, waiting while Koji and Navarre buried the last of the bandits. His wounded leg throbbed, and it made walking or even standing more than difficult. He suspected Koji's shoulder ached as well, but since Koji lacked a hand on that arm, he hardly used it anyway.

The thuds of approaching horses drew Tor's attention to the road.

Moments later, soldiers in chainmail and yellow tabards rode into view. The lead rider slowed to a stop at the edge of the clearing, his eyes narrowed as he surveyed Tor and the camp.

"What happened here?"

"Who are you?" Tor asked.

"Lieutenant Trotter of High Wizard Uxalti's personal guard. Now, I suggest you answer me before I have my archers stick quills in all of you until you resemble bloody hedgehogs."

"Bandits attacked us last night."

Trotter grimaced. "Search them and the camp. Kill anyone who resists."

Eight soldiers dismounted and drew their swords while a dozen others leveled loaded crossbows aimed at Tor and his companions.

Tor's expression darkened. "Why kill us? We have done nothing other than protect ourselves."

The man in charge, the wings on his helmet marking him as an officer, rode closer. "We have been tracking you."

"Tracking us?"

"Yes...and the graves you left behind."

One of the soldiers surrounding Koji and Navarre shouted, "Lieutenant! I found fresh graves."

Among the men standing near Tor, one lifted the tarp in the wagon bed and gasped. "Look, Lieutenant, two more bodies in the wagon."

The lieutenant rode his horse over and stared into the wagon bed. "That poor woman...just think of what she must have endured." Trotter suddenly snarled. "Arrest them! I want them shackled, gagged, and brought to Lamor for execution."

"You don't understand," Tor said. "This man hired us as bodyguards to protect him and his wife."

"Yet, they are dead while you three live."

"It was the bandits, they..."

"Lies!" the lieutenant roared.

Tor gripped his spear and stepped down from the wagon, using the shaft to steady himself. He did not realize a soldier was behind him until the pommel of the man's sword struck his head and the world went black.

~

At the brink of consciousness, Tor lingered, unable to fully rouse himself. The sounds of a city teased him beyond the steady clopping of hooves. His face felt flush, his dangling head swinging with each stride of the horse until it stopped. His eyes blinked open, but the cloud in his mind left him disoriented. Rough hands gripped him by the upper arms, carrying him into a shadowed doorway.

Soldiers hauled him down a curved stairwell, the constant jostling drawing his awareness through the fog. They dragged him into a cell, and someone knelt on his back, pinning him down while the shackles were removed from his wrists. When his wrists were freed, the soldier removed his knee, stepped out of the cell, and slammed the door closed.

Tor lay on a pallet in the cell, and his eyes drifted closed as the darkness reclaimed him.

~

"Tor."

Someone called his name.

"Tor. Are you awake?"

His eyes blinked open to a dimly lit room. He held a hand to the back of his head and felt a lump. It was tender to the touch. With the required effort, he crawled to his hands and knees.

"Tor?" It was Koji's deep voice.

"Yeah. I am alive." Tor groaned as he staggered to his feet. Pain shot through his wounded thigh, causing him to stumble against the door.

"Alive is good. However, you may not be for long."

His hands gripped the bars in the cell door window, and he pressed his face against them. "Where are we?"

"The dungeon below Lamor Castle. They think we are bandits."

Memories of the prior night flooded through his mind...and he recalled finding Hiranya's corpse. "We can explain what happened at our trial."

"There will be no trial, not according to Lieutenant Trotter. We are to be hanged in the morning." Koji's voice lowered in volume. "I am afraid this is the end for us."

Tor had escaped difficult spots in the past, but now he struggled for a means to solve this puzzle. "Where is Navarre?"

From farther away, he heard Navarre's voice. "I am here. For now."

A door down the corridor squeaked as it opened. Someone descended a staircase. The sound of footsteps drew closer. A man in a black cloak entered the chamber, his hood covering his head and leaving his face masked by shadow. The man slowed until he stopped outside of Tor's door, staring at him.

"My, my," the man said, "you have gotten yourself into quite the pickle."

With his head pounding, stomach growling, and mouth dry, Tor lacked the patience to humor anybody, so he went directly to the point. "The trouble was caused by others. We are innocent bystanders who Lieutenant Trotter chose to condemn in order to boost his own standing."

The man chuckled. "Of that, I have no doubt."

Tor frowned. "You believe me?"

"I have no reason not to believe you."

"In that case, can you explain the situation to High Wizard Uxalti?"

"I cannot."

Tor sighed. "Then why are you here?"

"I cannot because the wizard is currently incapacitated, as is everyone else in the castle."

"What does that mean?"

The man ignored Tor's question. "I have come to offer you a purpose."

Suddenly wary, Tor asked, "What sort of purpose?"

"Come and work for me, and I will see you exonerated."

"What sort of work?"

"I have a need for men of your talents, men who have faced darkspawn and survived, men who have been hardened by hardship in the Murguard."

"Soldiers retire from the Murguard every year."

"But how many can read ancient Hassakani?"

How does he know about that? "Few, I would guess."

"In addition to purpose, I offer you fame and fortune. It will be a risk-laden life, but that is nothing you three have not already endured."

With near certain death hanging over him, Tor knew he had little room to negotiate. "I cannot speak for my companions, but if you free us, I am yours."

Koji said, "My place is at Tor's side."

From the farthest cell, Navarre added, "As is mine."

"Splendid." The man lowered his hood to reveal a mature face framed by gray hair and a neatly trimmed beard. His gray eyes sparked with an intensity Tor could not ignore. "My name is Vanda. I will come to retrieve you in the morning."

"We are to be hanged in the morning."

"Then I had best not be late."

Still wary, Tor said, "Just know that if you ever betray us, I *will* kill you."

Vanda chuckled. "Now *there* is the spirit I was expecting."

The man walked off. Tor wondered if he would ever see him again.

LEANING BACK in his chair with a wry smirk on his face, Tor continued his story. "Of course, Vanda did return the next morning, but not until Koji, Navarre, and I were standing on the gibbet with a noose around each of our necks."

"You were that close to execution?" Borgli snorted. "You must have pissed yourself."

"I was on the brink of doing so when Vanda rode into the square on a two-wheeled cart pulled by a mule. In the cart were two rough-looking men, their wrists and ankles bound. High Wizard Uxalti was upset at the interruption...until the men on the cart began to confess, explaining they were the last two members of the bandits behind the murders and that we were innocent." Tor shook his head. "Whatever Vanda did to them, those men were far more afraid of him than they were of replacing us on the gibbet.

"We were freed and brought to Vanda's manor. Once our wounds had healed, we set out on our first quest, which resulted in two prized possessions – my ranseur and Koji's enchanted gauntlet. However, that is a tale for another day." Tor stood. "Now, I believe it is time for a nap. A soldier learns the value of sleep, and quiet days like this are rare in our profession."

"I agree," Koji said as he rose to his feet. "Besides, we are to dine with Vanda tonight, and that never occurs without a reason."

The dwarf frowned at his empty tankard. "But I only just started drinking."

CHAPTER 12
DINNER GUEST

Standing before his open wardrobe, Tor dug through it until he found a double-breasted black coat. He slipped his arms in and began securing one row of gold buttons and then the other, stopping mid-chest so the lapel hung loosely. He turned to the mirror and examined himself.

Brown eyes stared back at him. Sometimes, those eyes seemed foreign, as if they belonged to a stranger. The lines at the edges spoke of his age, but few could guess at the horrors those eyes had witnessed. His shoulder-length brown hair, still damp from the bath, was combed back, and his beard was freshly trimmed to follow the sharp lines of his jaw. He straightened the collar of his coat and turned to examine himself.

Red and gold dragons twisted around both sleeves from his shoulders to his elbows, giving the coat a striking appearance. Likewise, a gold stripe ran up the outer seam of each leg of his breeches. He squatted and slid on his boots, the black leather covering his calves and the bottom of his breeches. Then he stood before the mirror again, scrutinizing his appearance.

Satisfied, his gaze shifted to the window where the yellow glow of Lord Jakarci's magic flickered across Lamor. Near the harbor, the golden blaze of Bal burned brightly atop the Obelisk of Devotion. Although it was too distant for him to hear, he knew the people of Lamor were chanting to their god and wizard lord. Tor rarely joined in those chants, an act many wizard lords would consider treasonous, but hidden high on the hill in Vanda's estate, nobody would know whether he was participating or not.

Koji, on the other hand, seldom missed an opportunity to pray.

Tor rounded his bed, opened the door, and stepped into the hallway. As expected, the room across from his was empty. The one beside it, however, should have been occupied.

"Where is that dwarf?" He stomped to the end of the corridor and threw open the door to the baths.

The entire bathing room had been carved out of the rocky hillside. Fed by hot springs, the pools themselves consumed most of the space. Pale blue light from an enchanted lantern hanging on a hook beside the door illuminated the room and its lone occupant.

Tor said, "Koji and I left you in here a half an hour ago. You were supposed to dry off and get dressed."

As naked as the day he was born, Borgli stood at the edge of the pool, steam swirling around him as he wrung water out of his thick red beard. "The heat of the bath was so soothing...I lingered for just a bit before climbing out of the water."

"A bit? You call thirty minutes a bit?"

"Well, we dwarves live a long..."

"Yes, I know you live longer than we humans," Tor snapped. "That doesn't change the nature of time. Thirty minutes is still thirty minutes!"

The dwarf cranked on his beard again, sending a trail of water falling into the pool. "I'll dress quickly."

"Just be sure to wear the stuff I put out for you."

Borgli grimaced. "I'd rather wear my own stuff."

"Your own clothing won't be dry until morning at the earliest."

"It would have been dry had you not forced me to wash it."

"While you might not care that you smelled like a rusty sword that had been pulled out of someone's arse, the rest of us have fully functional noses. Your clothes needed washing even more than ours."

Borgli wrapped a towel around himself and walked past Tor. "Yeah, yeah. I've heard your bellyaching before."

"And you'll hear it again if you aren't upstairs in five minutes."

The dwarf stepped into his room, the only one that lacked windows, and turned back toward Tor. "I'll be there." The door slammed shut, ending the conversation.

Tor sighed and climbed to the main level. The golden glow of devotion made it easy to navigate without any added lighting. He ascended another flight, opened the trapdoor at the top, and stepped out on the roof.

Far across the rooftop plaza, Koji knelt beside the railing, chanting while staring toward the glowing obelisk. "...watch over us, guide us, and lead us into a better future."

The beam of light shining on the obelisk suddenly faded, and the golden flames snuffed out. The night felt even darker after losing that light. Although blocked from view by the cliff wall looming over the rooftop, on this night, the ever-present moon shone brightly and bathed the city in its pale light.

Tor crossed the rooftop as Koji stood. "Do you feel better now?"

His enormous friend turned with a grin. "You know I always feel better after prayer."

"Yeah, yeah." Tor had heard it a thousand times. "It gives you a sense of balance against the lives you have taken."

"Someone has to honor the dead, even if they are darkspawn."

Tor rolled his eyes. "Well, Devotion is over, and Vanda is expecting us."

"I am ready."

Side by side, they crossed the rooftop before Tor stepped ahead of his friend and led the way downstairs.

The main floor was dark other than indirect moonlight seeping through the windows. With his hands in front of him, Tor felt blindly along a table beside the wall until he gripped a smooth glass orb. He picked up the orb and set it in the sconce on the wall. Purple light bloomed from it and a dozen others spread across the apartment.

Borgli emerged from the other stairwell, stopped at the top, and gave Tor a flat-lipped glare. The coat he wore hung down past his knees, and his hands were lost somewhere in the sleeves. Likewise, his trouser legs were piled atop each bare foot.

Koji chuckled aloud, but Tor took care to hide his smile.

"I can't wear this!" Borgli growled. "I look like a child dressed in adult clothing."

Tor recovered first. "Well, you won't fit into my clothes, not with that belly of yours."

"We dwarves put pride in our bellies."

"Pride or not, Koji's clothing is the only thing we have that will fit you."

Koji said, "Perhaps we can modify it quickly."

With a raised brow, Tor looked at him. "If we shorten the arms and legs, you won't be able to wear them any longer."

"To tell you the truth, I haven't worn that outfit in years."

"Fine." Tor drew his dagger as he approached Borgli. "Let's make this quick. We will be late as it is."

∽

Tor carried the orb in one hand. Its glow had slowly dwindled since Tor had removed it from the wall sconce, but it still gave enough light for Tor to lead Koji and Borgli along the curved rock corridor connecting the guest house to Vanda's manor. They emerged just outside the dining room, where Tor placed the orb in another sconce, its light blooming at contact.

He paused in the dining room doorway, surprised by what he saw. Vanda stood before the burning fireplace, and he was not alone. A young woman stood beside him.

Her brown hair spilled over one shoulder, her slightly angular eyes and tanned skin speaking of her as Balmorian. Rather than wearing a dress, the common garb for females, tight, brown breeches clung to her long, lean legs and a green leather vest, cinched at the waist, covered her upper body. Beneath the vest was a cream tunic unlaced to leave her collarbone exposed. A thick black belt and black riding boots completed her ensemble.

The woman's dark eyes met Tor's. She frowned as those eyes scanned him from head to toe. "Who is this?"

Tor said, "I was about to ask the same question."

Vanda turned toward Tor. The sorcerer wore a black doublet trimmed in silver. "Ah. Finally. You are lucky. If I did not have a quest that I needed to discuss with you, dinner would have already begun." He put a hand on the woman's shoulder. "I want you to meet Taquell Tarpon. Taquell, this is Tor Ranseur."

"Truly?" She arched a brow. "I expected someone more...impressive."

Such dismissals irritated Tor. He had heard the same before and the comments only became more frequent as his fame spread. "And I would expect a young woman to show respect toward her elders."

She snorted. "You expect wrong. Respect is earned, and I've seen nothing to show you deserve it."

Fists tightening, Tor bristled until Koji rested his heavy paw on his shoulder.

"Easy, Tor," Koji said in a soft voice.

The woman looked Koji up and down. "And who is this oversized lunkhead?"

Vanda said, "This is Kojinko Maulo. Like Tor, he is a Murguard veteran and a seasoned adventurer."

Her gaze shifted to Borgli, who stood at Tor's other side. "And the walking beard?"

"The name is Borgli Handshaw." Borgli stroked his damp facial hair. "I am flattered that you are impressed with my beard."

The woman snorted. "If you say so."

"Enough banter." Vanda clapped his hands, the sound echoing in the chamber. The candelabras on the dining table ignited with flame. "Let us sit, eat, and have a civil discussion.

The wizard claimed the seat at the head of the table, as he always did. Tor sat beside him with Koji on his other side. The woman sat across from Tor, Borgli beside her.

She narrowed her eyes at the dwarf. "Be sure to keep your hands to yourself, little man."

"I am no man." He thumbed his chest. "I am a dwarf and among the tallest of my kind."

The woman chuckled. "Yeah, right."

"He truly is a dwarf," Tor said.

"Dwarves are the subjects of bedtime stories."

"Just because you have not seen something yourself, does not mean it doesn't exist, Taquell."

"I prefer you to call me Quell."

"Quell?" Tor frowned. "That means to quiet something. It's not a name."

"And Tor is?"

"It is short for Victor."

"And Quell is short for Taquell. What is the difference?"

Vanda sighed. "I asked for a civil conversation. If you two will not comply, I have ways of silencing you."

Tor clamped his mouth closed. His nostrils flared, but he said nothing. Likewise, Quell crossed her arms over her chest, and she pressed her lips together.

Approaching footsteps drew Tor's attention to the entrance as Ivanka and Goren walked in, each with a tray filled with food. The scent of spiced lamb tickled Tor's nose and caused his mouth to water.

"Excellent," Vanda said as the pair set the trays on the table and began passing the food down. "Let us eat and then we will discuss business."

"Business?" Tor asked.

"Of course. You didn't think Quell joined us merely for our company?"

Tor chose two pieces of flatbread before passing the bowl to Vanda, all the while staring at Quell. *What business could we have with this impertinent young woman?*

He would soon find out.

∽

Tor sipped his wine while waiting for Vanda to finish eating. He had watched Quell during the meal but was sure to look elsewhere when her eyes shifted toward him. From her appearance and mannerisms, he attempted to discern her background.

The woman was brash, poor-mannered, and unrefined, leaving him thinking she would fit better in a guard's barracks than high society. Her attire was better suited to riding a horse or hiking in the woods rather than life in a city. He judged her age to be in her early twenties, twenty-five at the oldest. Her intelligent responses spoke of an education, but her sharp tongue said that she lacked discipline.

Vanda set down his fork, took a drink of wine, and leaned back in his chair. "Among the most satisfying aspects of this life is the pleasure found in a delectable meal."

It was just the kind of strange thing Tor had heard from Vanda again and again.

"If you say so," Quell said. "Now, if you are finished, can I explain to these two why I am here?"

The sorcerer nodded. "As you wish."

"Wonderful."

Tor agreed, for his curiosity was raging.

"I am looking for my father," Quell said.

Brow furrowed, Tor asked, "Your father?"

"Yes. He disappeared in mid-summer."

"Your father has been missing for eight weeks?"

"Do you have rocks for brains? I just told you as much."

Tor scowled at her. "He likely fled to escape your tongue."

Borgli burst out laughing.

She pressed her lips together. "Do you want to fight, you horse's arse?"

"I'll..."

Vanda slapped the table. "Enough! You two will get along, or I'll put a curse on you that sends flaming pain through your groin every time you try to relieve yourself."

Tor had seen enough to Vanda's sorcery to believe it was possible. "I apologize. Please continue."

"Fine." Quell nodded. "My father's name is Joaquin Tarpon, and he acted as Lord Jakarci's Master Ranger for fifteen years. Ten years ago, when my mother died, he abdicated his position to raise me at a cabin in the mountains of Eastern Balmoria. As the years advanced and I grew older and more capable of protecting myself, he would leave me alone for days or a week or two at a time. When he returned, I always asked him about those trips, and he would wave them off as simple hunting expeditions. I knew he was hiding something, but I had no idea what.

"When his latest trip lasted thrice as long as any prior outing, I grew concerned. Winter is soon approaching, especially in the mountains, so I grew increasingly troubled, my worries about his welfare gnawing at me until I could take it no longer.

"I went into his bedroom and searched and searched for clues as to where I might find him. On my fifth visit to the room, I grew so angry, I flipped his bed over, which uncovered a loose floorboard hiding beneath it. When I lifted it, I found a journal. The handwriting inside it was his.

"The entries in the journal began just two years ago, the final entry recorded the day before his departure. I read through the journal again and again, and while I can make sense of parts of it, much of the information is disconnected and often confusing. So, I gave up on unraveling the mystery of the journal, locked the cabin up, and set out to find someone who could help me find him.

"As I traveled through Balmor, and when others learned of my problem, all said the same thing. You need to seek out the adventurer, Tor Ranseur. If anyone can unravel the clues in the journal and locate your father, it is him.

"So, I journeyed to Lamor in search of this fabled man. Three days past, I visited this house but was told Tor was on a quest, and I would have to wait until his return. That brings us to today.

"My father is still missing, his journal remains as cryptic as ever, and I fear I am running out of time."

Tor had listened carefully to her account to better understand her background and situation. Numerous unanswered questions remained, the primary one demanding to be asked. "I still don't understand why you think I can help you. My profession is to seek out ancient ruins and to recover relics from the past, not to find missing persons."

Quell pushed her chair back, stood, and walked to the corner of the room, where a longbow and quiver rested against the wall. She picked up the quiver, reached inside, and removed a small book before walking back. With an underhand toss, she sent the book to land on the table between her plate and Tor's.

"What is this?" he asked.

"My father's journal."

The book, with its plain brown leather cover, was barely larger than Tor's hand and no more than an inch thick.

"And why does that matter?"

"In it, my father mentions the discovery of an ancient temple, a place of worship he believed once belonged to someone named Urvadan."

Borgli gasped while Tor's gaze snapped to the girl.

She nodded. "Yes. I speak of the Dark Lord. I fear my father found this temple and whatever was waiting inside it now has him."

CHAPTER 13
A MYSTERIOUS JOURNAL

A stunned silence hung in the air. Tor's mind raced as he recalled tales of the infamous Dark Lord.

"The Dark Lord's tower is in Murvaran," he said, "far to the northeast and on the other side of the Great Peaks. Your father would have needed to travel to Kyranni, journey through the Fractured Lands, and then continue, the gods only know how far, deep into the Murlands. It would be a long and perilous journey, and with all the darkspawn he would encounter, there would be little hope for one man to survive."

"I thought the same at first," Quell said, "but upon further reading, I found mention of an ancient temple from before the Great Cataclysm. My father surmised that Urvadan abandoned it when he built the tower as his new home in Murvaran."

"I recall reading about an ancient temple dedicated to the Dark Lord. The text I found claimed that it was a place his worshipers visited to bring gifts to garner his favor." Tor frowned in thought. "If this discovery is true, I cannot imagine what artifacts might be found in a temple once occupied by a god."

Vanda picked up the journal and stood. "I believe it is time to retire to the parlor. Now that everyone understands the situation, we should discuss how to proceed."

Rising to his feet, Tor asked, "You want us to help her?"

Vanda stopped in the doorway and turned back with a steely look in his gray eyes. "Oh, yes."

"Why?"

"Because my"—he shook his head— "Urvadan's temple, if this man has truly found it, might hold relics of power the likes of which we have never before seen."

The sorcerer disappeared down the corridor, and Tor shot Koji a questioning look.

Koji shrugged. "The sorcerer is strange. We already knew this."

"Yeah." Tor pushed his chair in. "Yet, sometimes, he is even stranger than usual."

Quell retrieved her bow and quiver, slipping both over her shoulder before securing them on her back. "You heard the strange old man. Let's go make a plan."

As she walked past, Tor gripped her arm and spun her around. They were the same height, so glaring into her eyes took little effort. "What do you mean when you say, 'Let's go make a plan'?"

"I wish to know what you intend."

"I intend to figure out where this temple is hidden, find a way in, and recover whatever I can from it. That includes your father...if he is there and alive. That is all you need to know."

"Sorry. I need to be included in the plan and made aware of the details."

He rolled his eyes. "Why?"

"Because I am going with you."

"What?" His voice rose an octave. "I am not about to play wet nurse to a snarky young brat."

Her eyes narrowed. "Brat?"

"What I do is dangerous. I lost a member of my team just last year. I don't want to be responsible for you."

"I can take care of myself. I am a skilled hunter who has killed rock wolves and tracked moarbears." Quell poked him in the chest. "I *am* going with you. Unless you are willing to kill me, there is nothing you can do to stop me." She jerked her arm from his grip and walked away.

When her footsteps faded, Koji said, "I like her."

Tor shot Koji an incredulous look. "Why? She is stubborn, mean, and disrespectful."

"She has spirit and is willing to challenge you when you insist that your way is the only way."

"You know how poorly that works in the military."

"We are no longer in the military, Tor. Yes, you are still our squad leader, but we are people, not soldiers."

Koji walked off, and Tor turned to Borgli. "I suppose you like her as well."

The dwarf grinned. "She is filled with fire and fury, which reminds me of my mother."

"Your mother?" Tor pressed his palm to his forehead. "I am surrounded by misfits, rebels, and drunkards."

"You are the one who recruited me. I said I was willing to fight and use my skill to help you, but I never promised to agree with your opinions."

Deciding to move past the discussion, Tor turned away. "Come along. Let's see if we can inject enough sanity into this plan to keep us all alive."

Following the dark corridor, Tor led Borgli to the parlor at the front of the house, where glowing orbs of purple light rested in wall sconces, providing light. Vanda, Quell, and Koji stood beside the round table in the middle of the room. Tor and Borgli joined them to form a large circle with the crystal ball in the center.

The sorcerer set the journal on the table. "During Quell's last visit, I was able to briefly peruse the journal. As she described, it appears to detail clues that lead to the location of an ancient temple. The key piece I was able to glean was a reference to Zialis, so I will use that as our starting point."

Vanda produced a small vial from his pocket, removed the stopper, and poured crimson liquid into his hand. The tiny pool shimmered in the light, which indicated to Tor that it was wizard blood. The sorcerer set the capped vial aside, rubbed the blood across both palms, and then held them out, just inches from the crystal ball.

A spark of light bloomed in the heart of the milky globe. The spark divided into many, swirling in a flat, expanding plane. That plane reached the surface of the globe and expanded beyond it, stretching until the outer edge mirrored that of the table below it. A blurred image began to form within the light, gradually coalescing into a map of stunning detail. It gave Tor the impression that he was a bird in flight, thousands of feet above the land. A river running from the mountains in the east meandered through thick forests before passing beneath a stronghold and then spilling into the sea. Tor recognized the structure as Fralyn Fortress – a unique landmark, serving as a bridge as well as a stronghold of unequaled importance.

Quell gasped. "It is eastern Balmoria."

"Very good, my dear. This is the Serpent River with Fralyn Fortress at one end..." Vanda's finger followed the river eastward until reaching a valley near the river's origin. "And this is Zialis." He moved his finger farther east until it hovered over the towering white-capped peaks. "These are the Great Peaks, the spine of our world. They divide the wizardoms from the darkspawn ridden Murlands."

In his mind, Tor pictured the lands that extended beyond the man's view.

Orenth, from whence he had just come, lay to the south. Below Orenth and the mountains that hid Oren'Tahal was Pallanar, the southernmost wizardom – and the coldest. West of Orenth, both

Farrowen and Ghealdor were sandwiched between the inner seas and the Horizial Ocean. In the north and northwest were the rest of Balmoria, the jungles of Kyranni, and the deserts of Hassakan. The Fractured Lands, a network of narrow canyons, bordered eastern Kyranni and provided the bridge between the wizardoms and the Murlands, where darkspawn roamed. The Great Peaks were said to be otherwise impassable. Yet, monsters roamed a portion of the land between Zialis and the Great Peaks, which was known as the Wilds, making the city and the lands to the east dangerous.

Quell said, "I have studied my father's journal for many hours. In it, he references a place I know...a place in the Wilds."

Tor arched a brow. "You have been east of Zialis?"

"Me? No. But my father has told me stories of his journeys, and in one of them, he mapped out a place he had visited, marked by a feature called the Dragon's Snout." She pointed to a mountain peak just east of Zialis. "He described it as a rock feature on the eastern slope of this mountain, where it juts out to overlook a valley below the Great Peaks."

"What else can you tell us?" Tor asked.

She dropped her arm to her side. "In truth, not much. My father grew increasingly guarded over the past year, sharing little of his travels other than to warn me of the dangers found in the Wilds and how those dangers have grown worse over recent years. That is why the other notations and references in the journal are unfamiliar... except for that one thing. Worse, the latter entries are written in a language I don't understand."

Tor shot an arched brow toward Vanda.

The wizard nodded. "Yes. Ancient Hassakani." He dropped his hands to his sides and the map of light disappeared.

"Did you translate any of it yet?"

"I did not have the time." With a blood-coated finger, Vanda slid the journal toward Tor. "Take it. You will have time on the ship to study and translate it yourself during your voyage to Fralyn."

"I'd rather take the time to study it before I go, so I can be prepared."

"I have already made your travel arrangements. You four depart tomorrow at dawn. Autumn is fast approaching, and it is already cold in the mountains. You must make this trip before the first snowfall. Take what you anticipate needing when you pack tonight." He pulled a leather pouch from his hip and dropped it on the table, the contents clinking noisily. "The funds inside are enough to buy horses and provisions in Fralyn. Good luck."

The sorcerer walked off. Once again, Tor had more questions than answers.

CHAPTER 14
HORIZON CHASER

Waves licked the pilings supporting the pier, the rush of churning water all but masking the thumps of footsteps as Tor, Koji, and Borgli approached the waiting ship. The name painted on the stern said *Horizon Chaser*.

"This is it," Tor said aloud as he raised his gaze to the sky. Although the sun remained hidden behind distant peaks to the east, the bright blue above him signaled dawn's breaking. "Where is she?"

A snicker came from behind him. "She has been right behind you the entire time."

He turned to find Quell standing in the middle of the pier with a smirk on her lips. Part of him had hoped she wouldn't show, but another part was curious to see how she would handle the hardships that were likely awaiting them.

"If you are trying to prove something to me," Tor said, "don't waste your time. I am not impressed by stunts like this."

Quell sauntered up to him, her eyes narrowed. "I don't need approval from you or anyone else. I was trained by the greatest ranger of our time. My father had faith in me, and that is worth far more than the approval of Tor the Dungeon Crawler."

Tor's fists tightened. He considered his profession to be one of honor – the man who recovered lost relics from dead civilizations and brought them to the world of the living. He despised when others accused him of being a grave robber or used the term *dungeon crawler*. "Call me that again, and your time in this venture will immediately end."

She chuckled and looked at Koji. "It appears I struck a nerve."

The big man nodded. "He hates being called that."

"Good to know."

Tor turned toward the ship. "Let's board, so we can be away." He glanced over at Borgli and spied trepidation in the dwarf's eyes, as he had expected. Hoping to reassure the dwarf, he clapped a hand on his shoulder. "You survived the last voyage. This will be no different."

"I pray to Vandasal that it is so. It is not death I fear, it is the method by which it comes. Give me a good fatal battle wound, and I'll enter the afterlife satisfied. Drowning...not so much."

"This is a short trip. We should land at Fralyn tomorrow afternoon. After that, it'll be weeks before you are forced to board a ship again."

Tor led the way up the plank. Borgli followed next, his expression determined as he balanced with his arms out. Once Quell and Koji were on board, they clustered together on the deck just strides from the plank.

A man approached them. He had a red bandana tied to his head, the color a hard contrast to his tanned skin and dark beard. Tor surmised the man was roughly ten years his senior, but it could have been less depending on how hard life had been on him. "Who goes there?"

"I am Tor Ranseur. This is my crew. I believe you have been paid to provide us passage to Fralyn."

"Aye. I am Bahna, captain of *Horizon Chaser*." The man's gaze slowly took them in before landing on Quell, who he openly appraised. With a bulbous nose, a thick black beard, and a portly stomach, few would call Bahna an attractive man, even without the ugly scar on the side of his head. "I was told to expect four passengers but was not informed one would be such a fetching lass."

"Careful, you nasty old pirate." Quell stepped up to him and snarled. "This lass bites, so I suggest you and your crew look elsewhere for your conquests."

Bahna grinned, revealing a missing tooth. "And feisty too. I like that."

Tor put a hand on Quell's shoulder and pulled her back a step, drawing the captain's attention. "When do we depart?"

With apparent reluctance, Bahna tore his gaze from Quell to nod at Tor. "If you have your things, we can set sail straight away."

"We are ready to depart. The sooner we reach Fralyn, the better."

Bahna cupped his hands around his mouth and hollered, "Pull the plank and push off! Prepare to set sail!"

Tor asked, "Where are our quarters?"

The captain gestured toward a nearby staircase descending below the deck. "The door at the end of the corridor leads to your cabin. The others are occupied by crew."

"Great. We will get settled."

Tor descended the steep staircase, followed the dark corridor past four closed doors, and turned the knob of the last door. It opened to a cabin with bunks to the left and right and a table against the wall across from the door. A pair of chairs rested beside the table.

"Someday, I'd like to find a ship with spacious cabins and beds large enough for two."

Koji grunted. "I'd settle for a bed I can actually fit in without curling up on my side."

Borgli set his pack on a lower bunk before sitting on it. "I don't think this is so bad."

Tor rested his weapon against the wall and claimed a chair. "That's because you are half Koji's size, and you don't mind your own flatulence."

Quell remained in the doorway, scowling.

Tor asked her, "What's wrong with you now?"

She shook her head. "I just realized I am stuck in a tiny box with you three for the next two days."

"Did you think it was all fun, adventure, fame, and glory? I warned you about the hardships we face in this profession. If you want out, you had better get back on deck and tell Captain Bahna before we leave the harbor."

Her hands went to her hips. "You would like that, wouldn't you?"

"Actually, I would."

She stepped into the room, slammed the door, and approached the bunks across from where Borgli sat. After removing her bow, pack, and quiver, she slid them under the bunks. Then she stepped on the lower bunk and hopped with ease onto the upper one, where she lay down with her hands folded behind her head.

I guess she isn't leaving. Oddly, Tor realized he was not disappointed.

～

As he had much of the afternoon, Tor sat on the ship's deck, his back leaning against the wall between two doors – one leading to Captain Bahna's cabin, the other to the ship's galley. The clanking of dishes and banging of cabinets came from beyond the latter door.

Dinner had been a modest affair consisting of spiced lamb, red peppers, potato, and onions on wooden skewers. Even so, it was one of the best meals he had eaten on a ship.

Above him, a strong wind stretched the ship's white sails and drove *Horizon Chaser* at a brisk speed. Puffy clouds painted pink by the setting sun eased across the blue sky, outpacing the ship as they drifted east. That wind tried to snatch the pages of the journal in Tor's hands, attempting to flip them or tear them from his grip.

The journal stirred an odd juxtaposition of interest and frustration, of tantalizing clues and bewildering contradictions. He had been studying it since they set sail that morning, moving around the ship seeking privacy and enough light to read while avoiding direct sunlight.

Approaching footsteps caused him to look up and find Quell standing over him.

"Do you mind if I join you?" she asked.

So, she can be polite. He flipped the red ribbon dangling from the binding, so it lay across the page he was reading and closed the book. "Have a seat."

Quell spun around, squatted, and sat beside him, her eyes narrowed as she stared into the distance. "This is only my second time on a ship. I was a girl during my last journey. It had seemed so romantic, so adventurous—I stood at the bow gripping the rail the entire day."

"Only a day?"

"Yes, down the sound from Balmor to Harken. When we reached the mouth of the sound, and I caught my first glimpse of the sea, I stared in wonder at its vastness. While the sound is a large body of water, there is no point where you cannot see the other side. The sea, however..."

"It can be daunting. The ocean more so."

She sighed. "I have spent my entire life in Balmoria, living in the capital city when I was young and the remote, unpopulated mountains for the past twelve years. The forest, I know well. The sea, not so much. I also don't interact with people very often, so I am unused to it... having spent much of my life either alone or with my father. He was a quiet, independent man who left me to my own devices. I was sometimes included in his trips to Zialis, but most often, I was alone. Much of this occurred while I was growing into womanhood...unguided, but who could I turn to with any questions I had?"

"What are you saying?" He suspected she was trying to apologize but wanted to hear it from her.

Her gaze dropped to her hands, one kneading the other as they rested on her knees. "There are times when I respond poorly to people. Often, when this happens, I know I am being difficult or even mean, but I can't find it in me to stop. It is like a nicer, more compliant version of myself is trapped within my head and watches while the sour version snaps at others with or without provocation."

He considered how to reply before saying, "There are times I allow irritation or frustration to influence my behavior. In hindsight, I know I behaved poorly, but by then, it is too late. All I can do is apologize and try to do better next time."

A smile cracked her face as she gave him a sidelong look. "My father once said I could goad a stone into reacting in anger."

He smirked at the comment. "I am not surprised."

"I...apologize."

"I do as well."

Quell took a deep breath. "Good." She finally turned to look directly at him, her eyes sincere. "I will try to do better, just don't expect me to be all smiles and batting eyelashes...or to fall for your charms."

He arched a brow. "You think I am charming?"

She gave him a level look. "You are old enough to be my father."

"I am only thirty-seven."

"And my father is forty."

"Fair enough," Tor chuckled. "Besides, I don't need the complication of you pining after me. This quest will be difficult enough without that."

"Speaking of our quest, you have spent the entire day with your nose in that journal. I was hoping you might have gleaned something useful from it by now."

He looked down at the closed journal in his hand. He twisted it while eyeing the leather cover. "It is difficult to follow. Your father makes notes in the old language amid the new, which only adds to its complexity. His sketches, while intriguing, have no context, so I can't make heads or tails of them."

"Surely, you have learned something of import."

Tor flipped the book open and paged through it until he found the page. The sky had darkened enough to make it difficult to read. "Here, where your father mentions the dragon's snout, he follows with a notation written in the old script, which I have translated. It reads, 'In the ever-present mother's beaming smile, the dragon's snout will point the way to a path of shadow.'"

Quell frowned. "What does that mean?"

He replied with a shrug. "I don't know, but it is clear that the noted landmark is the starting point of a path that leads to something."

She rolled her eyes. "I already said as much."

"Yes, but you lacked the detail that traces the route in addition to following notes that mention a hidden canyon, a serene lake, and, finally, a plaza of death."

Her brow furrowed. "I don't know what any of that means."

"Neither do I, but I am hopeful it will make sense once we advance beyond the dragon's snout." Stars glimmered in the southeast, and the full moon seemed to brighten as the sky darkened. Tor pulled his feet beneath him, pushed off the wall, and stood. "Today's wind was brisk, and Captain Bahna claims we should reach Fralyn by noon tomorrow, which puts us hours ahead of schedule."

"What then?"

"We procure horses and provisions for the journey, and then we set out for Zialis."

CHAPTER 15
FRALYN

Horizon Chaser *sailed up the throat of the Serpent River, the Novecai Sea behind them and their final destination ahead. The ship rounded a bend, and the tree-covered riverbanks gave way to the first signs of civilization.

Cabins and farmhouses stood on the southern bank, each with a small wooden dock jutting into the water as a marker. Outside of one such building, a woman stood beside a clothesline, hanging freshly washed garments. She finished and paused to watch the ship sail past before retreating to the rear door of her cottage.

Tor stood at the starboard bow with Borgli on his left. The dwarf's knuckles were white as he gripped the teak railing. To Borgli's other side stood Koji, who was focused on reassuring his stout companion that all was well.

Quell, positioned at Tor's right, leaned close. "You should be proud of me."

"Why?"

"For all those snide comments I've kept at bay while watching our miniature walking beard whimper in fear."

Tor sighed and whispered back. "He is afraid of drowning. Don't you have any fears?"

"I am afraid of turning into a softhearted little girl like Koji."

"Heh." Tor had thrown more jibes at Koji about his soft core than anyone. "I find that unlikely to ever happen."

"That is a relief."

Koji clamped his bare hand on Borgli's shoulder. "You are doing great, my friend. If you ever feel yourself ready to panic, close your eyes and imagine you stand above land rather than water."

The dwarf nodded. "I cannot allow my fears to defeat me."

Despite the urge to ask why Borgli waited until they reached the river if he wanted to face his fears, Tor decided to accept any progress as a positive sign.

The ship eased around another bend, and the city of Fralyn came into view.

The harbor was a modest size with two piers and an array of docks for smaller craft. Similar to most other seaside cities, a wall divided Fralyn from the harbor. Clay-tiled roofs were visible beyond the wall, and a blocky, five-story keep lay at the heart of the city, its battlements visible above all else. A narrow spire stood in front of the structure as the tallest point in the city. Once nightfall claimed the area, that spire would ignite with the emerald flame of Oren, since Fralyn City lay on the Orenthian bank of the river. Despite everything the city had to offer, another structure competed for Tor's attention and easily won, for just upriver from Fralyn was a massive, towering citadel spanning the entire width of the river.

Larger than any other castle, Fralyn Fortress dwarfed the neighboring city that shared its name, looming as a dark monolith in the heart of the Serpent River Valley. Even from a mile away, the stronghold demanded respect – hundreds of feet wide and many times the length, with blocky towers rising into the sky.

The fortress also acted as a bridge since it physically connected

Orenth to Balmoria, making it the only means, other than by boat, to cross the river within thirty miles of the coast. The Maker-built structure was larger than some cities. More importantly, whoever controlled the fortress controlled the river, for it was nigh impossible for unwanted watercraft to pass beneath it without notice.

"This is our destination?" Borgli asked while staring toward the approaching pier.

"Yes." Tor clapped the dwarf on the shoulder. "Let's retreat to our cabin and retrieve our things."

Borgli nodded. "The sooner we are on solid ground, the better."

As Tor led the others toward their cabin, a thought occurred to him. He stopped and turned to Borgli. "Please tell me you know how to ride a horse."

The dwarf shook his head. "We have no horses in Kelmar."

Tor's chin dropped to his chest. "Great. Another challenge to endure."

∼

Frustrated, his patience worn down to a thin shell, Tor rode a chestnut stallion down the road back to Fralyn. He held the reins attached to the stallion's bridle comfortably in one hand, while the reins of the piebald mare trotting beside him remained tethered to his saddle. The last remnants of daylight lingered in the western sky, and the approaching night had begun masking his surroundings in gloom.

He turned at the split in the road – one direction would take him up a ramp that led to the dark interior of Fralyn Fortress, the other to the city where his companions waited. Upon the city walls, he spied a soldier lighting torches, and he slowed the two horses to a walk. Koji rode behind him, seated on a dark brown workhorse and trailed by a gray mare with a white streak down its chest.

As Tor approached the gate, he focused on the faces of the guards on duty, recognizing them from earlier that day. "Ho!" He pulled his horse to a stop just strides from the two men.

The guards stepped closer, one noting, "You're back."

Tor nearly snapped at them before biting his tongue. *Treating them poorly will do you no good.* It was one piece of the valuable wealth of wisdom he had gained over the years. After a calming breath, he said, "It took more time, more coin, and more convincing to purchase four horses than I'd expected."

The other guard said, "I'll say. You said you'd be back in an hour when the sun was still high overhead. it's now sunk somewhere below the horizon."

The afternoon had not proceeded as planned. Numerous farmers had turned down Tor's offer of gold before he found one who would sell a single horse. By then, it was mid-afternoon. Procuring three more consumed the rest of the day. He had been close to giving up hope and taking a barge upriver, but that would only delay the need for mounts until reaching Zialis.

Tor said, "I am well-traveled, but I have never visited a city where no horses were for sale. We had to travel ten miles outside the city and visit twenty-one farms to find four suitable steeds."

"Bad news – the Orenthian army came through last fall and procured every available horse."

"Why?"

"Who knows? Those haughty snobs from Tiamalyn don't tell us city guards anything. They just ride about with their chins high, refusing to even look us in the eye...like we were slugs rather than humans." The guard spat in disgust.

Tor leaned to the side and spat. "A pox on them all." Siding with the guards was likely to earn him their favor.

As he expected, the guards nodded while voicing their agreement.

Tor waited a beat and said, "If you've no other questions, we could use an ale or three."

"Our shift ends after Devotion, and we are off to the Bloody Knuckle Tavern ourselves."

Tor knew the tavern, and the name had been earned, which meant it was the type of place he wanted to avoid. Enough trouble would find them as it was. "You men have a good evening."

He and Koji rode at a walk, crossing the square inside the gate and following a street that ran parallel to the riverfront. Enchanted lanterns at each street corner illuminated the way. After passing three intersections and a few dozen people on foot, he turned down an alley and emerged in a gravel yard between a building and the city wall. A dark outbuilding stood against the city wall at the back of the yard. The building had walls on three sides, the side facing the yard open except for posts positioned every six feet. He and Koji dismounted and tied the horses to posts in the building, leaving the reins long enough for them to reach the hay and water troughs waiting in the shadows.

They then headed toward the back door of Ed's Stumble Inn. When Tor opened it, he was greeted by raucous laughter and chanting. He followed a short hallway that opened to a taproom thick with patrons. All were facing the bar, upon which Borgli stood, his hand gripping the shaft of a long, curved horn. Quell leaned over the railing of the loft above him, pouring a tankard of ale down the large end of the horn. The inn's patrons cheered as the dwarf downed the ale coming out the bottom. With the tankard empty, Quell grabbed another full mug and began pouring it into the horn. The crowd chanted and cheered as Borgli continued to drink.

Tor shot Koji an annoyed glance before pushing his way through the crowd. He knew some of the men might get upset, but when they spied Koji in his wake, they were unlikely to pick a fight. Upon reaching the stairs, Tor raced up and pushed past the patrons occupying the loft. He stopped a stride from where Quell stood with her back to him. He counted nine tankards on the table, all of them empty. Beside the mugs was a small glass filled with dark liquid. He picked up the glass and gave it a sniff. It smelled of anise. *Swoon*. He gripped Quell by her shoulder and turned her toward him. Her eyes widened in surprise.

"What are you doing?" he demanded.

"Borgli is trying to win a bet."

"A bet?'

"To down ten tankards of ale without stopping for a breath."

Tor closed his eyes for a beat before speaking. "You two were supposed to procure provisions and wait here without causing trouble."

"We did."

"This *is* trouble." He motioned to the cup of swoon. "What is this?"

"That is for me. I am not overly fond of ale."

"Well, Borgli is about to get a surprise." He poured the glass of hard alcohol down the horn, leaned over the railing, and waited.

The dwarf chugged and swallowed gulp after gulp, draining the horn until the swoon reached him. His eyes suddenly bulged, and he tore his mouth from the horn. He coughed, spluttered, and staggered a step, appearing as if he might fall off the bar. His fist thumped against his chest as the crowd quieted, all eyes on Borgli while he blinked with bleary, red eyes. When the dwarf's mouth opened, Tor feared he might vomit on the crowd below him. Instead, he let out a mighty belch, its timbre low enough to shake the room.

The crowd burst out in laughter. Numerous men exchanged coins they had won or lost on the bet. Borgli knelt on the bar and accepted a stack of coins from the barkeep.

Quell tapped Tor's shoulder, drawing his attention away from the scene below. "I was looking forward to that drink, but with the coin we just won, I can buy myself another."

"How much did you win?"

"We had ten silver pieces left after we bought the provisions you requested. Two were spent on these drinks and the food we consumed before this all started. The rest was placed on the bet, so we turned eight silver marks to sixteen."

Tor grunted. "That is exactly how many you started with."

"So, you aren't mad?"

"When I asked you to avoid trouble, I also meant to avoid attention. This little stunt is exactly the opposite of what I wanted. That said, a little extra coin won't hurt, especially now that we need to room here tonight."

"What took you so long anyway?"

He grimaced, his ire again rising.

Koji answered for him. "Finding horses proved to be more challenging than expected."

A voice arose from the din of the crowd, singing a song unfamiliar to Tor. The voice was low, gravelly, and while the singer likely attempted to carry a tune, he failed miserably. *Borgli.*

Tor sighed. "Let's go get him before he finds more trouble."

He eased between the people in the loft and descended to the main floor with Koji and Quell in his wake.

The crowd had disbursed and spread throughout the inn. In the center of the room, Borgli stood on a table with a mug in each hand. He swayed as he sang, spilling ale with each movement but appearing oblivious to the puddles forming on the table. He stumbled, stepped on a wet spot, and slipped as his foot shot out from beneath him. With a roar of surprise, the dwarf flopped on his back and dumped both full ales onto the patrons occupying the table behind him. He rolled sideways, fell off the table, and disappeared.

Eight rough-looking men, all with wet splotches on their faces and tunics, stood, their expressions like thunderclouds.

"By the gods," Tor swore. "Now, he did it." Over his shoulder, he said, "Come on, Koji. We've a mess to clean up."

Borgli staggered to his feet and looked up as one of the upset men stepped before him. He narrowed his eyes and stared up at the man. "You seem to have spilt on yerself, mister."

The man growled. "You snide little piece of crap."

His fist struck Borgli square in the face. The dwarf stumbled a step, shook his head, and grinned. "Let's play."

Releasing a roar, the dwarf ducked low, charged the man, and wrapped his arms around his legs. Although the man stood a foot and a half taller than Borgli and likely outweighed him by a hundred pounds, Borgli picked him off his feet and slammed the man down on a table. The table tipped over onto a startled couple. The woman screamed, the man roared, and a melee broke out.

A pair of men grabbed Borgli, one holding each arm. A third punched the dwarf in the face twice before Tor reached him.

Coming at the man from behind, Tor hooked the man's arm as he was winding up for another punch. Tor then rammed his hip into the man's back while bending forward. The man flipped over him and landed on his knees. Tor followed with a swift kick to the chin, snapping the man's head back and knocking him out.

Koji strode into the angry mob and threw a punch. His gauntlet-covered fist struck a man in the back, driving the wind from the man's lungs while launching him into his companion. The first man slid to the floor while the others backed away from the giant Kyranni.

Tor punched one of the men holding Borgli, knocking him backward. The dwarf shook his arm free and spun toward the other man holding him. Borgli grabbed a fist full of the man's beard and yanked his head down. A crack resounded when Borgli rammed his forehead into the man's face. The man staggered and fell when Borgli kicked the back of his knee.

Tor dispatched a third man with a punch to the gut before slamming his face against a table. The man slid to the floor. Tor spun around, ready for the next brawler. None came.

Koji stood over five men, three groaning as they held their heads, the other two unmoving. Borgli staggered and slowly turned while holding his fists out before him. The crowd stood in a broad circle around the downed men, some cheering, others watching with gaping eyes.

Quell strolled through a gap and stopped beside Tor while looking down at the unconscious man at his feet. "That was fun. I was afraid I'd have to jump in and save you guys, but you seem to have cleaned up fairly well."

A bright green light glimmered outside, drawing all eyes to the window.

"Devotion begins," someone said.

All the patrons headed out the door until only Tor, his companions, and the six unconscious men remained.

The barkeep leaned over the bar, his face drawn into a scowl. "I want the lot of you out of here."

Tor approached the bar. "Listen, Ed, we did not start that fight."

"The drunk one poured ale all over a table of men. If that didn't start it, what did?"

Without bothering to hide his sigh, Tor replied, "Listen, our stuff is already stored in our room upstairs, and we need a place to sleep. Let us stay here, and I'll give you an extra five silvers."

The man frowned for a beat as he considered the request. "Fine, but I want you upstairs, and I don't want to see the drunk one down here again until morning."

The sound of chanting came from outside as the people in the streets began offering their prayers to Horus, wizard lord of Orenth.

Tor dug out the silver pieces and dropped them into the man's hand. "We'll head upstairs right now."

"Good. Now, off with you. I need to partake in Devotion in case any guards step inside before it is over."

Tor reached out, grabbed Borgli by the beard, and pulled him toward the stairs.

"Ouch!" Borgli whined. "What are you doing?"

"I am putting you to bed before you cause any more trouble."

"Trouble? That was the most fun I've had in a decade."

Quell chuckled. "I'll admit, it was entertaining."

"Don't encourage him," Tor grumbled.

CHAPTER 16
HORSEMANSHIP

The inn's stable yard was dark, the sky to the east glowing with the first moments of daylight. Tor stood beside the gray mare, the most docile steed among the four he had purchased the previous day. Koji and Quell each already occupied a saddle, Koji on the enormous workhorse and Quell on the piebald mare. Both watched as Tor gave Borgli riding instructions.

"To mount your horse, you grip the saddle horn like this." Tor demonstrated the action. "Put your foot in the stirrup and push off the ground. Once you are up high enough, swing your leg over and slide into a sitting position." He sat in the saddle and noticed Borgli scowling. "What's wrong?"

The bleary-eyed dwarf said, "You are treating me like I am a child."

"You said you've never ridden a horse before. I am trying to give you some instruction."

"In a condescending manner."

Tor pressed his lips together. "You are just grumpy because you are hung over."

"I am not. We dwarves are a hardy folk and can handle our alcohol."

With a calming breath, Tor continued. "Once you are in the saddle, you grip the reins in one hand. They are used to turn and to stop your horse."

"What can I use to stop your mouth?" the dwarf grumbled.

Quell snickered, and Tor shot her a flat look that caused her to cover her mouth.

Anger stirred in Tor's stomach. Unable to hold back any longer, he snapped. "Listen, you insolent runt. I am trying to help you." He took another deep breath and continued his instruction. "When you ride, you want to relax and shift your weight with the rhythm of the horse. Don't fight it, or you will be in for a bumpy ride."

"I'll bump your arse right off that thing if you call me a runt again."

Again, Quell laughed, and this time Koji chuckled along with her.

Tor threw his hands in the air. "That's it. I am done." He slid off the horse and walked up to his own mount. Once in the saddle, he said. "If you think you can ride, do it. I want to be away from Fralyn the moment the city gates open, which occurs at sunrise."

"Fine." Borgli grumbled.

The dwarf walked up to the horse and eyed it with a grimace. After a moment, he reached up, grabbed ahold of the saddle, and put a foot in the stirrup. He jumped up and tried to swing his leg over. It didn't make it. Instead, he kicked the horse in the flank, startling it and causing it to shift nervously. Borgli's hands slipped, and he fell backward, landing hard on his backside.

Quell laughed heartily.

Tor smiled in satisfaction. "My, Borgli. Your horsemanship skills certainly leave an impression."

The dwarf made a fist. "Shut it, Tor, or I'll shut it for you."

Rather than poke the bear again, Tor fell silent, watching as Borgli climbed to his feet and approached the horse. Again, he gripped the saddle and stepped into the stirrup. With a jump, he pulled himself up and atop the saddle, only he was now on his stomach. The dwarf kicked and squirmed before he was able to turn and pull a leg over. When Quell burst out laughing, Tor found it impossible not to join her, but Koji's bellowing laughter drowned them both out.

Borgli stared down at the horse. "Something is wrong."

Quell said, "You are supposed to be facing the horse's head, not its arse."

The sight of Borgli sitting backward in the saddle was one to remember, and one that was further fueled by the bitter scowl on the dwarf's face.

∽

THE FIRST RAYS of the sun shone between two peaks to the distant east, far beyond the walls of Fralyn. A bell rang, and the portcullis began to rise. The moment it was high enough, Tor urged his horse into a trot and rode through the city gate with Koji at his side. Just behind them, Borgli rode beside Quell, whose smirk remained on her face as she watched him struggle. The dwarf bounced uncomfortably and gripped the saddle horn as tightly as he had the ship's rail when they pulled into port.

The road ran parallel to the river, drawing them closer to the dark towering fortress that spanned from the Orenthian riverbank to the Balmorian riverbank. At the split in the road, one route meandered uphill as it headed deeper into the Orenthian countryside. Tor turned his horse toward the river, where it climbed a stone ramp leading toward the dark maw of a tunnel. Manning the ramparts above the tunnel were archers in yellow tabards.

A quartet of guards stood just inside the open portcullis. Each wore a pale gray and yellow tabard over chainmail. A black emblem in the shape of a bee marked the left side of their chests.

Tor stopped his horse, and Koji and Quell followed his lead. Borgli, still gripping the saddle horn, rode past the guards.

"Stop!" a soldier shouted.

Over his shoulder, Borgli howled. "I don't know how."

"Stop or you will be arrested!"

Tor sought to stave off an issue. "I will pay for his crossing."

The guard watched Borgli with a furrowed brow. "He has no imports to declare?"

"No. None of us do. We are simple travelers who seek to cross into Balmoria."

The man turned toward Tor. His eyes scanned the three of them before settling on the weapon on Tor's back. "What sort of weapon is that?"

"It is a ranseur."

The guard rubbed his jaw. "I've heard that name before somewhere."

Tor just wanted to keep moving, so he dug out his coin purse rather than give the man a reason for a longer discussion. He also did not want the guard to realize who he was until the crossing was ensured. "How much do we owe you?"

"One silver per horse."

Extending a hand toward the guard, Tor dropped the coins into the other man's hand. "I can see why Balmoria thrives. It is at the expense of everyone else."

The man eyed the coins before stepping back. "Holding this fortress has its benefits."

"Give my regards to High Wizard Greehl."

The guard frowned. "You know him?"

"We have some history."

"What is your name?"

Tor nudged his horse into a trot and spoke over his shoulder. "Tor

Ranseur." The shocked expressions on the guards' faces were the last thing he saw before turning forward.

Down the dark confines of the tunnel, they rode. Wide enough for two wagons to pass each other, the tunnel's brick walls curved at the top until they met one another to create an arch. Narrow openings lined the sides of the tunnel, and although it was too dark to see what waited on the other side of the wall, Tor knew the design was to allow archers and spear bearers to hide on the other side and attack enemies trying to pass through. In the apex of the arched ceiling were sporadic trapdoors, murder holes to attack those trapped in the tunnel's confines.

In the distance, daylight at the other end of the tunnel called to Tor, begging him to kick his horse into a gallop and race toward safety. He resisted the urge and focused on the bouncing silhouette in front of him.

Soon, Tor drew even with Borgli and gave him a sidelong smirk. "Since you are such an expert rider, I suspect you will want to go faster once we reach the other side."

"Faster?" Borgli groaned. "My brain is rattled, and my arse is sore."

As they neared the end of the tunnel, the surroundings grew brighter, allowing Tor to get a better look at Borgli. *He looks miserable.* Suddenly, Tor felt sorry for him.

"That is because you are riding horribly," he said.

The dwarf's chin dropped to his chest, his groan turning to a whine. "I know."

They rode beneath the second portcullis, exited the tunnel, and descended the ramp to the Balmorian side of the river. Tor reached out, snatched the reins from Borgli's grip, and pulled both horses to a stop.

"What's wrong?" Borgli asked.

Koji and Quell rode down the ramp and stopped just past Tor and Borgli.

"Listen to me." Tor looked Borgli in the eyes. "We have ridden one mile, and you are already miserable. It is only going to get worse, and we have a hundred miles to go."

The color drained from Borgli's face. "A hundred miles?"

"Will you try to follow my instructions? If you don't, your arse is going to hurt so badly, you won't be able to sit for a week."

Borgli nodded. "Yes. I will do anything you say."

Tor climbed down and turned to Koji. "You two might as well dismount and take your horses down to the water for a drink. We are going to be here for a while."

~

Carrying an armload of wood, Tor ducked beneath low branches and entered the clearing where they had decided to make camp. Koji was kneeling near a ring of blackened rocks, snapping branches over his knee and then stacking them in the fire pit.

Tor dumped his load beside Koji. "Where is Quell?"

Koji shrugged. "She said she needed to stretch her legs."

"While I don't blame her, night is fast approaching, and I don't want to have to hunt her down in the dark."

"She grew up in the forest, remember?"

"True." Tor recalled her father being a ranger. "Hopefully, her training is more than a youthful boast."

"Where is Borgli?" Gripping a loose corner, Koji peeled pale bark from a branch and tossed it into the fire pit.

Lowering four full waterskins off his shoulder, Tor sat on a fallen log. "After we refilled the skins, he opted to remain at the river."

"What for?" Koji dug his flint and striker from the pack beside him.

"Although his riding improved as the day advanced, his arse is sore. He hopes the cold water will numb it."

"He is bathing in the river and isn't worried?"

"Yes. The river is particularly wide here, so the current is gentle in this area and the depth near shore is only a few feet."

"But the water is snowmelt." With rapid downward strokes, Koji raked the striker across the flint.

"Oh, it is bitter cold for sure."

"It'll numb more than his arse."

A grin stretched across Tor's face. "And will likely shrink some of his parts."

Koji chuckled as a spark shot off the flint. He leaned in and blew on the spark, igniting the bark. Carefully gripping the burning bark by an unaffected corner, he positioned it beneath the pyramid of broken branches. The flames licked the wood, and the fire began to spread. Satisfied, Koji rose to his feet, dusted his hands off, and sat on a log across the fire from Tor.

The duo stared into the fire while the crackling of flames and popping of burning wood rose above the steady rush of the nearby river. All the while, the sky darkened as night chased dusk westward.

Curious, Tor broke the silence. "What do you think of this?"

"Think of what?"

"Traveling with Borgli and Quell."

The towering warrior furrowed his brow while running a hand over his bald pate. "This is our second journey with Borgli, and while his aversion for ships and his lack of experience with horses are inconveniences, I like him. It feels like..."

"Like it did before Navarre died?"

"Yeah. Sort of, but...yeah."

"And what of Quell?"

"She was prepared to challenge you at every turn at first, but that seems to have calmed."

"For which I am thankful."

"And her bow could be useful. There were many times Navarre's archery skills saved our arses."

"But we have yet to see if her skill approaches his."

"I doubt she is carrying that bow around just to impress others."

"True, but there are archers…and then, there are marksmen."

"Or markswomen?"

Tor frowned. "I don't think that is a word."

"Well, as you know, female Kyranni warriors are just as fearsome as males."

"I am well aware that Balmoria and Kyranni embrace women who can fight, and while I hail from the southern wizardoms where such ideas are uncommon, those prejudices were pounded out of me long ago."

A woman's voice came from behind Tor. "That is a relief."

He turned as Quell entered the firelight. Her bow rested in one hand. A pair of grouse dangled upside down from the other. She tossed the birds, which landed between Tor and Koji, just inches from the fire. "While you two were jabbering, I caught us something better to eat than jerky."

Koji turned and began digging through his pack. "Yes. Much better. I packed a seasoning that will cause your mouth to water. It is perfect for wild foul."

"Are you the cook?"

"I found out long ago that when you eat as much as I do, it is best if you also know how to cook." He pulled the leather pouch from his pack, along with a small pan. "Does anyone object to beans with the bird meat?"

Quell sat beside Tor and rested her bow against the log. "Do I have a choice?"

Tor replied, "You could choose to not eat the beans. Other than dry bread and jerky, we have no other food to choose from."

"Beans it is." She smirked. "I'll just be sure to sleep far from Borgli. Even without that type of fuel, he can burn the hair right out of your nostrils."

"That's the truth."

She frowned. "Speaking of which, where is the hairy dwarf?"

"Right here," said a gravelly voice coming from behind Koji.

Borgli stepped out of the trees and entered the clearing. He carried his clothing and armor in his arms, masking much of his upper body, but it was clear that he was stark naked. He circled the logs and approached the fire before dropping his belongings and holding his hands toward the flames.

Between blue lips, he said, "That water is freezing cold."

Smirking, Quell said, "I noticed."

The dwarf followed her gaze and looked down. "Oh. Yeah. I should probably get dressed."

Tor chuckled. "While you've enough hair that someone might think you an ape, I think clothing is a good idea."

Borgli squatted, found his breeches, and began to apply that good idea.

〜

His stomach sated, Tor took a swig of water and stared up at the stars. "That was a mighty fine meal for a night on the trail. Thank you, Quell, for snaring the birds."

"Don't thank me. Thank that oversized brute for his skill at cooking."

"Oh, I am used to Koji finding a way to turn boring food into something interesting. He isn't as skilled as Goren, but he is not half bad."

Borgli rubbed his stomach, now covered by his brown tunic. "Aye, it was a fine meal, only lacking ale to make it better."

Tor arched a brow. "Didn't you have enough last night?"

"Yes, but last night is not tonight. I am ready for another go."

The comment caused Tor to shake his head. "I am afraid you are going to cost me more than you are worth."

"Just wait until you see me in battle." Borgli lifted his hammer off the ground and caressed it. "Tremor and I will lay waste to our enemies. You'll then see my worth is tenfold of my consumption."

"Well, if that is true in addition to your rock-shaping skills, I will learn to adapt…provided you can learn to properly ride a horse."

The comment caused Borgli to frown. "I thought I did well today."

"You certainly did far better after we crossed the river…and after you accepted Tor's help," Koji said

"Speaking of the crossing," Quell commented, "that fortress is unlike anything I have ever seen."

Tor nodded. "It is one of a kind, to be sure."

"When we spoke to the guards before crossing, you told them to give your regards to High Wizard Greehl."

"I did."

Koji grinned. "I'm sure it'll irritate Greehl once he learned we rode through the fortress, right beneath his nose."

Quell's brow furrowed. "Does Greehl miss you so much?"

Tor snorted. "If Greehl had his way, Koji and I would be strung up and tortured right now."

"Oh, now I sense a story I must hear."

After brief consideration, Tor nodded. "Our contentious relationship with Greehl began four years ago. Back then, Koji and I had another partner named Navarre. He was a skilled archer and a good friend."

"What happened to him?"

"Our profession is dangerous and comes with a cost. While it should have been my debt to pay, Navarre paid for it. I…" The memory was still too painful. "That is a story for another time." He took a deep breath and continued. "During one of our adventures, we came across the original plans for Fralyn Fortress. Driven by a powerful interest in such things, I studied these plans for days before I came across a notation about a secret chamber. What was hidden in the chamber was not discussed, but I was curious as to whether this chamber had ever been discovered and what, if anything, might have been found inside.

"So, we journeyed to Fralyn Fortress and requested an audience with Greehl – the high wizard of the fortress. Rather than invite us inside, he and his guards met us in the tunnel. I explained the situation and my desire to explore the citadel, but he laughed in my face. While this was before my fame began to spread, I still considered the response rude. We were turned away and told never to bother the high wizard again.

"Greehl did not know who he was dealing with, for once my mind is set on something, I find it impossible to let it go. Thus, Koji, Navarre, and I gathered in a private room at the very same inn we departed from this morning. There, we devised a plan to sneak into the most daunting stronghold in the Eight Wizardoms."

CHAPTER 17
FOUR YEARS AGO

Beneath the cover of darkness, Tor stood at the Serpent River's edge. Hours had passed since nightfall, the night particularly dark with the moon masked by a cloud-covered sky. He stared toward Fralyn Fortress, a half-mile downriver, the amber glow of torches visible on the ramparts. Although guards were posted at all hours, at the midpoint between dusk and dawn, most soldiers manning the stronghold slept while those on duty struggled against the grogginess that dominated such hours.

"It is time." Tor turned toward the shadows of his two companions, both taller than him, one the size of a giant, the other lean and lithe. "Let's slide the boat into the water. Koji, you are at the oars. Navarre, you come in last and take the forward position."

"Right," Navarre moved to stand before the bow of the rowboat.

Koji gripped one rail and Tor the other as together they pulled the boat toward the water sliding it backward down the riverbank. When the stern began to float, Tor climbed in, followed by Koji. Navarre grunted, pushed the boat from shore, and jumped in, rocking it until he settled. After placing the oar pins in place, Koji began to row with long, easy strokes.

The rowboat moved toward the opposing riverbank while the current pushed it downstream. When they reached the middle of the river, Tor signaled and Koji turned the craft, so the bow was aimed toward the fortress. The watercraft drew closer to the quiet citadel, allowing Tor a view of the arched openings beneath it. He counted the thick supports between each arch and stopped at number eight – the center support.

He pointed, giving Koji a silent command. The brawny man rowed in response, altering the vessel's path. When Tor made another motion, Koji ceased rowing. The current carried the boat downriver, the night still other than the rush of flowing water.

The rowboat drew within two hundred feet of the fortress. In the bow, Navarre held his longbow ready as he scanned the ramparts high above him. At a hundred feet, no soldier had reacted. No calls had been issued. When the boat had moved within a dozen strides of the structure, Navarre shouldered his bow and stored his arrow back in the quiver on his back.

The boat, still caught in the current, drove directly toward a fifty-foot-wide support. Moments before it crashed into the brick wall, Tor waved urgently. Koji lowered the oars and rowed backward with one long and powerful stroke, slowing the craft to half its speed. Just before the bow struck, Navarre leaned out, placed his palms against the brick support, and braced himself, straining to slow the boat until the bow struck the brick with a soft tap.

Koji stored his oars and Tor dug out the rear fender as the current turned the craft. Before the side of the boat could strike the support, Tor had the fender over the side to absorb the impact. In the bow, Navarre flipped another fender over the rail and wedged it between the support and the hull. Pinned there by the current, they moved on to the next step in their plan.

While Tor and Navarre undressed, Koji used one oar to hold the boat in place. Water flowed past them, routing to either side of the support and leaving a calm pool where the boat rested.

As soon as he was down to his breeches and boots, Tor pulled his light rod from his pack and held it in one hand. "Ready?" he whispered.

Navarre, his lean form also naked from the waist up, nodded. Tor grabbed the coiled rope from the bottom of the boat and grunted as he lifted the anchor dangling from it. He then sat on the rail, took a deep breath, and tipped backward into the water.

As the anchor pulled him down, Tor looped his arm around the rope and used his free hand to twist the brass end of the light rod. A pale blue aura bloomed, illuminating his immediate surroundings. Kicking to drive himself downward faster while the anchor continued its descent, he swam and held the light toward the brick wall. Fifteen feet down, he spied a dark opening. A splash stirred the river's surface as Navarre followed him.

Just before Tor drew even with the opening, he released his grip on the rope and used his arms to swim toward it. The current caught him and shot him forward into a tunnel two feet wide and three feet tall. Dark water-stained brick swept past him, and he suddenly realized if the outlet was too small for him to fit through, he could be trapped; the current was too powerful to swim against.

The narrow surroundings fell away. The water around him widened as the current slowed. His lungs begged for air, demanding he swim toward the surface, but he pushed such demands aside and held his light toward the opening. Moments later, Navarre emerged from the black maw, his cheeks puffed as he swam toward Tor. Both men kicked and stroked, struggling to surface while their lungs screamed for relief.

Tor's head burst from the water with a deep gasp. The surface was calm, his surroundings pitch black. While still panting to reclaim his wind, he raised the hand holding the light rod. The enchanted object painted the area with soft light.

The pool occupied the bulk of a dank rectangular chamber with a high ceiling. The walls were slick with moisture, and black mold coated many of the stone blocks. Two pairs of shackles hung from chains over pulleys mounted to the high ceiling, the chains gently swaying ten feet above Tor's head. A dark doorway waited to one side of the room. There was nobody in sight.

Tor swam to the side of the pool, reached up to the stone block pool deck, and pulled himself onto it. He crawled on his hands and knees, water dripping off him to pool on the floor, and slowly caught his breath. Beside him, Navarre staggered to his feet, and Tor followed suit.

"What is this place?" Navarre asked between panting breaths.

"Judging by the shackles, pulleys, and chains, I'd say it's an interrogation room."

"By threatening captives with drowning?"

"Yeah. They likely weigh them down and dunk them below the water until they either talk or die."

"And they call darkspawn monsters."

"Humans are no angels, but at least we don't eat each other."

"There is that."

"Come along." Tor held the light rod up and headed toward the doorway.

An ascending stairwell waited just outside the chamber. He flicked a finger toward Navarre's knife before he detached the bola from his own belt. Tor led the way up a dark stairwell, rising two full stories, holding his bola in his hand; Navarre also had his knife ready. A short corridor at the top brought them to a closed door. Tor put his ear to the door and listened. Voices came from the other side.

"I hear two men talking," Tor whispered.

Navarre moved beside the door and held his knife up. "Ready when you are."

Tor turned the knob, eased the door open, and spied a pair of guards standing a few strides away, one facing his direction, the other with his back to the door. Both wore yellow and gray tabards over chainmail. Their helmets lacked the wings of an officer. Tor yanked the door completely open, spun his bola, and sent the cord flinging toward the guard facing him. The guard's eyes grew wide, and his mouth opened to call for alarm, but the bola struck him before a sound emerged. The cord caught the man across the mouth, and the weighted disks at the ends of the bola whipped around his helmet. The moment the first disk touched the man's cheek, he collapsed with a clatter.

The other guard spun around but Navarre was there to cover the man's mouth with one hand while the other hand drove his dagger deep into the man's armpit. The guard stiffened, stumbled, and fell to the floor. With the two men dispatched, Tor looked around to ensure they were alone.

They stood in a dark corridor stretching in both directions, running parallel to the bridge tunnel. The same narrow openings Tor had seen while riding through the tunnel were visible on the nearest wall while shelves filled with arrows, spears, and other weapons lined the opposite wall. A ladder beside the shelves led to a circular opening in the ceiling. Nobody else was in sight.

"You are wearing that one's uniform," Tor said, pointing toward the dying guard.

"But it's going to be full of blood."

"You should have thought of that before you stuck a knife in his ribs."

"What would you have me do?"

"Something less bloody."

Navarre grimaced. "Thanks."

Tor squatted beside the man held in the stasis spell. "Sorry about this, but I can't have you calling for help when the spell wears off." He lifted the man's head, pulled his helmet off, and slammed his skull against the floor a resounding crack.

The man's eyes closed, but his body continued to shake until Tor unwound the bola from his face.

"Let's pull them back through the doorway before we strip them down."

"Then what?"

"Then, we find the hidden chamber."

CHAPTER 18
STILL FOUR YEARS AGO

Dressed as Balmorian soldiers, Tor and Navarre climbed a long stairwell, their chainmail clinking with each step. Tor gripped a spear while Navarre had elected to carry a sword, but the weapons were intended to help them blend in more than anything else.

The staircase brought them past numerous landings and closed doors before they reached the top. Tor opened the door and stepped into a corridor that was dimly lit by a torch on the wall. He followed the corridor while recalling the construction plans he had spent so many hours studying.

A temple dedicated to Bal was located on the sixth floor, where they now stood. The temple was situated over the center of the river. Somewhere within it was a hidden passage to a secret chamber...at least, according to the notes on the drawing.

Tor passed two doors before coming to an alcove with double doors made of dark stained wood. The top of the alcove formed an arch ten feet up. "This must be it." He pushed a door open and stopped to survey his surroundings.

Stars in the night sky were visible through windows in the ceiling three stories above him. Ornate columns lined the chamber's interior, casting shadows in all directions. A brazier burned at the far end of the chamber, giving light to a towering statue of a perfect, muscular male figure that stood with his arms extended. Bees the size of watermelons surrounded the man's shoulders and arms. And while the statue was crafted with incredible detail, the face and groin were both featureless.

On each side of the room was a fountain with a sculpture depicting a string of bees in flight. Water poured from those statues and into small pools at their bases, the sound of running water filling the otherwise empty chamber.

"This is it. Close the door." Tor approached the statue on the dais, staring up at it.

The door clicked behind him, and Navarre's heels marked him crossing the floor until he stopped at Tor's side. "This is Bal?"

"It would appear so."

"I've been to temples in four wizardoms. Each god is unique, but I notice that none have faces."

Tor had noticed the same thing. "Or genitals."

"If I had to go without one or the other, it might be a difficult decision."

"Not a choice I'd like to make."

Navarre shrugged. "Well, you are not a god, so I don't expect you will have to make it anytime soon."

"I've other problems to deal with, such as where we find the hidden chamber. According to the plans"—or at least according to how Tor interpreted them— "the chamber should be directly below the dais."

Tor squatted before the three stairs rising to the dais, so his eyes were level with the tiled floor of the platform. With narrowed eyes, he examined the surface, searching for any oddities. The dais itself was eight strides across and just as deep. A stone altar stood at the front and the statue of Bal loomed at the back, the towering figure secured to the wall right behind it.

Seeing nothing of note, Tor stood and climbed the dais. He circled behind the altar, scrutinizing every detail. It was made of black marble with golden striations, the polished surface providing a dim reflection of his own visage.

He patted the altar. "Help me move this."

Navarre ascended to join him, his expression doubtful. "I think you have me confused with Koji. This thing must weigh two thousand pounds."

"I was thinking three, and while I'd love to have Koji's muscle with us right now, he is too big to blend in, and he would have hated that swim we had to take earlier."

Chuckling Navarre positioned himself beside Tor. "This is true."

With his hands against the end of the altar, Tor said, "On three, we push. One. Two. Three."

The two men shoved, putting their weight into the effort. The altar did not budge, and their feet slid backward along the smooth tile.

"Again."

The second and third tries yielded the same result.

Panting from the brief exertion, Tor backed away. "That is not going to work."

"It is a heavy piece of marble. It we could break it into sections, we could move it without much trouble."

Tor grinned. "What a wonderful idea."

"You intend to destroy the altar?"

"Yes."

"But you would need a sledgehammer, and all we have is a spear, a sword, and a couple of knives."

"You need to think bigger." Tor turned toward the twenty-foot-tall sculpture. "We are going to use that."

"What? Do you know how much noise that will make?"

"Go and bar the doors. That will buy us time."

Navarre seemed doubtful. "I hope you know what you are doing."

"So do I."

While Navarre tended to his task, Tor circled to the side of the statue to peer up at the narrow gap between it and the wall. Fifteen feet up, an iron bar anchored the statue to the wall, two feet away. An idea took shape. He dug out his bola and held it by one of the disks. He wasn't worried about contacting it since his ring disabled the enchantment's effect. With the bola dangling from his fist, he eyed the iron bar. A quick upward swing and a leap with his arm extended above him sent the far end of the bola cord whipping around until it snapped against the iron bar. The weighted disk wrapped around twice and struck the bar with a clang. Tor landed and stumbled backward before he caught himself. The dangling end of the bola swung back and forth like a pendulum, each stroke decreasing as its momentum was spent.

Navarre climbed the dais. "The door is barred. They'll need a battering ram to get inside."

"Good." He motioned toward the bola. "I need you to boost me up."

"Again, it would be nice to have Koji here."

"Just do it and stop your bellyaching."

Sighing, Navarre turned his back to the gap between the statue and the wall and squatted with his hands cupped together. Tor placed one foot in the man's clasped hands and held onto his head.

"Again, on three," Tor said. "One. Two. Three."

Tor pushed off the floor with his other leg, jumping to lighten his weight while Navarre stood, staggered, and finally stilled. With one palm against the wall and the other against the rear of the statue, Tor balanced on one foot and reached up, but was still a foot too low.

He pressed one boot against the back of the statue's leg. "Push me higher."

As Navarre pushed up on his foot, Tor stretched for the bola. His fingers wrapped around the cord, just above the disk, and he snatched it in his grip. He grabbed hold with his other hand and climbed, hand over hand, until he reached the bar. Holding tight, he pulled himself up while kicking and squirming until his upper body lay over the bar. With the statue and the wall to support him, he climbed on the bar and turned so both boots were planted against the statue's upper back while Tor's own backside was pinned to the wall.

"Here goes," Tor said before taking a deep breath.

Releasing a deep grunt, he pushed with all his strength. The bolts securing the bar to the wall loosened, causing dust to rain down. Again, Tor strained to extend his legs, and the bolts loosened further. On the third attempt, the bolts suddenly broke free, and the statue rocked forward. The weight then rocked back, driving Tor's knees against his shoulders. When it rocked forward, he pushed again, his teeth clenched. His straining groan became a rising roar. The statue tipped forward, the gap widening too much. Tor slipped and desperately reached for the bar sticking from the statue's back. He caught it and slammed against the statue as it slowly tipped forward.

The towering sculpture crashed down and struck the altar with a might boom, the impact tossing Tor free. He spun and landed on the dais, striking his rear, shoulder, and head before rolling to a stop. The room quieted until all he heard was his own groaning.

When Tor's vision cleared, he found Navarre kneeling at his side. "Are you alright?"

He sat up with a groan and pulled the helmet off his head. "My ears are ringing, but I am well."

"While I was never fond of helmets, better to have your ears ringing than your brains leaking out."

Tor chuckled. "True." He climbed to his feet and turned to survey the damage.

Pieces of the statue's shattered arms lay strewn across the dais while the statue's body was broken into three parts – head, torso, and legs. The head had ended up halfway across the room, but the torso leaned at an angle against what remained of the altar, its marble split apart with large sections shattered. The impact had shifted the altar so a third of it now extended over the top step. An opening in the floor beneath the altar revealed a steep staircase descending into darkness.

The rush of excitement caused Tor to scramble over to the altar, pausing briefly to retrieve his bola from the rod sticking out of the statue's back. The newly exposed opening was still too narrow for him to fit, so he pushed against the broken section. It shifted slightly.

He looked over at Navarre. "Don't just stand there. Give me a hand."

Both men pushed, and the altar section shifted a few inches. With the next push, the section toppled down the stairs, creating another ruckus and a boom that ended in a cloud of dust.

Navarre wiped his hands clean on his tabard. "What do you think is down there?"

"We are about to find out." Tor dug out his light rod, twisted the end, and it bloomed to life.

Shouts came from the corridor outside the temple. The doors rattled, but the bar held.

"Let's hurry before they find a way in." Tor climbed down into the opening, squatting low to get past the altar remains.

The stairwell led them to a small chamber under the dais, its walls no farther than five strides apart in either direction. In the center of the room, the sculpture of an arm extended from the floor. The hand was partially open as if reaching for the heavens. A jeweled object adorned the hand, consisting of a golden bracelet connected to a ruby ring with chains of gold.

"Is that it?" Navarre exclaimed. "After all we went through to get here, all we find is a Hassakani hand chain?"

Tor's brow furrowed. "Perhaps there is more to it than we suspect. After all, I thought Claw was a simple weapon when we discovered it. The same goes for Koji's gauntlet."

"That is true."

Tor approached the arm and slowly strolled around it, eyeing the area in search of anything nefarious. When he completed the loop, a boom came from above.

"Oh, no." Navarre peered up through the opening above him. "It sounds like they found a battering ram already."

"In that case, it is time to throw caution aside." Tor squatted and unclasped the bracelet, then carefully lifted it and the ring from the stone hand. Nothing happened.

"What if it had been a trap?"

"We've no time for traps, so I took a chance. Come on." He hurried up the stairs.

Another boom shook the room, the doors rattling from its fury, but the bar held.

Once they were back in the upper chamber, Tor pointed toward the window above the fountain. "Let's break it and get out of here."

Navarre hefted a chunk of broken stone, ran toward the fountain, and launched the chunk with a mighty heave. It smashed through the glass in a spray of shards. Tor hopped onto the edge of the pool, climbed the sculpture of the bees, and used his light rod to break off the remaining shards along the bottom of the window. He then climbed on the sill and peered down. A rampart waited a story below.

A boom came from across the room. The wooden beam barring the door split with a crack, and the doors swung open. A dozen armed guards stood just outside the room. "Get them!" one cried.

Tor stuffed both the light rod and the hand chain down the neck of his tunic, climbed over the sill, and gripped it before dropping down. His body swung around and struck the outer wall. There, he dangled by his outstretched arms for a beat before letting go.

His feet struck the stone ramparts, and he fell backward with the momentum. Quickly, he rolled aside and looked in both directions. Torches lit the area, but he saw no soldiers. Navarre landed beside him and rolled into a standing position. They both scrambled across the roof, heading toward the low wall bounding it. A Balmorian archer appeared at the broken window and took aim.

Tor watched the archer, waiting until the man's arrow stopped shifting before he dove aside. The arrow struck the low wall where he had been standing. A hundred feet away, a door opened, and soldiers poured out onto the roof.

"What now?" Navarre cried.

"Remove the chainmail. We are going for a swim." Tor yanked his tabard over his head.

"We are a hundred feet above the river."

Tor pulled the chainmail up. "I know."

By the time he had tossed the chainmail aside and reclaimed his light rod and the hand chain, the charging soldiers had covered half the distance. Tor climbed on the wall and hesitated for a beat. He stared down at the torchlit ramparts three stories below him. The dark river waited somewhere beyond those torches. He glanced toward the soldiers, now just strides away, and then he leapt out as far as he could.

The fortress walls sped past, and he cleared the lower ramparts by only a few feet before plummeting into darkness. He splashed into the water feet-first, keeping his arms pressed tight against his chest. His body shot down deep into the frigid river before it slowed. Tor then kicked and stroked toward the sky until he broke the surface with a gasp.

"Tor?"

He turned to find Koji in the boat no more than twenty feet away, but the current dragged at him. Navarre surfaced between them.

"Cut the anchor line!" Tor shouted as the current pulled him beneath the fortress.

He bobbed along the surface and stroked against the current to try and slow himself. The silhouette of a boat was suddenly coming toward him. Koji reached out, his bare hand catching Tor by the wrist. The big man hauled him out of the water until he was able to crawl over the edge and tumble into the hull. Moments later, Navarre fell against his side, both panting from the exertion and the chill of the water.

Koji reclaimed the oars and began to row with long, steady strokes. The boat emerged from beneath the fortress and angled toward shore. They passed a large warship moored along the battlements in the middle of the river. Then, the fortress and battlements were behind them. The shouts and cries of alarm echoed from the torchlit fortress as it receded into darkness.

~

THE WOOD HAD BURNED to embers by the time Tor finished his tale.

"What of the hand chain?" Borgli asked.

"As always, I brought it to Vanda." The old man was skilled at discerning the magical nature of artifacts, an ability Tor appreciated but found bewildering.

Quell rolled her eyes. "He meant to ask, 'Was it anything special?'"

"Oh. Yes. As I understand it, the hand chain holds a unique enchantment that bolsters the magic of the wizard who wears it."

She whistled. "I bet wizards would pay handsomely for something of that nature."

"Or kill anyone to get their hands on it," Koji added.

"What became of the artifact?" the dwarf asked.

"Two years later, a tall Hassakani wizard visited Vanda's manor. To my surprise, he gave the man the hand chain and told him to use it wisely until it was time to gift it to another." Tor recalled the visit as if it had occurred just days ago, for it was one of the strangest encounters he had experienced, which was saying something.

"What was this man's name?"

"The wizard went by the name Chandan."

When Chandan had departed, rather than saying goodbye, he had turned to Tor and said, "Until we meet again." Those words had stuck with Tor as both ominous and prophetic. He wondered when he would cross paths with Chandan again.

CHAPTER 19
ZIALIS

Taquell Tarpon sat with ease in the saddle while maintaining a stoic expression, hoping to hide her rising anxiety. The closer they drew to Zialis, the more real her gambit became. Eventually, Tor and the others would realize the truth of the situation. She only hoped that Tor would be deeply invested by then, and it would be too late for him to abandon their quest.

Varying shades of gray clouded the sky, masking the sun from view and leaving the forest road as dark as dusk. The threat of rain had increased as the day advanced. Quell, who despised riding in the rain, had begged Tor to push his crew in the hope of reaching Zialis before the threat was realized. A constant rotation of trotting, walking, and short gallops had allowed them to cover more miles than on a typical day. With few breaks, each too brief for anyone's liking, the journey was taking its toll on horses and riders alike.

The road followed the curving Serpent River, as it had since they crossed into Balmoria. The farther inland they rode, the more their surroundings changed – hills to mountains, warm coastal weather to cool mountain air, green leaves giving way to the yellows and reds of autumn. For the first two days, their heading was mostly eastward. Then, midmorning of their third day out of Fralyn, the river and the road turned north, informing Quell that they were nearing their destination. She just hoped to reach Zialis before the inevitable rain fell.

Riding at a trot, they rounded a bend, and a wall came into view. It stood three stories tall with spiked posts along the top. The wall began twenty feet into the river and ran across the land toward a mountain to the northwest. The road turned just shy of the wall, running parallel alongside it. Farms occupied fields amid trees on the western side of the road, opposite from the wall. They climbed a rise and caught their first glimpse of Zialis.

"There it is." A confusing concoction of relief and dread roiled in Quell's stomach.

With a wall of its own, a rarity for inland settlements other than capital cities, Zialis was built at the foot of a mountain with hillsides covered by green trees amid gray rock that matched the stones in the city walls. The settlement appeared more fortress than city, and for good reason.

Quell caught up to Tor and rode even with him while pointing northwest. "My father's cabin is on the western face of that mountain, an hour walk from the city."

Tor narrowed his eyes, staring in the direction she pointed. "Why not build it on the eastern face? Wouldn't that give you better weather conditions?"

Since most weather in the region originated in the seas before sweeping inland, Quell understood why Tor would ask why the cabin hadn't been built on the leeward side. The answer was obvious for anyone who lived in the region.

She gave a simple explanation, allowing him to deduce the rest. "It would, but the eastern face is outside the wall."

He frowned in consideration. "The wall runs from the river to the mountain face, dividing the Wilds from the rest of Balmoria. The city and everything on this side are protected."

Quell smirked. "You aren't as dumb as you look."

He snorted. "Thanks for that."

"Even with our cabin miles west of the wall, we still have darkspawn attacks on occasion. The last one came just before my father left." Images and sounds of the night flashed through Quell's mind. It had been a frantic and frightening skirmish that lasted for only a few minutes but felt like ten times as long.

"Goblins?" Tor asked.

"Yes. Perhaps a dozen of them."

"Was there a shaman as well?"

"Thankfully, no, so the monsters were disorganized. My father and I picked them off from the roof of our cabin. The next morning, we created a pyre and burned the remains."

Quell hoped that the knowledge that she had faced and fought darkspawn would give Tor additional confidence in her as a member of his quest. She had heard stories of untested soldiers freezing in fear during their first darkspawn battle.

"Good thinking. Sometimes..." Tor visibly shook with a chill. "There are worse things out there than goblins."

"So, I've heard."

They continued past a farm where a man stood on a plow drawn by a pair of oxen. Rows of tilled soil crossed the field in his wake. West of the farm loomed thick forest, its green canopy stretching as far as the eye could see.

On the other side of the road, they passed pale sections in the wall, visibly newer than the grayed and weathered stone blocks surrounding those areas. Those sections had been repaired after a darkspawn attack that had included a pair of ogres. Quell recalled seeing one of the monstrous corpses when visiting the city the following morning – eight feet tall with shoulders as broad as a wagon bed, gray-green skin, sharp teeth jutting up from an underbite jaw. It had left her with nightmares for much of the following two years.

They approached the city gate, which stood open and manned by ten guards in gray and yellow tabards – four of them archers on the wall, with the other six standing with halberds at their sides. The middle two guards lowered their halberds at an angle until the blades stood only inches apart, blocking the path.

Quell and Tor stopped their horses a few strides from the guards, one of whom she recognized.

"Good afternoon, boys," Quell said.

"State your name and your business in Zialis," one of the guards said.

"Don't pretend you don't know me, Ollison."

The man, roughly her age, grinned. "What brings you to the city, Quell?" His gaze turned to Tor. "And who are these three?"

Bitterness from her last visit to Zialis remained, causing her to thrust her chin at the man. "What brings me here is my business. As for my companions, have you heard of Tor Ranseur?"

The other guard frowned. "Isn't he the one who got in a mess up in Harken regarding a grave robbery?"

Tor groaned and slapped his forehead. "That was a misunderstanding."

Ollison chuckled. "I heard High Wizard Shambor was quite upset."

"He was and it nearly cost me"—Tor glanced toward his lap— "my pride. Thankfully, we got the situation sorted before things went too far."

"Well, we burn our dead, so you'll find no graves here."

Tor rolled his eyes. "I don't care about your blazing graves. We are here to speak with High Wizard Z'Kawl and to spend the night before we move on."

"Is the high wizard expecting you?"

Quell had expected the question and prepared her response, playing the first card in her hand. "No, but he will see Tor Ranseur."

"Why?"

"Because he is on a quest of great import. Besides, he is going to help me find my father."

The guard's brows rose. "Your father still hasn't returned from the Wilds?" He shared a look with his companion. "In that case, he is likely..."

She snapped and tore the bow off her shoulder. "Say *dead*, Ollison, and I'll put an arrow through your throat."

Ollison blinked and cleared his throat. "Well, I was going to say he is badly in need of a bath."

The heat of Quell's anger cooled but remained a simmer. "We have wasted enough time with you two. Unless you intend to poke me with one of those oversized skewers, we are heading into the city and meeting with Z'Kawl."

She spurred her horse into a walk. Tor, Koji, and Borgli followed her into the city.

Rather than a square waiting inside the gate, which was common in cities across the eight wizardoms, a corridor ten strides wide ran toward another open gate. Openings, too narrow to climb through, were spaced along the stone walls running the length of the corridor. Tor stared through one as he rode past and spied daylight on the other side.

They passed through the second gate and came to a broad intersection with a narrow street straight ahead and another street to the left. To the right was a closed gate. The walled-in corridor beyond it led to a gate that faced east. In the corner of the city, between the two walled-in corridors, stood a barracks. It was a curious design for a city but made perfect sense for a fortress. Stationing the guards between the two entrances kept response time to a minimum.

Quell noticed Tor examining the two entrance corridors. "Are you wondering about the baileys?"

"I haven't seen them used in a city before."

She nodded. "When darkspawn attack, the defenders often open the outer gate and allow the creatures to storm in. Then they slam the portcullis down behind them, trapping them in the bailey corridors. Archers and spear bearers man the windows in the walls and attack through them to slaughter the trapped monsters."

Borgli stroked his beard while nodded. "They utilize an ancient dwarven defense technique."

Koji grunted. "Many castles have baileys."

Tor added, "Didn't you notice a similar design when we passed through Fralyn Fortress?"

The dwarf said, "I was too focused on trying not to fall of my horse to notice. Regardless, we dwarves invented it first."

A flash of light came from the horizon. Moments later came a boom of thunder.

Tor said, "Let's see if we can get an audience with Z'Kawl."

Borgli asked, "Why do we need to see this man?"

Quell explained, "Our final destination lies somewhere to the east, and in order to enter those lands, we need his permission. Without it, our risks more than double."

"Why?"

She turned her horse. "Because Zialan warriors patrol those mountains."

Borgli shot Tor a questioning look. "What kind of warrior?"

"You'll see," Tor replied.

Spurring her horse into motion, she led the others at a trot, passing shops with apartments above them. Ahead, the Obelisk of Devotion jutted above the rooftops, providing a landmark to guide them.

The road turned and turned again before opening to a square with the obelisk standing in the center. A castle surrounded by a moat waited beyond the spire. The castle was located at the edge of the city, where the moat turned to flow between the castle and the city walls. Square towers stood at each corner of the castle and a blocky keep occupied the center of the complex.

A drawbridge, ten feet wide and thrice as long, spanned the moat. Quell took the lead as the group rode up to the bridge, crossed it, and emerged in the castle bailey. Armed guards in the gravel yard eyed Tor and his companions as they rode past.

Quell turned and led them to a building standing beside the castle wall. The building was open on one side and consisted of half a dozen stalls. A pair of men dressed in gray sat at a small table in the end stall, both rising as she dismounted.

"I am here to request an audience with the high wizard," she said.

One of the guards gazed at her with narrowed eyes, "Aren't you Ranger Tarpon's daughter?"

"I am."

"Didn't Z'Kawl throw you out a few weeks ago?"

Quell clenched her fists and her cheeks warmed. "He did."

"And you wish to see him again?"

"The circumstances are different this time." She handed him the reins. "Take care of our horses. We will be back for them soon."

Wishing to avoid any further questions from the guard or, more importantly, from Tor, Quell stormed off, expecting the others to follow. She passed through an arched opening and approached the main keep, where a pair of armed guards in chainmail beneath yellow and gray tabards stood beside massive, metal-reinforced doors of dark oak.

"State your business," one of the guards said. The man was no older than Quell.

"You've known me for ten years, Nathan." She kept her tone even to hide her mounting irritation. "You also know why I am here."

Nathan's gaze flicked to the other guard. "I am on duty, Quell."

"Your duty is not so serious that you can't treat me like a person."

His eyes found the floor. "I am sorry about your father."

She stiffened, not wanting to hear such condolences. "He is missing, not dead."

The man's eyes widened. "I did not mean…"

The other guard chuckled. "She has got you all twisted up, Nate."

Tor interjected, "We've just arrived in Zialis after days of traveling from Lamor. Can you escort us to the high wizard?"

"I can bring you to Chancellor Fosston," Nathan said. "The Chancellor will decide if you warrant a meeting with His Grace."

At the mention of Fosston's name, anxiety fluttered in Quell's chest. She prayed the wizard would not send her plans into disarray.

Tor said, "Let's go see this Fosston, then."

Nathan nodded to his companion. "I will return momentarily." He then turned, opened the door, and led them inside.

The castle interior was dark, dank, and sparsely decorated. Notably, it lacked the opulence one expected from the manors and palaces occupied by the ruling wizard class. A narrow corridor thick with shadow led them deeper into the keep. After passing a half dozen doors, some open, others closed, Nathan stopped them outside one that stood open a crack. There, he knocked and waited.

From inside the room, a nasally male voice asked, "What is it?"

"Sorry to bother you, Chancellor. Visitors have arrived and requested an audience with His Grace."

"Send them in."

Nathan pushed the door open and stepped aside. Tor strolled into the room, gave it a cursory glance, and turned his focus on the lone occupant.

With dark hair slicked back and his brow arched, a man in his late thirties turned from the window. The man wore dark gray robes with yellow emblems embroidered along the lapel, cuffs, and hem. A yellow sash completed his outfit. The man stood a few inches shorter than

Quell and weighed no more than she did. He stroked his long drooping mustache while surveying Tor, Koji, and Borgli. The action made it impossible to miss the gaudy gold rings adorning three of his fingers.

The wizard's gaze settled on Quell, and his smirk melted. "Did you misunderstand the high wizard's command, Miss Tarpon? I thought his rejection was clear, but then again, your family is not known for their intelligence or obedience."

Quell had expected resistance from Fosston. The man was insufferable even without the grudge he held toward her, but with it...

Her eyes narrowed, and her lips tightened. "I understood him perfectly. He is unwilling to commit soldiers to assist in my search, so I found help elsewhere."

The chancellor turned toward Tor and his companions, eyeing them briefly before gesturing toward Koji. "The big one looks like he might be formidable, but these other two are unlikely to offer much help when you are assaulted by a horde of darkspawn."

"I *will* find my father."

"If you do, I suspect it will be his corpse." Fosston's smirk returned.

Quell clenched her fist and made a move toward the wizard but stopped when a hand clamped down on her shoulder. She looked back to discover it was Tor, who said, "We request an audience with High Wizard Z'Kawl."

"And why would the high wizard agree to see you?"

"My name is Tor Ranseur. My crew and I have come seeking the Dark Lord's temple."

The color in the man's face drained away.

CHAPTER 20
PERMISSION

Tor stood resolute, waiting for Chancellor Fosston's reply.

After a quiet, uncomfortable pause, Fosston said, "I thought the temple was only a myth."

It was a sentiment Tor had heard on countless occasions regarding just about anything outside of everyday life. "Anything can be treated as a myth until someone proves it true. In fact, many people in the southern wizardoms doubt the existence of darkspawn because they have never seen them."

"Nobody in Zialis would cast such doubt. We have suffered their attacks more than anyone...other than Murguard soldiers such as yourself."

"So, you do know of my reputation."

The wizard nodded. "I wonder how much of it is true and how much is pure embellishment."

"I suspect some of both," Tor replied. "The tales people tell are often based on truth and then altered to fit their own preferences. Each subsequent person stretches it further until the story only vaguely resembles what truly transpired."

Fosston cast Quell a grimace. "This is something I know all too well."

While curious about why the wizard disliked Quell, Tor remained focused on his own agenda. "Can you get us an audience with Z'Kawl? Autumn winds push the warmth of summer aside and the snows of winter loom, especially in these mountains. The sooner we set out, the better our odds of avoiding travel through snow."

The wizard glanced toward Quell, his lips tightening when their eyes met. "I will secure you an audience. The rest is up to you."

"That is all I ask."

"Wait here."

The wizard walked out, leaving Tor and his crew alone.

Tor turned to Quell, whose steely gaze remained on the empty doorway. "He does not like you."

She snorted. "And I don't like that arse hat much either."

"Do you have some history with him?"

"My father does."

"Why does he hate your father?"

"Fosston used to be chancellor for Lord Jakarci in Balmor. My father caught Fosston doing something embarrassing and disgusting. When he informed Jakarci, Fosston was banished to Zialis for life."

Zialis was among the most dangerous places in the world to live. For a wizard used to finery, it was remote and lacked the sophistication found in the capital city, only making the situation more distasteful for someone like Fosston.

Tor asked, "What did he do to earn banishment?"

She smirked, "He was caught molesting the wizard lord's prized sheep."

"Sheep?" Borgli burst out laughing.

Tor had heard tales of lonely soldiers in the wild resorting to unsavory outlets for their urges, but for an educated, prominent wizard to do so when living in a large city with plenty of other forms of entertainment... He shook his head in disbelief.

The dwarf was still laughing when Fosston reappeared in the doorway.

The wizard frowned. "What is so funny?"

"Nothing," Tor said.

"Nothing baaad," Quell added with a grin.

The wizard's face darkened, and he glared daggers at her. "His Grace is waiting for you in the dining room. Show yourself there. You know the way." He thrust a finger toward the door. "Now, out of my office before I forget myself and unleash a spell on the lot of you."

Tor turned from the wizard to hide his grin. *His anger simmers. Better to avoid bringing it to a boil.* He led them out of the room and paused in the corridor, waiting until Quell reached him.

"I assume you know how to find this dining room," Tor said to her.

"Follow me." She walked past him and headed for the stairwell.

One flight up, they followed another corridor to an open doorway bracketed by two guards.

"His Grace is expecting us," Quell said.

The men stepped aside, leaving the doorway open. She swept past the guards, and Tor followed with Koji and Borgli straggling behind.

Like the rest of the castle, the dining room was dark. Its walls were made of dull gray stone, and its rugs black, maroon, and gold. The weapons hanging on the walls made it appear more like an armory than a dining room. The dark, clouded sky visible through diamond-paned windows added to the already ominous ambience.

A black table stood in the center of the room surrounded by ten chairs, three of which were occupied by men sitting in the warm aura of a candelabra. One wore black robes trimmed in gold and appeared to be in his forties, whom Tor assumed was High Wizard Z'Kawl. The man with his back to the door looked to be a decade younger than the wizard and was dressed in a dark gray uniform with yellow stripes down the arms and legs, marking him as an officer in the Balmorian army. The third man's hair was gray, and his eyes were alert and burned with fire. His long hair was tied back in a tail save for two stray strands adorned with black beads that dangled near his ears. Atop the man's head was a leather headband that came to a point in the front. The man wore gray and brown leather armor and was strangely the most impressive of the group, which was interesting, considering his company.

Their quiet discussion ceased the moment the wizard noticed the new arrivals.

Z'Kawl frowned. "Taquell Tarpon. You appear to be as stubborn as your father."

She pushed past Tor and approached the table. "My father would call me resilient."

"And I would call you pig-headed."

"Let's see what you say when I return with him at my side."

The wizard's face darkened. "I have not yet consented to your request."

"You said you would not allow me to go alone. Worse, you would not provide an escort. Well, I have found one."

Z'Kawl turned his attention on Tor. "You are Tor Ranseur?"

"I am."

"I pictured you to be more…impressive."

Such comments were common, and Tor refused to allow them to affect him. "I strive to appear less spectacular than I am in reality. It encourages others to underestimate me and allows me to blend in when I wish to avoid undue attention."

"Yet, your reputation makes you somewhat of a…legend. Although, some would call you a villain."

Tor's lips tightened. "I am no villain. I lead a team of salvagers who strive to recover relics from the past."

The wizard laughed. "What do we care about the past?"

"For one, we could try to learn from it. Why repeat the errors of our forebears?"

"That is a fair point."

Tor looked around, took a step closer, and lowered his voice. "Don't forget that the legends of ancient history are based on truth. There are lost artifacts that hold more power than you can comprehend."

The uniformed officer snorted. "I have heard such rubbish in fireside tales meant to frighten children."

"Such as stories of the Dark Lord's temple?"

The man laughed. "Exactly."

Tor turned to the wizard. "We believe Quell's father discovered its location and journeyed to the temple but has yet to return."

"I thought the temple was a myth."

"Ancient history describes it as a place his worshipers would visit and leave items of power as gifts. When the cataclysm struck, the temple was demolished, and the Dark Lord built a tower in Murvaran." Tor tilted his head. "What if it wasn't destroyed? What if it was merely buried only to be found now, two thousand years later?"

Z'Kawl rubbed his goatee in thought. "Very well. I give my approval for you to venture into the Wilds. However,"—he leaned forward and grabbed Tor by the wrist— "whatever you recover from the temple comes here afterward. If there is something of value...something I can use to help protect my people, it will be mine."

Tor tore his wrist away and glared at the wizard. "My team and I are funded by a party who claims the right to anything we recover. That is non-negotiable."

A palpable tension filled the room as the wizard glared back at Tor. Finally, Z'Kawl nodded. "You go on your quest. Perhaps you will even find Ranger Tarpon, but if you wish to have any hope of surviving the Wilds, you will accept my offer of an escort, led by my son, Grazal."

Tor frowned. "This venture will be dangerous and will lack the niceties you wizards are used to enjoying."

"Don't worry about Grazal. Growing up in Zialis hardens people. He is no pampered wizard, and unlike most who graduate from the University, he has experience in battle."

While Tor preferred limiting his party to his own team, he also realized that traveling in the Wilds presented significant risks, particularly if they happened upon a large group of darkspawn. The added advantages of having a wizard on his side were too great to dismiss. "Fine. Your son and an escort may join us, but no more than two dozen soldiers. If the party grows too large, it'll slow us down and attract undue attention."

"Agreed. There is only one last issue to address." Z'Kawl turned toward the gray-haired warrior seated at the table. "Chieftain Hajako, do you agree to allow this quest on your lands?"

The warrior examined Tor with narrowed eyes. "The Dark Lord's temple is a legend in my tribe, passed down from our ancestors. Do you truly believe you can find it?"

"I believe Taquell's father found *something*. With the clues he left behind, I am hopeful we can find it as well...whatever it is."

"I have known Ranger Tarpon for a decade. He is an honorable man and among the few who has been allowed to freely venture through the Wilds on his own. If he claims to have discovered the location of this lost temple, that is good enough for me."

Z'Kawl smiled. "Wonderful." He turned toward Tor. "I will have my men prepare for the journey."

"How quickly can your son be ready to depart?"

"He will meet you inside the city gates at dawn."

"Good. Now, if you will excuse us, I would like to find rooms at an inn before the rain strikes."

The man in the uniform shook his head. "You'll have to sleep elsewhere. Zialis only has two inns, and both are currently occupied by my men – at least those I could not house here in the keep."

Z'Kawl added, "Captain Nuclezi is visiting from Balmor. His troops take priority. I am sure you understand."

Tor frowned. "Where are we to stay?"

"I suggest you travel out to Miss Tarpon's quaint cabin. After all, you are her guest, are you not?"

Quell glowered at the wizard but, thankfully, kept her tongue leashed.

"We will return at sunrise." Tor turned and left the room with his companions following.

Concerns about the quest consumed Tor's thoughts as he navigated the castle, stepped outside, and retrieved his horse. He led his crew, mounted, across the small city and through the southern gate where he drew his horse to a stop.

As Quell stopped beside him, Tor asked, "Where to?"

She pointed northwest. "We follow a narrow trail around that farm and through the forest. It is no more than four miles."

"Good. Let's see if we can get there before the rain hits."

A bolt of lightning shot down from the clouds and struck somewhere north of the city. Booming thunder rumbled, and rain began to fall.

CHAPTER 21
THE WILDS

Quaint was an optimistic term for Quell's cabin, far more favorable than what Tor would have used. While larger than a ship's cabin, this one proved worse because there were only two beds. Of course, Quell slept in hers, but Tor offered the other to Koji, knowing that the man was too big to sleep on a chair or the sofa. Tor turned to find Borgli strewn out on the sofa, which left only the chair. Covered by a blanket on his lap while his feet rested on the dormant fireplace hearth, Tor had done his best to rest, but it was a struggle, his discomfort causing him to wake frequently. When he spied the first hints of daylight outside the window, he tossed the blanket aside and woke everyone else up.

Minutes later, still bleary-eyed from a poor night of sleep, Tor rode down a shadowy trail in the twilight of predawn. Mud and puddles covered much of the trail, but at least the rain had stopped. It had taken most of the night for Tor's clothing to dry after getting caught in the prior evening's storm.

The trees parted to reveal a sleepy farmhouse amid a field bordered by a split rail fence. The trail ran along the fence line and toward the city of Zialis, its walls illuminated by torches although the city remained asleep.

They rounded the corner and sighted the gate, the portcullis still down and guarded by ever-vigilant soldiers. Tor slowed his mount to a walk.

He watched Quell riding beside him, her face resolute as she gazed toward the wall separating them from the Wilds. Memories of the prior evening's visit to the high wizard replayed in his head and awoke a concern he had dismissed at the time.

"You never told me that Z'Kawl denied your request for help before you came to me."

She frowned. "He was unwilling to risk his soldiers to try and find my father."

"But now..."

"Now, the great Tor Ranseur has come seeking a fabled temple that contains untold secrets."

Tor narrowed his eyes. "You hoped to use me to gain the high wizard's favor."

Quell snorted. "Don't pretend there is nothing in this for you. Finding the temple might be your greatest discovery. Regardless of what wealth it contains, your fame will further swell. Isn't that what you wanted?"

"Do you think me so vain that all I care for is fame?"

She arched a brow. "Please, enlighten me. What do you care about?"

"I spent a third of my life fighting against the Dark Lord's minions. Thousands of good, brave soldiers died at my side during that span. Yet, what else can we do? If we abandon the Fractured Lands, the monsters will run rampant across the Eight Wizardoms."

"What does that have to do with your current profession?"

"I seek relics that can be used in the war against the Dark Lord."

"War?" She laughed. "What war?"

"The war to come, the final conflict between good and evil as foretold in the prophecies of the Seers of Kelmar."

Borgli blinked. "You know of the prophecies?"

"I do." Tor turned back toward Quell. "The Dark Lord's temple is said to contain his greatest treasures, not treasures of wealth but of power. If we can retrieve those artifacts and use them against the Dark Lord, it may be enough to turn the tide in our favor."

"So, you don't care about fame?"

Koji laughed. "While what Tor says is true, he also enjoys the fame he has gained. Lucky for him, I am here to ensure his head does not inflate so much that he cannot fit through the doorway."

The dwarf chortled, Quell chuckled, and Koji grinned broadly. Tor shook his head and smiled despite the slight against him.

Through an opening in the clouds to the east, morning light shone, signaling dawn's break. A bell rang, and the portcullis lifted, its chains clanking noisily in the stillness. Simultaneously, the inner gate at the far end of the corridor opened to reveal a squad on horses, waiting.

"There is the rest of our party." Tor urged his horse into a walk and passed through the outer gate unchallenged. As he rode through the corridor and approached the second gate, he surveyed the waiting riders.

Chieftain Hajako sat on a black steed. At his side was a male warrior with black beads in the thin braids framing his face. Like Hajako, the hilt of a katana stuck up above the warrior's shoulder and his dark eyes lacked emotion. Small metal plates covered much of his body like scales.

On one side of the chieftain were twenty soldiers dressed in gray and yellow tabards over chainmail. Six carried bows, six spears, and the rest shields while swords rested in their scabbards. Seated on a white stallion on the other side was a young man in dark gray robes. *That must be Z'Kawl's son, Grazal.* His dark hair was slicked back like the high wizard's, but unlike his father, Grazal's face was clean shaven and decidedly handsome.

"You must be Tor Ranseur," Grazal said.

Tor pulled his horse to a stop. "I am."

"I am Grazal, son of High Wizard Z'Kawl." The wizard turned toward the soldier on the horse beside his. Unlike the others, a pair of metal wings adorned the helmet on the man's head. "This is Lieutenant Heizer. These soldiers report to him, and he reports to me."

"In that case, you had best all remember that I lead this expedition. You agree to this, or you will remain behind."

Grazal scowled. "As I was told. I just hope you know what you are doing."

"I have more experience than you might guess, which brings with it wisdom. Wisdom includes knowing when to rely on the experience of others. Thus, for the first leg of this journey, I will defer to Chieftain Hajako's direction." He turned toward the Zialan chief. "Are you ready?"

Hajako nodded. "Let us be off. If we travel swiftly, we can reach the Zialan Stronghold before the sun sets. It would be unwise to be out in the Wilds after dark." He waved to the guards in the tower over the other inner gate. The portcullis lifted, and the party entered the corridor leading to the east gate. The second portcullis opened, and they continued past it, into the land known as the Wilds.

East of the wall, a road divided a broad swath of open land, hundreds of feet across. A half mile to the southeast, the clearing terminated at the river. In the other direction, the clearing ended at a steep, rocky cliff. As far as Tor could see in both directions, clusters of bones and skulls lay nestled in the long, yellowed grass. It was a somber scene and reminiscent of the battlegrounds in the Fractured

Lands. Unwanted memories began to invade Tor's thoughts, forcing him to turn from the bones and peer toward the waiting forest.

Hajako said, "Be wary once we reach the wood. While darkspawn despise daylight, the gloom of night lingers in the forest. Sometimes the darkspawn do not retreat to their hiding places until the sun is a quarter of the way into the sky."

Tor shared a knowing look with Koji. The jungles near the Fractured Lands held similar dangers.

The road entered the shadow of the forest, and Tor immediately had the sensation that someone was watching him. He reached over his shoulder, gripped Claw by the shaft, and pulled the weapon free. Others reacted similarly, everyone riding at attention with their weapons ready.

~

THE SURROUNDING forest encroached on the road until it became a narrow trail that gently turned north and climbed toward a saddle between two mountains capped by bare gray rock. As the elevation increased, the gaps in the trees broadened, alleviating the creepy sensation that dominated much of the morning. At mid-day, the party crested the saddle and stopped in a small clearing to rest their horses.

Across the meadow, an angled rock outcropping rose a hundred feet above the saddle. Tor gestured toward it, "Koji, I want to get a better view of our surroundings."

"I am with you." Koji knew the dangers of going off alone in hostile territory.

The two of them crossed the field, both quiet until they drew near the landmark.

"I'll survey our surroundings," Tor said. "You patrol the bottom and let me know if you spy any trouble."

Before Koji could reply, Tor began climbing. The red-tinted rock had a dimpled surface, making it easy to grip. Still, he maintained three points of contact and took care to ensure solid footing during the climb. Suddenly, Quell appeared, climbing past Tor. With skill and ease, she scrambled up the rock and stood at the top, waiting while Tor completed his ascent.

"Your age slows you down," Quell said.

Tor stood upright and dusted off his hands. "I was simply being cautious. Had I reason to rush, I would have been up here much faster."

She smirked. "If you say so."

Although clouds blanketed the sky, Tor held a hand over his eyes while peering out into the distance. A forest valley lay before him; it was surrounded by mountains, steep cliffsides, and rocky ridges. The shape of the land made the valley a natural funnel with the saddle where Tor now stood and a canyon at the far end the only ways in or out. Steep, rocky cliffs overlooked the canyon, making it appear more like a corridor carved into the mountain.

Quell's arm extended toward the canyon. "Do you see that rock pile in the far gap?"

"I might be older than you, but my eyes are as sharp as ever."

"That is the Stronghold."

Tor frowned. "It doesn't look so daunting."

She shrugged. "Twenty miles of distance will do that."

"I'm surprised darkspawn are able to get through that gap."

"That canyon is a mile wide and is assaulted too often to repair the walls that once spanned from cliff to cliff. Thus, the Stronghold only slows their advance."

"You've visited it before?"

"Yes. Once with my father. Three years ago, at a time when darkspawn sightings were less common than they are now. The Stronghold...is not what you expect."

"What does that mean?"

She gave him a sidelong look, her mouth turned up in a smirk. "You'll see."

He shook his head. "You can be so annoying at times."

"As my father told me a hundred times over." Quell turned and looked down at Koji "We should climb down. We have a long ride across this valley."

Sighing, Tor nodded and began his descent.

CHAPTER 22
THE HIDDEN VILLAGE

With the skies darkening, the sun somewhere behind the mountain to the west, Tor and his party continued down a lightly traveled, wooded valley trail. The entire journey had given Tor a strange feeling, but it had taken him hours to identify what felt so odd. When they were halfway across the valley, he realized he had not seen or heard any signs of wildlife. No rabbits. No squirrels. Not even a single bird. Each time they stopped, the silence was thick and haunting. The sensation only became more dominant as it grew darker.

The valley floor shifted to an incline, and the trail became a series of switchbacks that climbed the wooded hillside. When the ground leveled, they emerged from the forest and came to an open meadow bordered by steep cliffsides with piles of fallen rock at the foot of both cliffs. The trail ran down the center of a canyon, heading directly toward a strange formation of granite boulders, each the size of a house. Some were stacked on others, bridging gaps and creating what almost appeared to be a manmade structure, except the boulders were far too large to make that possible.

Chieftain Hajako pulled his horse to a stop just shy of the boulders. Tor and the others reined in their mounts and gathered near him. As the noise of hooves settled, the rush of water drew Tor's attention. He turned his mount to face the northern canyon wall where a waterfall tumbled hundreds of feet into a pool. The water then fed a stream running along the canyon in the opposite direction of the one they came from.

"Remain here," Hajako dismounted. "The Stronghold is filled with traps. I wish to ensure that all is as it should be within."

Tor frowned. "I only see a stack of large, randomly-arranged boulders."

"The boulders make the Stronghold"—Quell gestured toward monoliths— "along with the tunnels beneath them."

"People live in there?"

"Nobody lives there. However, the darkspawn do not know that."

Minutes passed before Hajako emerged from the boulders. He was not alone.

A quartet of warriors surrounded their leader. All had long hair with a string of beads on each side of their faces. Three were male with lean, athletic builds. The fourth was female and not much older than Quell. Unlike the others, the beads in her braid were gray instead of black.

"All is set." Hajako mounted his horse. "Darkness is nearly upon us. Best if we leave before it gets too late."

The man spurred his horse into a trot, and the four warriors ran with him, two at each side. Grazal and the Balmorian soldiers followed, leaving Tor and his crew at the back. Confused but aware that it was not time for questions, Tor urged his horse into motion.

They followed the trail to the pool's edge and slowed to a walk. There, Hajako turned sharply, nearly doubling back as he followed the shoreline. A narrow path at the foot of the cliff took them around the pool and up a rocky slope, toward the waterfall. Just before reaching the falling water, Hajako dismounted and waited for the others to do the same. The four Zialan warriors ducked into the shadowy recess behind the falls and disappeared. Hajako, Grazal, and the soldiers followed, each leading their mounts in single file.

Tor looked back at Borgli. "Do you fear falling water like you do the sea?"

The dwarf grunted. "You'll fear my fist up your arse if you ask me that again."

The comment caused Quell to chuckle as she led her horse after the others. Tor and his crew followed through the mist and into a cavity between the rock wall and the falls. The path expanded and turned, becoming a tunnel five strides wide and just as tall. There, the female warrior waited with a torch. In the light of torches deeper in the cavern, the rest of the party climbed a sloping tunnel.

"My name is Ekaji." The young woman wore a serious expression. "I am to escort you to our village. Is that the last of you?"

Tor looked back and peered around Koji as Borgli rounded the turn. "Yes. This is it."

"Good. Follow me." She turned and headed along the tunnel with her torch held high.

Gripping the reins in one hand, Tor walked up the gentle slope, curious to see where it would lead them.

～

THE TUNNELS WERE MORE extensive than he had anticipated, with a myriad of twists, turns, and branching paths, all of them ever rising. After thirty minutes of climbing, the floor leveled out, and light came from ahead. Surrounded by a palpable aura of anticipation Tor led his mount toward the tunnel's end.

The rocky ceiling fell away to reveal the evening sky with the last remnants of daylight to the west and the full moon to the northeast. Between the two horizons stood a towering, snowcapped peak. Tor's gaze lowered to take in his surroundings.

The ground gently sloped from the mountain to a drop off a few hundred feet from where Tor stood. A stream ran down the slope and disappeared over the edge. The upper portions of the slope were covered in the green of crops, meadows, and trees, while the lower portion was largely barren rock. Built within the barren region and nestled beside the stream, was a torchlit village.

Six men with short hair ran in, bowed to Hajako, and then began collecting the horses. The Zialan chieftain waved for everyone to follow, turned, and marched toward the village.

No wall surrounded the village, which was unexpected. Instead, broad torchlit streets ran between log buildings, the largest of which stood in the center of town. Hajako climbed the front steps of the large building, opened the door, and led them inside.

Tor entered to find a long, open room with a vaulted ceiling supported by log posts and beams. A large fireplace stood at each end of the space, but the room was otherwise vacant.

Hajako said, "This is the common house. You will camp here for the evening. Be happy you have a roof, for the nights bring a stiff chill this time of year. Enjoy your evening. You will sleep beneath the stars after this.

"A meal will be coming shortly." Chieftain Hajako closed the door, leaving them alone.

∽

HOOTS AND HOWLS INVADING Tor's dreams caused him to wake. His eyes flashed open to a dark building, the sounds coming from outside.

Darkspawn. Those same cries had woken him on countless nights during his time in the Murguard. Immediately, he reached for his weapon, its cool, smooth shaft giving him a sense of comfort despite his racing heart. He crouched and looked around the dark room, illuminated by indirect moonlight seeping through the windows. Another round of hoots, howls, and shrieks echoed outside. The others sleeping in the common house – his team, the wizard, and the Balmorian soldiers – all stirred. Some leapt to their feet while others looked around in fear.

"Koji," Tor said in a soft voice.

"I hear them, Tor."

"You and I are going outside."

"What about me?" Quell asked.

"Do as you wish but do so quietly."

She slid her quiver over her shoulder and picked up her bow. "Then, I am coming with you."

"I am coming as well," Borgli declared, his hammer in his grip.

"Fine." Tor turned to Grazal. "You and your men are to remain here unless you hear cries for help."

"My magic can help—"

"Your magic is of no help to me if you are dead. I am only going out to investigate." Tor headed for the door.

He opened the door and peered around. Nothing moved. Hoots and howls continued from the south.

Over his shoulder, he whispered, "Follow me but remain quiet."

He headed down a torchlit street toward the frightening sounds. At the village edge, he paused and listened while searching the area. Pale moonlight illuminated the rocky surface, but nothing moved. A terrifying shriek echoed in the night. Tor waved for the others to follow and advanced toward the sound, slowing as he approached the end of the plateau. He eased up to the cliff edge and peered down.

Hundreds of wiry creatures ran along the canyon floor, some gripping swords, others bows or spears. The monsters rounded the pool, heading for the pile of boulders. The first goblins disappeared into the Stronghold. Snaps and pops arose, followed by screams. A burst of fire erupted and billowed into the air, briefly illuminating the surrounding boulders. Burning goblins screeched and flailed before falling dead. The scene continued for some minutes until a cluster of goblins gathered beyond the stronghold and encircled a solitary figure. Despite the dim lighting and the distance, Tor knew it must be a shaman.

The goblin magic user chittered in its odd language. The surviving goblins burst into a run toward the forest and the valley leading to Zialis.

Only after the monsters faded into the distance and the night fell silent did Tor turn to the others. "This gives you a clue of what we face out in the Wilds. We must travel by day and be vigilant at night." He then noticed the look of concern on Quell's face. "Are you well?"

She shook her head. "There were so many, and my father traveled alone. This is far worse than I imagined."

Tor clapped his hand on her shoulder. "Do not give up hope yet. These monsters are not familiar with strategy, nor do they study human behavior. That provides a distinct advantage to those of us who understand darkspawn and their tendencies. I suspect your father has utilized that advantage as well."

She nodded, but her eyes continued to stare down into the canyon.

︴

Tor woke again to noise, but this time it was the clang of steel on steel. The soft light of the impending dawn waited outside the windows, so darkspawn were the unlikely culprits. Still, he gripped Claw, waved for Koji to follow, and crept past the waking soldiers.

He opened the door to find a pair of Zialan warriors sparring near the stream. Each held a katana, their swords moving too quickly to follow. Rapid clangs resounded as the warriors sliced, blocked, spun, and parried. Compelled toward the fight as if it were a gorgeous vista, Tor approached the sparring area. He settled twenty strides from the warriors, fascinated to witness a duel with real weapons rather than wooden replicas. His companions gathered around him, all watching the furious fight.

One warrior was Hajako, who dressed in simple black robes that flowed with each movement. The other was Ekaji, the female warrior who had escorted them through the tunnels the prior evening. Unlike the Zialan chieftain, she wore dull gray scaled armor with darkened metal panels on her shoulders, forearms, and chest.

Hajako moved with speed and grace unrivaled for someone his age. The woman possessed incredible reflexes, reacting and blocking blow after blow, which was fortunate since her moves were initiated slightly late, proving she lacked the chieftain's anticipation. The warriors twirled their katanas, slicing and blocking in a steady flurry of clangs. The conflict was evenly matched until one warrior made a mistake.

The woman spun and swept her leg in a tripping maneuver, but Hajako leapt, her foot passing beneath him as her sword came around. Rather than landing on his feet, Hajako dropped to his knees and ducked his head. Her katana swept over him, and he thrust with a twist. The woman tried to move, but her weight had shifted too much to one leg. His blade bit into her thigh. She grunted and staggered backward.

Hajako stood and lowered his blade. "You lose, Ekaji."

She held one hand against her wound, her steely gaze glowering back at him, but she kept silent.

"You will remain here and continue to train."

Her lips tightened and she snapped. "I am finished with training. I wish to fight."

"You have yet to achieve the black." He shook his head. "You are not ready."

"I—" She stopped when he raised a finger.

"You will do as I say. Now, visit the healer to tend to your wound. This conversation has ended."

Obviously disgruntled and with blood running down her breeches, Ekaji limped off.

During the duel and following conversation, villagers, both male and female, children and adults, went about their morning as if nothing of interest had occurred.

Hajako turned, his eyes meeting Tor's. The warrior chieftain slid his blade into the scabbard on his hip and walked over. "The day breaks, adventurer. I trust you slept well."

Troubled thoughts had plagued Tor – shadows and monsters stalking him throughout the night. Such nightmares began years ago, but the late-night darkspawn sighting had made them worse.

"Well enough, I suppose," Tor lied.

"Breakfast will arrive at the common house shortly. Once you are finished eating, my warriors will escort you down to the canyon floor. From there, you are on your own." He removed the twisted armband from his bicep. "One of you, wear this. Zialan warriors wander the Wilds. Should you come across any, this will inform them that your presence in the Wilds is welcome."

Tor accepted the object and turned it over in his hands. It was made of twisted bronze wire and had an ornate spiral shape in the center of the coil. "Thank you."

"Eat quickly. The sooner you depart, the farther you can walk before it grows dark."

"Walk?"

"The horses will remain here. The terrain beyond this canyon will be challenging enough on foot and is nigh impossible on horseback."

When the Zialan leader walked away, Tor turned to his companions. "I don't suppose any of you wish to wear this."

Borgli snorted. "My arms are too muscular to fit it."

"As are mine," Koji said.

"Sorry." Quell shook her head. "It clashes with my outfit."

He sighed. "I figured as much. Let's pack up so we can set out when we are finished eating."

CHAPTER 23
TROUBLE

Tor and his party, including Grazal and his soldiers, emerged from the tunnels beneath the waterfall and circled the pool. While shadows still clung to the canyon, the skies were the pale blue of morning, and a halo of sunlight framed the slope of the eastern peaks beyond the far end of the canyon.

Warriors already worked within the Stronghold, dragging goblin corpses from the field of boulders before piling them on a flat, blackened rock near the far cliff wall.

He turned to his escort, the same female warrior Hajako had defeated in the morning duel. "What are they doing?"

Ekaji peered across the canyon. "On the mornings after a darkspawn attack, we burn the bodies and rearm the traps hidden in the Stronghold."

Tor recalled her desperate fight with Hajako. "Why did you duel your chieftain?"

She frowned. "I wish to see more of the world. He does not think I am ready."

"I know something of fighting. While you lost that duel, you would have bested most soldiers."

"We are not most soldiers. We are Zialan warriors. It is a high standard. Until I achieve the black, I am stuck here, as commanded by Chieftain Hajako." She turned toward the boulders. "I have escorted you as far as I am allowed. From here, you are on your own. Be well and take care to find a defensible location before darkness falls."

She walked off, passed into the shadows of the boulders, and was gone.

Grazal harrumphed. "The Zialans are a strange lot."

"They are," Tor agreed. "Enough about them. We have our own quest to pursue, so let's be off." He walked along the pool, heading toward the eastern end of the canyon.

The others fell in line behind him – Koji, Borgli, Quell, Grazal, Lieutenant Heizer, and the rest of the soldiers, their chainmail clinking with each stride. While Tor preferred to travel in quiet and not alert any lurking enemy of his presence, he was saddled with the wizard and his guards. Worse, he worried they might turn out to be more necessary than he had hoped.

The pool fed into a stream, which flowed along the base of the northern cliff and gently meandered eastward. A broad trail of trampled grass and dirt ran parallel to the stream. Tor and his party followed the worn path for a mile before the canyon walls opened up to present a broader view. He approached the edge of the drop and stopped to survey the latest vista.

The rising sun, positioned between two peaks to the east, shone down on a forest-covered valley. Just to his side, cascading water tumbled hundreds of feet down a steep hillside to feed a stream before it was lost in the dark trees. Towering, snow-capped peaks and incredibly high ridgelines surrounded the valley to complete the stunning vista.

"Such a shame," Koji said.

"What's a shame?" Borgli asked.

"That such beauty is hidden away from the eyes of those who might appreciate it."

Quell said, "Do not allow the serene landscape to fool you. This land is infected with darkspawn." She indicated a saddle to the northeast, far across the valley. "When I visited here with my father, this is as far as we went. According to him, that saddle is the only other way out of this valley. While standing in this very same spot, he told me about a landmark called the Dragon's Snout and said it was located on a mountain face overlooking the saddle."

Tor squinted, his focus on the bare rocky portion above the forest and below the snow. "That mountainside is easily twenty miles away."

"Yes. My father told me that it consumed a full day for him to cross this valley."

"In that case, we had best hurry. I want to be out of the forest before the sun reaches the western peaks. If we are caught among the trees while the shadows are thickening, we risk a darkspawn attack."

He took a deep breath and began the steep descent down the rocky hillside. The footing was difficult and forced him to place each step with care. The forest waited far below, the trees masking whatever might be lurking in their shadows.

∿

The day passed more quickly than Tor would have liked. He tracked the sun's journey across the sky while he and his party traveled in the opposite direction. Twice, they stopped to refill their waterskins in the stream, the second time just before the flowing water turned north and faded into a dark, underground cavern.

The forest proved a challenge as well. The undergrowth, boulders, and fallen trees often forced Tor to alter his path. From time to time, he would put Koji in the lead. The Kyranni warrior's skill with his machete held value beyond his ability to use it in a fight. He hacked and slashed his way through all the vines, ferns, and shrubs that seemed to have them trapped.

And so, they gradually advanced across the valley floor. By the time they began up the incline at the other end, the afternoon shadows amid the trees had begun to swell. Pressed by need and a sense of urgency, Tor kept a steady pace despite the panting breaths and burning thighs plaguing him and the rest of his party. The trees, shrubs, and rocks forced him to blaze his own path, often going at an angle that turned to a switchback when the incline became too steep. The sun slipped behind the peaks to the west, and Tor urged the members of his party to push forward despite their rising exhaustion. The valley behind them was draped in shadow by the time the trees fell away to reveal open ground covered by rocks, shrubs, and yellowed grass. They had reached the saddle.

Nightfall was fast approaching when Tor climbed a massive boulder to get a better view of his surroundings. He scanned the open ground of the saddle, in search of a safe place to hole up for the evening and was not surprised when Quell scrambled up the boulder and stood at his side.

"There it is!" She pointed to the northeast. "See that rocky point jutting from the face of that mountain?"

Scanning the rocky slope, Tor spied a rock formation that stuck out from the hillside. The pair of rounded boulders above it and the flat surface that broke inward elicited an image matching the description of the distinct rock formation.

"The Dragon's Snout," he said.

"It must be," she agreed.

He reached into his pack, dug out the journal, then opened it to a page marked with a red ribbon. His finger slid down the page until he found the passage he sought.

"In the ever-present mother's beaming smile, the dragon's snout will point the way to a path of shadow."

"Yes." Quell said. "Since you translated it, I have considered that passage a dozen times over and came up with nothing. What does it mean?"

"It means we are going for a climb."

"Up there?"

"I've done..."

A distant howl rang out. Hoots followed, the sounds rising in volume.

Tor spun around and looked down, as the wizard and warriors below him, their eyes round with fear, searched their surroundings. "We need to reach higher ground." He pointed toward the mountain on the north side of the pass. "Head that way. Quickly!"

Quell was halfway down the boulder by the time Tor started his descent. When he was ten feet from the ground, he leapt, landed in a squat, and ran after the others.

They raced across the open ground and up the shallow slope at the foot of the mountain. Tor spied a large rock outcropping and angled toward it. "This way! Toward the boulders!"

The others altered their path to follow him. A hundred simultaneous hoots drew Tor's attention as a mass of wiry gray bodies burst from the trees at the far end of the pass. Fueled by desperation, he ran faster and reached the rock outcropping before anyone else. Slowing as he rounded it, he spied a pocket between the boulders, the opening no more than ten feet across. He rounded the boulder in the center and found a similar opening on the other side. At the rear of the pocket was a slanted rock surface, easy to climb and leading to the top of the outer boulders, which stood fifteen feet tall.

He quickly began issuing orders. "Everyone, dump your packs here behind the middle boulder. Quell, you and the archers take position atop the boulders. Grazal is with you. Borgli, Koji, and I will guard this entrance. Heizer, I need you and your swordsmen to take the other opening. Put your spearmen in the middle, half behind you and half behind me. They can thrust between the warriors at the fore and attack any monster that draws close enough."

Rather than argue, as Quell often did, she raced into the opening and scrambled up the angled rock. The wizard and the other archers followed, splitting into two groups so Quell and three archers stood on one outer boulder and Grazal and the other three archers stood on the other.

Tor tossed his pack aside, pulled his weapon from its holster, and stood ready. Koji, with his machete in his bare hand, stood to one side while Borgli, gripping his war hammer, positioned himself on the other. A trio of spearmen took position behind them.

By then, the goblin horde was only a hundred strides away. The monsters, armed with anything ranging from rusty swords to broken tree limbs, came toward them with frantic fury in their oversized eyes.

"Archers!" Tor paused until the host was close enough to make an easy target and then bellowed, "Loose at will!"

A rapid string of thwaps came from above him. Arrows sailed and struck the monsters in the vanguard. Seven fell to the onslaught, and the next creatures in line tripped over the fallen, their limbs failing as they shrieked. Two bolts of lightning arched out in a *V* as Grazal launched a magic-powered attack. Each bolt struck a charging goblin, causing them to arch their backs in pain. Electricity arced from goblin to goblin, spreading until two dozen fell to the ground, their bodies on fire.

Hooting wildly, the remaining monsters circled around their dying comrades and raced forward. Another flight of arrows struck, taking six more monsters but leaving dozens still charging.

"Launch maneuver," Tor announced. It was a risky move, but he and Koji had experience with it.

"I'm ready," the Kyranni warrior nodded.

"Don't let them kill me, Borgli."

"What?" the dwarf asked.

Out of time, Tor raised his weapon over his head, wound back with both hands gripping the shaft, and thrust his body forward, using his momentum to catapult Claw at the charging horde. With its shaft parallel to the ground, the ranseur hurtled forward and struck the two monsters in the front. The weight of the enchanted weapon, easily exceeding a hundred pounds for anyone not wearing the magical ring linked to it, drove the monsters back, felling a few goblins to each side and a dozen others unlucky enough to be directly behind them.

With a narrow window to operate, Tor darted forward, ducked below a clumsy sword strike, and gripped his weapon. He looked up as a wild-eyed goblin raised an axe, ready to drive it into his skull.

~

Realizing that Tor was in trouble, Borgli rushed toward the goblins, released a roar, and swung. His war hammer sped past Tor and connected with the attacking goblin's ribs, breaking bones while launching the creature sideways into another monster as it regained its feet. The two went down in a heap.

"Get back!" Borgli bellowed, raising Tremor high and swinging again.

His hammer smashed through a sword, shattering it when a goblin raised it for a block. The hammer crashed down on the monster's head with a tremendous crack. The creature crumpled to the ground.

Borgli took a few steps back and waited as another pair of monsters rushed toward him. As the creatures closed the gap, he swung his hammer, the heavy weapon striking one of the monsters in the shoulder and launching it into the other, causing both to tumble in a twisted ball.

∽

Koji stood ready as Tor shuffled back. A goblin with a spear thrust its weapon at Tor's chest. With a mighty, downward chop, Koji's machete lopped off the spear tip. The impact of the blow caused the goblin to stumble. Koji took advantage of the opening and followed with a mighty punch. His gauntlet struck the creature's head with a loud crack, launching the creature into two others.

Another pair of monsters rushed in, their red-tinted eyes wild. Using his gauntlet, Koji knocked aside the sword strike from one monster while slashing at the other, his machete drawing a red gash across the goblin's chest. The wounded creature squealed and fell back, allowing Koji to focus on the other. The darkspawn swung again. This time, its blade clanged as it hit the machete. Koji followed with a punch. His metal fist slammed into the goblin's face, which launched the wiry creature off its feet to smack into the next cluster of monsters.

∽

Tor battled in the middle, with Koji to one side, and Borgli to the other. The three fought frantically while arrows from above pelted the crowd of goblins, slowing them briefly before they charged back in.

Tor thrust, swung, and scooped with his weapon, using the tines on one end and the claw on the other to break swords, crack heads, and sweep feet beneath enemies. Borgli hammered the charging monsters, breaking weapons, skulls, and bones as he swung again and again. Koji fought with calm concentration, severing enemy limbs and cracking monster skulls. The battle was frantic, and corpses began to pile up, forcing the three warriors backward.

One of the archers on the boulder above cried out just before his body struck the ground beside the dwarf. An arrow stuck out of the man's eye while the other gaped toward the stars above.

The distraction nearly cost Tor, who twisted to avoid a spear thrust just in time. The attacking creature was met by a spear wielded by one of Heizer's soldiers. Tor thrust a boot heel at the monster and pushed it off the spear shaft. Suddenly, there were no monsters attacking. Then he noticed more serious trouble.

A few hundred feet away, a fire burned in the long grass below them. Standing at the far side of that fire was a single goblin wearing a necklace of bones and a loincloth. The goblin hopped, waved its arms, and chanted wildly while a crowd of goblins lurked behind it, at the edge of the firelight.

"Shaman!" Tor shouted. From his experiences in the Murguard, Tor knew that goblins were a mindless bunch and likely to flee an armed enemy when not under the influence of a shaman. To make matters worse, shaman magic was boosted by fire, which made the creature twice as dangerous. "Kill it!" he bellowed.

~

STANDING fifteen feet above the ground, Quell and the other archers loosed repeatedly, wounding and killing charging goblins. When Tor shouted to alert them of the shaman, Quell adjusted her aim. The creature was farther away than the others, but it was a shot she had made dozens of times. She raised her bow, adjusted for the wind, and loosed at the same time as archers around her.

A volley of arrows sailed toward the monster, but the creature waved its arms and sent a wall of fire shooting upward from the fire. The arrows struck the wall, burst into flames, and fizzled to the ground, leaving the goblin magic user unharmed.

On the boulder across from Quell, Grazal waved his hands and thrust forward. A bolt of wizard lightning sped across the open space, but instead of striking the shaman, the electricity bent and connected with a metal rod planted in the ground just strides from the creature. The shaman responded by shrieking out something and raising its hands toward the sky. A swirling ball of red, crackling magic appeared above the shaman's raised hands. The creature thrust forward. and the magic missile hurtled toward them.

"Take cover!" Tor shouted from below.

Quell looked from side to side, but there was nowhere to hide. The only choice was to jump down, but the ground in front of the boulder was littered with weapons and corpses of dead monsters. That moment of hesitation cost her.

Sizzling crimson energy struck, sending shoots of pain down her extremities. Her arms and legs locked up, her muscles contracting as her entire body cramped. She fell onto her side and shook violently.

∼

Tor darted between two soldiers still gripping their spears, made a desperate dive to the ground, and rolled into a recess beneath one of the boulders.

From his back, he spied Grazal atop the opposite boulder, his hands raised as he called upon his magic. The enemy missile struck an invisible shield, hovered for a breath, and then burst into a thousand crimson sparks that rained down. When a spark touched Grazal, he stiffened and collapsed. The same thing happened to the three spearmen near where Tor hid. Both Koji and Borgli now lay on the ground in one direction, as did Heizer and the soldiers protecting the other gap. All shook violently while red sparks sizzled along their skin.

Tor crawled out to discover that he was the only one not in the grip of the shaman spell. Still beside the fire, the shaman now hopped in glee. The creature spied him, barked orders, and waved. Half of the remaining monsters – more than a dozen – charged toward Tor.

He looked down at Koji, Borgli, and the others, who shook in the agony of the evil stasis spell. Even Quell and the other archers were caught in the shaman magic, their bodies twitching violently on top of the two boulders.

"I can't fight them all alone," Tor mumbled aloud. "By the gods. What do I do?"

CHAPTER 24
THE DRAGON'S SNOUT

Tor held his weapon ready and strode out beyond Koji, his body still trapped by the shaman stasis spell. He took care to remain within the funnel of the two boulders. If any of the monsters got behind him, it would likely be the end of Tor and his crew.

Shrieks filled the night, followed by clangs and death cries. Tor then spied a skirmish among the goblins near the shaman. A silver blade flashed in the firelight, cutting down creature after creature. Before Tor could identify the warrior wielding the blade, the charging monsters were upon him.

Tor brought Claw around with a tremendous swing, extending his arm while gripping one of the tines, using the length of his arm and the extended weapon to keep the monsters at bay. The claw end dug into a goblin torso, the momentum of the swing lifting the creature off its feet and smashing it into a neighboring monster. With a flip of the weapon, Tor gripped the shaft in both hands and blocked a sword strike. He twirled Claw again and knocked a spear thrust aside. A twist and a jab brought the claw end around and struck a creature in the face, knocking its teeth out in a spray of blood. A sword came at him again, but he caught it between Claw's tines, then twisted and snapped the blade in half. A backhand swing drove the tines through the attacking monster's throat.

Three more monsters replaced the fallen, all coming at him at the same time and forcing him to retreat. He tripped over Koji's leg, fell backward, and struck the ground hard. The goblins coming at him suddenly stopped. They lowered their weapons, their oversized eyes widening. Unwilling to miss the opening, Tor reacted with a wild swing. The claw end of his weapon careened through the scrawny legs of the three goblins, breaking bones and sweeping them off their feet. Screeches filled the air as the monsters still standing turned and bolted off into the night.

On his knees, Tor flipped Claw end for end and used the tines to skewer each of the three writhing goblins, killing them. Shrieks of terror reverberated in the night as they faded into the distance. He stood and turned his focus on the silhouette beyond the burning grass.

Dressed in dark leathers, a warrior with a lean build, long hair, and a katana stood over the slain shaman. Half a dozen other bodies lay strewn about the area while the remainder of the goblins had fled. The figure turned and rounded the fire, allowing Tor to see a face for the first time – a female face. *It is Ekaji, the Zialan warrior who escorted us this morning.*

She squatted beside a dead goblin and wiped the blood from her blade with the creature's loincloth.

A voice came from behind Tor. "I h...h...hate that s...sp...spell."

He turned to find Koji sitting up with his hand against his forehead. "At least it is not fatal. So long as you don't get poked while you are incapacitated."

"Yeah. Th...thanks for that."

Borgli sat up and put his hand against his forehead. "I f...f...feel like my b...br...brain is about to explode."

Tor squatted beside the dead archer and cleaned his own weapon on the man's tabard. "Much like a hangover, you are experiencing a side effect of the spell. Give it a few minutes, and you'll feel better."

Ekaji slid her sword into the scabbard on her back as she approached Tor. "You fought well but were destined to die had I not killed the shaman."

"Yes, well...thank you for that."

"Killing the vermin is why my people exist. I do it out of duty and nothing more."

Borgli picked up his hammer and stood. "You sound like a fun drinking companion."

Ekaji narrowed her eyes at him. "Are you making a joke of me?"

"Would you know a joke if you heard one?"

The woman made a fist and stepped toward the dwarf, ready to fight.

Tor held his ranseur in her way, stopping her. "We are not your enemy, Ekaji."

She did not look at Tor, but she stepped back and relaxed her fists. At the same time, the soldiers on the ground and those on the boulders began to move.

Quell rolled over and looked down at Tor while holding a hand to her head. "Y...y...you f...f...forgot to warn me about g...goblin magic."

"Sorry." Tor shrugged. "I suggest you watch out for goblin magic."

She gave him a flat-lipped look. "Thanks."

Ekaji smirked. "You are funny."

"I'm glad you think so." Tor recalled the morning duel with Hajako. "Didn't your chieftain forbid you from joining us?"

Her smirk melted. "I do not agree with his decision."

"Won't that cause you trouble?"

"When I return, I suspect it will."

"Yet, you are here anyway."

"I saved you, didn't I?"

"I wasn't complaining. However, if you intend to join us, you must agree to follow my orders. I cannot have you risking our lives or impacting the success of our quest."

She crossed her arms, her gaze meeting the faces of the others as they gathered behind Tor. "Your strategy against the darkspawn was impressive, even if you neglected to address the shaman and nearly died."

Tor was about to retort, but she continued.

"You proved both intelligence and battle experience. I will agree, so long as you consider my advice when given."

Wishing to put the issue behind him, Tor nodded. "Fine." He turned toward the others. "Is anyone injured?"

Grazal rubbed his shoulder. "Just bruised from the fall when the stasis spell struck."

Numerous others expressed bearing similar bruises.

Heizer said, "Malin's hand requires bandaging." He then gestured toward the dead archer. "And Torstan is dead. Otherwise, my crew is well."

Tor peered up the mountainside. "In that case, we are climbing. It will be difficult, but I want to camp on higher ground and do so before we encounter anymore darkspawn."

"More climbing?" Borgli groaned.

Quell said, "It is preferable to dying."

"Barely."

"Everyone grab a pack." Tor bent and picked one at random. "We'll head up at an angle toward the eastern slope. Climbing will be easier in the moonlight."

Without waiting, he circled around the rear side of the boulders, choosing to avoid the dead goblins, and climbed the rocky rise.

A GASP ACCOMPANIED each step and sweat beaded on Tor's forehead despite the evening chill. In the light of the round moon, he climbed at an angle, using Claw for support each time he encountered loose footing. His thighs burned, and he longed to rest, but he pushed himself forward and demanded the same from every member in his party.

They marched in single file, first Tor, then his crew, the wizard, Heizer and his soldiers, and finally, the female Zialan warrior at the rear. Nobody spoke. Even if they had the breath to spare, it risked attracting attention. The hoots and howls echoing in the valley below were constant reminders of the dangers surrounding them.

An hour after leaving the scene of the battle, Tor crested a rise and strode across a flat ledge thirty strides long and half as deep. A wall of rock blocked the west wind, softening its bite. His gaze rose to the hillside above him and settled on the dragon's snout, now no more than five hundred feet away.

Quell stopped beside Tor and followed his gaze. "There it is," she said between gasps.

Koji stopped at Tor's other side and bent over to rest his hands on his knees while panting for air. At his side, Borgli leaned on the bigger man and wiped his brow. Grazal came next, followed by Heizer.

"We will camp here for the night," Tor announced. "Heizer, set up shifts for watch. Three soldiers per shift. The rest of you should get as much sleep as possible. We leave at daybreak."

Heizer asked, "What about *your* crew?"

"I need them sharp minded, so they sleep while I climb up for a look around."

Quell asked, "You are climbing to the snout now?"

"We are too close to wait until tomorrow. Besides, I wouldn't be able to sleep without knowing what is there."

"I am coming with you."

Tor did not argue. Truthfully, he was happy to have her along. "Koji, you are in charge while I am away. See that everyone is settled. No fires. We don't want to attract any attention."

Koji nodded. "I will see it done, Tor. Good luck to you."

"Thanks." He waved for Quell to follow. "Our climb is not yet over."

"Let's go," she said with a firm nod.

He walked the length of the shelf and began another ascent.

~

AFTER A DOZEN ZIGS AND ZAGS, twice being forced to backtrack after reaching a spot too steep to climb, Tor finally reached the height of the dragon's snout. He then worked his way along the daunting slope, stepping with care as he approached his destination. Twenty minutes after leaving the rest of his party, he and Quell climbed onto the outcropping of rock known as the dragon's snout.

Pale moonlight paved a path across a rocky shelf sixty feet wide at the base and twice the length. The rock narrowed the farther Tor walked out until it was no more than ten feet across at the tip. He turned toward the mountainside and the pair of rounded formations overlooking the snout. Oval-shaped recesses in the rock gave the impression of a pair of eyes, the rounded rock above them brows. *It is like the mountain itself is watching me.* Curious, he approached the formation and felt around in the recessed areas. The rock felt solid and unremarkable.

"Do you see anything of note?" he asked over his shoulder.

"No. To tell you the truth, I have no idea what we are looking for."

He turned toward her and recalled the passage from memory. *In the ever-present mother's beaming smile, the dragon's snout will point the way to a path of shadow.* "There must be a clue in your father's notes."

"I know. But what is the *ever-present mother*?"

Tor rubbed his bearded jaw while slowly strolling down the snout.

He stopped and looked up at the moonlit mountain. "I don't see a smile. Even if the dragon could smile, the mouth is beneath the snout. We already checked there and found nothing."

"Although, it was dark under there with the moon blocked by the rock above us."

"True." He turned toward the moon. "At least we don't have a cloudy night, or we'd not even have the advantage of the moonlight." His eyes widened. "Moonbeam!"

"What?" She spun toward him.

"The moon. Unlike the sun, it never leaves the sky. It is always in the same location, only masked during a cloudy night."

She frowned. "Everyone knows that."

He rolled his eyes. "It is ever-present."

Her eyes turned round in realization. "The moon is the mother."

"In her light, the snout will point the way." Tor walked toward the tip and looked down. A three-hundred-foot drop led to a steep hillside covered in a thousand feet of rock before turning to thick forest. Miles of trees covered a valley leading to the foot of another towering peak, even taller than the one above them. "If we are supposed to search down there, this could take a while."

"But why the moon? If we were supposed to just go in the direction the snout pointed, we could do that during the day."

"True."

He turned and noticed the outline of shadow on the mountain across the saddle to the south. A distinct point jutted out from the shadow, appearing like a dragon peering out of a cave.

"Look." Tor gestured toward the shadow.

Quell followed it and said, "It is the snout, outlined by the moon."

"Which never moves, so neither does the location of the shadow."

A smile spread across her face. "The shadow of the snout points the way."

Tor eyed the mountain and noted the rock formations near the shadow. "Mark the location well. Tomorrow, you and I are leading the others across the saddle and up the opposite hillside. If your father's notes are true, the path to the temple begins there."

CHAPTER 25
THE HIDDEN PATH

Early the next morning, Tor rallied his party. After a brief meal consisting of dried meat, dried fruit, and bread too dry to eat in normal circumstances, they descended the steep hillside. The pace was faster than the ascent but limited by less-than-ideal footing. By the time the sun peered between the two peaks to the east, they stood at the battle scene from the prior evening. It was a grizzly sight and a stark reminder of what dangers lay ahead.

Two vultures picked at the corpse of the human archer. Yet, the birds avoided the dead darkspawn. The monsters were unnatural, their meat rancid and inedible, even for carrion. While the battle had been a victory and the corpses of forty-some monsters far outpaced that of the single dead human, the mood among Tor's party was somber. Nobody said a word, and he suspected all were eager to move beyond the scene and never look back.

They crossed the flat, open ground between the two peaks and approached the tree line on the eastern face of the saddle. Images from the prior evening flashed in Tor's mind – hoots and howls preceding the darkspawn bursting from the forest. While daybreak was upon them, a gloom remained in the trees, daring him to enter.

In the shadows of the tree line, he stopped and waited until the others were close. In a quiet tone, he said, "Remember what we faced last night. We don't know what lies ahead or where more darkspawn might be hiding. Remain quiet and do not stray from the group."

With Tor in the lead, followed closely by Koji, Borgli, and Quell, they entered the forest.

The ground immediately began to slope down toward the valley. Rather than descend, Tor walked parallel to the slope, his path gently turning from southeast to east as if rounding the rim of a bowl. A half mile in, he altered his path and began to climb. Soon, the trees parted to reveal a rocky hillside covered in long yellowed grass and sporadic shrubs. Hundreds of feet above him were a pair of boulders leaning against each other – his destination. Knowing there was no other way, he took a deep breath and began the climb.

∞

THE SUN SHONE down upon them, the chill of the night long forgotten by the time Tor and his party reached the pair of boulders he had noted the prior evening. He paused below them and turned toward his party as the line of people gathered around him.

"Drink some water but take care to ration it. We don't know when we will next be able to refill our skins. Rest here while my crew and I search the area. We won't be long." He waved toward Koji. "You, Borgli, and Quell are with me."

"What are we looking for?" Koji asked.

"You'll know when you find it." He rounded the boulders. "Spread out. Shout if you find anything of note."

Koji and Tor split off to the right while Borgli and Quell went to the left. The hillside was all rock and scrub. While the grass in the area was trampled, Tor found nothing else of note. After minutes of searching, worry began to claw at him. *What if we misinterpreted the clue? What if there is no temple?* As the doubts began to seat themselves in place, Borgli called out.

"Over here!"

Tor spun toward the dwarf, who stood a hundred feet away and a bit upslope from him. He began in that direction, followed by Koji. "What is it?"

"I sense a hollowness."

Quell, standing just below the dwarf, put her hands on her hips. "What the blazes does that mean?"

Borgli tilted his head, his gaze distant while one arm made a circular motion over the hillside. "There is a tunnel or cave here somewhere."

"And how do you know that?"

He puffed up and thumbed his chest. "I am a stone shaper. The best of my generation."

Quell shot a befuddled look at Tor as he drew close. "Is he making sense to you?"

Tor nodded. "Borgli has special abilities. Apparently, they include the ability to find a cave."

Borgli rolled his eyes. "I can feel the rock around me – its shape, its density, its harmony. When a cave is present, I feel a void in the elements I normally sense in rock."

"All right. Where is this cave?"

The dwarf closed his eyes, held his hands before him, and took a step to the east. "Near here."

Tor climbed up to the dwarf and walked past him, rounding a gently curved wall of rock obscured by a massive boulder. Three strides later, he discovered an opening. It cut back toward where Borgli stood before fading into darkness. Scrapes marred the rock, leaving pale streaks – a telling sign that goblins had passed by.

Digging into his pack, Tor found his light rod, activated it, and held it before him while easing into the opening. The gap turned into a tunnel ten feet tall and half the width. A dozen strides in, Tor stopped and turned back.

He emerged with a grin. "We found it. Quell, go fetch the others. We are about to go spelunking."

∼

THE PALE BLUE aura from the rod in Tor's hand ate away at the darkness as he advanced along the tunnel. More than once, he came across areas where weapons and claws had dug at the wall. Each was a reminder of the danger that might await them. On three occasions, the tunnel branched. Each time, Tor chose the left option, following the cryptic clues found in the journal. *Wrapped in darkness, the walls closing in, remain bold and silent. Hope is all you have left. Giving up cannot be right. Thrice, you must say this to yourself.*

Twenty minutes after they had entered the tunnels, the route turned and daylight whispered a promise of open skies. Tor lowered his rod and continued toward it with anticipation fluttering in his stomach. He emerged into sunlight, stepped out on a ledge, and peered down at a valley unseen by humans for thousands of years. *Except for Quell's father*, a voice inside told him. *Shut up and enjoy this*, he replied.

A small lake lay in the center of a wooded canyon bordered by steep, impassable slopes. The ridgeline above where Tor stood was the lowest point of the bowl surrounding the valley. The other points, snowcapped peaks connected to each other, all stood above the snow-line. The lone exception was a narrow crevice with a creek running through it. The creek heading east toward the Murlands.

At the south end of the canyon, no more than five miles away, a stone structure the size of a small palace backed against a steep cliff-side. An array of pillars stood before a flat-topped pyramid built from tan-colored stone blocks. The forest tightly surrounded the building on three sides, making it appear abandoned even from the distance.

"There it is," Tor said aloud.

Koji stopped at Tor's side. "My heart sings in response to such beauty."

Quell stood at Koji's other side. "If you begin to cry, I am going to poke you with my hunting knife. That'll give you a reason for tears."

Borgli chuckled and nudged Tor. "I like her."

Grazal appeared on the ledge and stared across the canyon. "It is true. It *does* exist."

Tor surveyed the land between the ledge and the canyon floor. "I see a trail leading down this hillside. We will follow it to the forest and visit the lake to refill our waterskins. Then, we head for the temple. I fear what will happen if we do not complete our business and get out of this canyon before nightfall."

Quell asked, "What if darkspawn wait inside?"

"Then, we will have a fight on our hands. However, this time we will surprise *them*."

~

It was mid-morning by the time Tor emerged from the forest and scrambled down to the lakeshore. He squatted and dipped his hand in the water. It was freezing cold. *Snowmelt*. He scooped a handful, lifted it to his nose, and smelled it. Nothing. The water was clear with large rocks visible in the bottom of the pool.

"It looks safe." He uncapped his waterskin, downed the rest of its contents, and dunked the skin beneath the surface. Air bubbled out as water filled the container.

The others drank their fill before refilling their skins, some then drinking again. He then stood and stared toward the temple, its upper reaches visible above the trees. The building stood a quarter mile away with untold secrets waiting for him somewhere inside. He dug into his pack, flipped through the journal, and found a drawing depicting the temple beyond a line of trees.

Quell leaned over his shoulder, looked at the image, and then lifted her gaze to the temple. "My father drew this while standing where we are now."

"I agree." Tor turned to the next page. It was where the truly confusing journal entries began.

Drawings of objects, strange runes, and squirrely lines filled page after page. Here and there, single word notes were written in ancient Hassakani.

"What do these notations mean?" Quell asked.

"I don't know yet. I am hopeful it will make more sense once we are inside." He stored the book before throwing the pack over his shoulder. "If everyone is ready, I'd like to start toward the temple."

Heizer nodded. "My men are ready."

"As am I," the wizard added.

"Good. Let's go."

After following the shoreline to the end of the lake, they climbed the grassy bank and faded into the trees. The undergrowth between the temple and lake was trampled – bent grass, squashed ferns, broken shrub branches, and footprints everywhere. Tor weaved through the trees, twice having to duck beneath a low branch before he reached the forest edge.

Stretched-out rows of stairs led from the forest floor to a plaza made of square stone tiles. Twenty-foot-tall columns bordered the plaza, leading up to the temple, which loomed over the surrounding forest. No openings were visible other than a dark doorway in the front of the building. In the heart of the plaza was a green-tinted, bronze pedestal molded in the form of three snakes twisted together. At the top of the pedestal, five feet above the plaza floor, a ruby nested between the open mouths of the three snakes. The ruby, approximately the size of Tor's fist, was worth a fortune and begged to be stolen... which is why Tor stopped just shy of the stairs.

He silently rubbed his jaw, narrowed his eyes, and surveyed the plaza.

Etched in each of the stone floor tiles were runes unknown to Tor. He examined the nearest tile, and the embossed symbol gave him a nefarious impression. His gaze lifted to the pillars, and he noted the tiny, diamond-shaped, mirrored panels mounted on the interior face of each column. Those tiles began just inches above the plaza floor and ran up to the top of the pillars.

"What are you waiting for?" Grazal asked.

"This is a trap."

"What makes you say that?"

"Because there is no forest growth on the plaza floor. I don't even see debris. After all of these years, wouldn't you expect it to be littered?"

The wizard frowned. "I suppose so."

Lieutenant Heizer said, "You can stare all you want, but I intend to claim that ruby for High Wizard Z'Kawl.

When the man climbed the first step, Tor reached out and grabbed his arm to yank him back.

"What are you doing?" the lieutenant said, outraged.

"Watch." Tor squatted and picked up a rock half the size of his head.

With a grunt, he heaved the rock past the columns. It struck the tiled floor, bounced, and landed on a neighboring tile. The moment it touched the second tile, the ruby came to life. A bright crimson glow arose from it, and beams of bright red light shot out from the jewel, reflected off the mirrored panels mounted to the columns. The light crisscrossed the plaza, the highest beams far taller than any man, the lowest at ankle height. When a beam struck the rock on the plaza, the rock flared with an angry glow and suddenly faded away. The light in the gem doused, and the beams disappeared.

Everyone stared at the vacant tile where the rock had once been. The eager soldier backed off the stairs but remained silent.

"How do we get past it?" Borgli asked.

"Grazal," Tor said, "I don't suppose you have any magic that would be useful here?"

The wizard shook his head. "The magic that vaporized the rock is unknown to me. I have no idea how to counter it."

Tor frowned. "What if you destroy the ruby?"

The wizard furrowed his brow, raised his hands, and launched a lightning bolt at the gem. Just before striking it, a red glow flared in the jewel and the lightning fizzled away.

Heizer suggested, "What if we throw rocks at it?"

"Try an arrow first."

The man signaled an archer, who raised his bow, nocked it, and loosed. The arrow sped across the plaza and disintegrated when it struck a crimson curtain near the ruby.

Tor sighed. "As I suspected. Some element of the magic protects the ruby from harm. We need to find another way."

"Another way?" Grazal asked.

He turned to Heizer. "Split your soldiers into two teams and walk the temple perimeter. You can lead one team. Grazal will take the other. Search for another way in. If you find one, return here to report. I suggest you do not try to enter the building, not if you want to live. Ekaji and my crew will remain here while I think on a way to get past this trap."

∼

Unable to think of anything else, Tor sat on a step and paged through the journal. Shade from the trees protected him from the mid-day sun.

His team sat on the stairs beside him while Heizer and his soldiers huddled together beneath the trees. Tor imagined their comments. *This is a waste of time. He does not know what he is doing. We should head home before we all end up dead.* He could not blame them. His frustration was growing as well.

Disgusted, he slammed the journal down to the ground. The book flipped over, falling open. The breeze blew the pages to a drawing of crisscrossed lines. The wind caught the next page and turned to another sketch of crossing lines. A third page followed, and something clicked in Tor's mind.

Leaning forward, he lifted the book, climbed up a step to get out of the shade, and held the book up to the sun. Folding the rest of the pages back, he lined up the pages of crossing lines, so the sun shone through the three sheets of paper. It revealed a grid, fifteen blocks across and twice as deep. Lines crossed the grid, moving first at an angle and then straight, an angle, straight again, and finally, after numerous turns, terminated at the far end of the grid.

He grinned. "It's a map to cross the plaza, and it starts with the same tile I had thrown the rock on earlier."

Quell leaned against his side and stared up at it. "It was there the whole time."

"Yeah. But he drew it on three different pages. The notes as well." Tor lowered the book. "Now I know what the words on the pages mean. The first says together. The third says view. The final page says sun."

"Together, view in the sun." Quell shook her head. "I never understood my father's fondness for riddles."

"He left you a journal filled with them."

"He wanted to leave clues others would not understand."

"Yet, you came to me."

She smirked. "I suffered through his riddles but was never skilled at deciphering them. You seem to have a knack for these things."

"We shall see." Tor turned toward the group of soldiers. "Lieutenant Heizer." The man turned toward him. "Have your men gather rocks, logs, and branches. We will need them for a test."

While the soldiers spread out and began to search the forest, Tor climbed down and picked up the lone visible rock, nearly as heavy as the last. He stood on the middle stair and concentrated on the target tile. He tossed the stone. It landed, bounced, and rolled, but never left the tile. Nothing happened.

Rising up a stair, he stretched to reach the stone, gripped it, and pulled back. Again, he tossed it, this time targeting the tile directly left of the previous one. The stone struck the tile, bounced, and by the time it settled, crimson beams of light had spread across the plaza. A beam struck the stone, and it vaporized.

Tor grinned as the light faded. "This will take a while, but I can get us across."

CHAPTER 26
A TOUCH CAN KILL

Tor bent over and tossed a broken branch. The thick wood struck a plaza tile ten feet away, bounced, and settled just before reaching the neighboring tile. Nothing happened.

"That is five tiles. The sixth is a bit far to reach without striking another, so it is time to go."

"Go?" Borgli grimaced. "We can hardly make it across from there."

"From now on, we will have to test as we go."

"We?"

"I'll go first. Each of you follow but take care to step only on the marked tiles. Heizer's men will pass us rocks and branches, so I can test each before I advance."

Borgli's eyes widened. "What if you hit the wrong square?"

"Based on what I have seen, the beams of magic don't intersect with the safe tiles."

The dwarf appeared doubtful but said nothing more.

Tor picked up a rock and stepped on the first tile, which was still marked by a stone. No angry glow arose in the jewel, and nothing happened to him. Another rock waited on a tile diagonal from the first. He stepped on the tile, and nothing happened. Koji followed, keeping one empty tile between them.

When Tor reached the last marked tile, he opened the journal, now modified so the map resided on a single page and located the noted tile. He squatted, softly tossed the rock, and leaned back. Nothing happened. Twisting, he reached back and accepted another rock from Koji.

It was a painstaking process – the chain of people extending as they slowly advanced across the plaza, continued for ten very stressful minutes. And then, Tor missed.

A tossed rock took an odd bounce and launched sideways rather than forward. When it rolled to the adjacent tile, the ruby came to life. An angry glow bloomed, and beams of deadly light shot across the plaza, bouncing from pillar to pillar, streaking past Tor and the others. One of the soldiers reacted. He shied away from a close beam and stepped back. A ray caught his ankle. His body stiffened, a glow enveloped him, and he was gone. The light faded, and the survivors shared a nervous glance.

"As I said," Tor announced, "remain on the marked tiles. Touch no others, regardless of what happens." He reached toward Koji. "Give me the next rock."

After a dozen more tosses, including one miss, Tor finally stepped off the last tile and into the alcove before the temple entrance. Moments later, the last of his party joined him. Once everyone was safely across, he turned toward a tall door masked in shadow. The door itself was made of stone and covered in strange symbols carved into the surface.

Tor paged through the journal and came to the final entry – an illustration of an object in the shape of a cross, each of the four ends raised with a three-dimensional symbol. After memorizing the four symbols, Tor examined the runes on the door, his fingers running over them until he located a glyph he recognized. He then spied the others from the drawing, one parallel to the first, the others positioned above and below while other symbols occupied the spaces in between. He pressed his palm to the center, but nothing happened.

"The cross must be a key," Tor muttered.

Quell said, "My father owns this artifact. He claimed that it, along with the legend of the temple, was passed down from his father and his father's father before that."

Tor turned toward her. "Why did you not tell me this before now?"

She grimaced. "I did not know what happened to the cross. Even so, I always considered it a simple trinket lacking purpose. How could I know you might need it?"

"Fine," Tor sighed. "When did you last see the cross?"

"A few weeks before my father left our cabin. I haven't seen him or it since."

Groaning, Tor said, "He likely has it, and if he is inside, we must find another way in."

Borgli shrugged. "I can get us in."

Tor's eyes widened in realization. "Of course. I should have thought of that. Will it take long?"

The dwarf waved it off, as if the request were inconsequential. "Give me a minute. Two at most." He approached the door, placed his hands on it, and slid his fingers into the stone.

"Whoa!" Heizer gasped and looked at Grazal. "How did he do that?"

The wizard furrowed his brow while staring intently at Borgli as he worked. "I have no idea."

Quell arched a brow. "Impressive, Borgli. I see there is more to you than a massive hammer and a pretty beard."

The dwarf grinned over his shoulder as he removed a melon-sized chunk of stone. "These fingers know how to tickle more than just the ladies."

She snickered. "Get us in there, and I'll buy you ale when we return to Zialis."

"If I wasn't motivated before," he dug a chunk out with a grunt, "I am now."

Ekaji stared out toward the plaza. "The day passes, and we have reached mid-afternoon. When darkness claims this valley, I believe we will have unwanted company."

Tor recalled the darkspawn markings in the tunnels and the footprints in the forest floor. "I suspect you are right. That is why we need to get inside, finish our business, and leave before nightfall."

Koji said, "I just hope no monsters lurk beyond this doorway."

Borgli dug another chunk of stone from the door. "I am working as fast as I can."

The group fell quiet, everyone watching while the stone-shaper did his thing. Soon, darkness appeared beyond the broken stone, the hole extending all the way through the twelve-inch-thick door. Borgli continued to remove sections of stone until the opening was two feet wide and three feet tall, the bottom edge a foot and a half off the ground. He then stepped back and dusted off his hands.

"There you go. Even the giant should fit through if he holds his breath."

Koji grunted. "Your belly is as round as mine."

The dwarf rubbed his sizable gut. "This is muscle."

"And my arse is made of gold," Quell countered.

Borgli grinned. "I'd like to see that."

She laughed. "You wish, you walking beard."

"Thank you." He preened a bit, stroking the thick ginger hair hanging down to his stomach.

Tor finished digging his light rod from his pack, squatted, and reached into the opening. Light bloomed inside, but the space was too large for it to reach the walls or ceiling. "I'm going in. Give me a few seconds to make sure it is safe."

He ducked his head into the darkness and examined the floor, finding bits of rubble resting on smooth, solid stone. The nearest wall, six feet to his left, looked innocuous. The opposite wall, ten feet to the right, mirrored the other. Tor eased through the opening, entered the temple, and then stood upright.

The air smelled stale, cobwebs clung to the corners, and a pair of beetles skittered away in fear of his light. Taking careful steps, his gaze scanning the floor and his surroundings, he advanced across the temple entrance hall. The light in his hand extended to reveal a pair of pillars covered with runes. An arch connected the pillars, carved in the strange symbols of an unknown language.

Tor turned back toward the entrance to find Quell climbing through. "You were supposed to wait."

"Nothing happened to you, so I figured I would be safe enough so long as I followed your lead."

"Huh. I expected a snide comment from you."

She grinned. "I had a few and managed to restrain myself."

"Perhaps you are growing up."

"Don't tell my father when we find him. I wouldn't want him to think less of me."

Tor chuckled. "Fair enough."

Borgli squeezed through the opening and joined them. He walked up to Tor and peered toward the opening between the pillars. "This place is massive. Much larger than it appears from the outside."

"How do you know?" Quell asked.

"I can feel it."

Koji, grunting and groaning, wiggled through the opening. The big man dusted himself off while Grazal ducked inside. Ekaji, Heizer, and the rest of the soldiers followed with everyone gathering between Tor and the door.

"In this space, we are beyond the entrance trap and out of the reach of darkspawn once nightfall comes." The light in Tor's hand illuminated the faces of those in his party. "While this chamber appears safe for now, there is still no telling what dangers might await us in the temple. Thus, I would prefer—"

A chill suddenly passed over Tor, his breath swirling in the air before him. Spurred by a sense of urgency, he reached over his shoulder, drew his weapon, and shouted, "Beware! Wraiths!"

Everyone reacted. Koji, Borgli, and Ekaji drew their weapons. The rest of the party looked around in alarm. A terrifying wail shook the room, causing heads to turn from side to side in search of the source. A dark, ghostly shadow emerged from a stone wall, reached out, and touched the back of a soldier's neck. The man stiffened and collapsed. Ekaji thrust with her katana, slicing through the wraith. The creature emitted a screeching wail and fizzled away.

"It killed Petris!" one of the soldiers announced as they all backed away from the corpse.

"Wraiths are the Dark Lord's tools." Ekaji held her blade up above her shoulder while staring toward the spot where the wraith appeared. "Just a touch will kill."

Tor spun slowly, his heart hammering in his chest. One hand held the light rod high while the other gripped Claw's shaft. "Use your weapons. Just as you die from a wraith's touch, the shades cannot abide the touch of steel."

Another phantom form emerged from the wall opposite the first. The wraith reached for Borgli, who stared in the other direction, unaware of the threat. Koji spied the shadow and his long arm swept above the dwarf's head. When his machete sliced the shadow, an ear-splitting shriek echoed in the chamber. The shadow popped and faded away.

All at once, more shades materialized, extending ghostly arms whose touch would kill.

Swords flashed, wails echoed, and men cried out. Tor continued to spin around, searching for an incoming attack. He raised his light high and spied a wraith coming down from above him. With a high thrust, he drove Claw's tines into the shade just before it reached Koji's head. A terrifying screech followed as the wraith dissolved. Then, as quickly as the attack began, it ended.

Although they had barely moved, Tor and the others panted from the tense anxiety. Four soldiers lay dead, while the survivors gripped swords, spears, or knives. In their center was Grazal, kneeling on the floor, his eyes filled with fear.

"Is it over?" Quell held her hunting knife before her while her gaze swept the room.

"I believe so," Tor said. "When one wraith wakes, so do those nearby."

Grazal asked, "What if others heard us?"

"From beyond this chamber?" Tor shook his head. "They only haunt the area where their human form died…the poor trapped souls."

"Trapped souls?" Quell asked.

"Yes. Bound here by dark magic."

"What of those we killed?"

"Released from their prison, but unable to move on to the afterlife."

"That is horrible."

"Blame the Dark Lord. It was his nefarious magic that created them in the first place." Tor looked down at the dead soldier at his feet. "We have now lost six of our crew. I pray we don't lose anyone else." The statement reinforced a decision he had been debating. "Which is why we split up here."

Grazal stood, his eyes still wild. "Split up?"

"Yes. Our group is too large. Deadly traps are bound to lurk beyond this chamber, and it will be easier to keep a smaller crew alive in those circumstances."

"What if you come across monsters?"

"I assure you, Koji and I have killed more darkspawn than the rest of you combined." His gaze shifted to Ekaji, and he gave her a nod. "Your blade may come in handy if we stumble across trouble." Everyone knew the reputation of the Zialan warriors and had witnessed some of that skill when she saved them the prior evening. "Quell, I suspect I cannot hold you back, so you are with me. Besides, an archer in the group might prove helpful. Borgli, you are coming with me as well. We will likely need your skills at some point, be it your hammer or your ability to shape stone." He nodded, feeling good about his decision. "The five of us will advance. The rest of you are to remain here. This entrance appears to be the only way out, so we will be back and will need your help once we are again outside...especially if it grows dark before we are out of this valley."

The scowl on Heizer's face made it clear he did not care for Tor's plan. Yet, he glanced at Grazal, making it clear he would defer to the wizard.

"You claim that the wraiths are gone?" Grazal asked.

"Yes, but others might wait for us in there." Tor pointed toward the dark opening between the pillars.

The wizard took a deep breath, his nostrils flaring while his gaze was one of determination. "I do not wish to be trapped in here when night falls. We will remain here until sunset approaches. If you have not yet returned, we will depart without you."

"Agreed." Tor did not know what waited for him, but he was confident it would not take them more than a few hours to address it. He removed his pack and set it against the wall. "Koji. The rations in your pack are sufficient." He handed the Kyranni warrior his waterskin. "This, along with yours, gives us sufficient water as well. Borgli, Quell, and Ekaji, leave your packs here. We will reclaim them on the way out."

His crew then followed him toward the pillars, where he stopped to give them another examination. Spying nothing of note, he thrust his weapon into the opening and jumped back. Nothing happened.

With a prayer on his lips, he stepped past the pillars and into a cavernous space. His light rod revealed a broad staircase descending into darkness, but he could see nothing else. After a backward glance to make sure the others were with him, Tor began his descent.

CHAPTER 27
A DEADLY DESCENT

Quell held her bow ready and prayed that they had seen the last of the wraiths. Unlike anything she had ever faced, the phantoms, their mere touch able to kill, terrified her. It did not help that her arrows were useless in such tight confines as the temple entrance. She could not blame Grazal for his behavior; it was obvious that he felt the same as she did. *At least I did not end up cowering on the floor.* The sentiment offered little solace, but it was something.

She and Koji descended the stairs side by side with Tor in the lead while Borgli and Ekaji brought up the rear. The pale aura of Tor's light rod only reached eight stairs below him before darkness consumed it. The staircase stretched to the left and right for as far as Quell could see. Above her, there was nothing but endless gloom.

After a descent exceeding a hundred steps, Quell spied something ahead. Tor slowed and Quell narrowed her eyes, attempting to make sense of it and then realized that it was the bottom of a boot. A man lay sprawled out, his head resting six stairs below his feet. From the stench, it was clear that the man had been dead for some time.

Tor stopped and looked around before reaching the man. "Don't move. Something killed this man."

Squatting, he appeared to examine the staircase, but Quell's attention was focused on the prone male form. The color of the boots, the cut of the coat, the brown hair peppered with gray – it was all too familiar. Emotions she had buried beneath a mound of hope suddenly burst forth and overcame her.

Quell rushed past Tor and squatted at the dead man's side. "It's my —" She covered her mouth as tears welled up, the word refusing to be said.

Tor sighed and finished her sentence. "Your father."

She nodded and closed her eyes tightly, attempting to contain her tears. Deep down, she had known for weeks that something bad had happened to him, but she repeatedly told herself to have faith. Caught between the two warring perspectives, she found herself unable to think of anything else. She had to know...and now that she did, all the pain of his loss poured out.

Tor descended a few steps and put a hand on her back. "I am sorry."

She stood and responded with a cracked voice. "I feared something had happened to him, but I still hoped otherwise."

"Hope is a valuable commodity and certainly better than giving in to despair." He looked down at the man. "I don't see any wounds. I wonder what..."

A bitter chill was Quell's only warning, causing her to spin around as a wraith reached out. She ducked and the ghostly hand swept over her. With an upward thrust, Tor drove Claw's tines through the shade. A bone-chilling shriek coincided with the wraith's demise. The air warmed, signifying the end of the threat. Still, Quell spun around, her eyes sweeping the dark surroundings in search of another threat while her heart pounded in her chest like a drum.

"I think we know what killed him," Tor said.

Koji patted her on the back. "Your father now has vengeance."

Vengeance, Quell had considered avenging her father if anything had happened to him, expecting it would provide a modicum of satisfaction. Instead, she felt empty. The wraith was only a tool of the Dark Lord, and its demise did not bring her father back. *It is the Dark Lord who must suffer.* The thought helped her push past her grief and grapple for resolve.

Quell dried her eyes, stared down the staircase, and saw the glitter of a reflection at the edge of Tor's light. She descended a few steps, eyeing the object. She realized what it was before she reached it. Squatting, she picked up the bronze cross and turned it over. Raised symbols stood out on each of the four ends of the object.

"He had the key with him the whole time." Tor sheathed his weapon, descended a few stairs, and took the cross from her. He examined it before staring into the darkness. "If he carried it into the temple, perhaps there is a use for it other than entering."

"What about my father?" Quell looked back at the man's body lying on the stairs. It felt so...wrong. "We can't just leave him here."

Tor turned back toward her. "I am sorry, but we will have to leave him for now and deal with him on our way out."

Her chin dropped to her chest, attempting to balance her feelings with logic. She knew Tor was right but could not speak it, so she nodded instead.

Koji stopped at her side and clapped a thick mitt on her shoulder. "You have my condolences, Quell."

"Ouch." Quell winced. "Careful, you big lummox."

"Sorry." He yanked his hand back.

She gave him a sad smile. "But thank you for the sentiment."

"I know well what it is like to lose one you love. My heart bleeds for you, and I offer my shoulder if you care to cry."

Quell rolled her eyes. "I take it back." She waved to Tor. "Let's continue before he tries to cradle me like a babe."

Tor grinned. "I would not put it past him."

"I was merely attempting to console her." Koji appeared hurt.

Borgli looked up at the tall warrior as he walked by. "If you try to rock me like a babe, I'll put a fist in your mouth."

Ekaji stood at the dwarf's other side, and when Koji shot her a look of appeal, she shook her head. "Don't even consider it unless you want to lose a limb...and I am not talking about your arms or legs."

Koji shook his head. "Nobody understands me."

The lighthearted moment helped to ease Quell's sorrow. "Don't worry about it, Koji." She gestured toward the stairs below. "Let's find out what drew my father here in the first place."

"Right, then." Tor raised his light rod and continued his descent.

The staircase soon ended at a floor of stone. Tor led the team across it toward a stone pedestal that appeared in the gloom ahead of them. The object stood eight feet tall and a foot wide. Quell and Tor approached the pedestal, the light revealing a grid of runes etched in the side facing them. Stopping a stride away, Tor looked down at the cross in his hand while Quell examined the runes marking the column.

"Here," Quell tapped on the pedestal. "This matches one of the runes embossed on the cross." She had spent enough time studying the cross to recognize the runes. "The others are here, here, and here," Quell said tapping on other runes located three spaces from the first one.

Tor nodded as Quell stepped back. She held her breath, the anticipation palpable as Tor brought the cross to the pillar. When the four matching raised marks on the cross met the recessed ones on the column, a click sounded, and the cross locked in place. The top of the pedestal began to glow with an amber aura. As the glow pulsed and grew brighter, Tor backed away.

Suddenly, a beam of light shot up from the pedestal. Hundreds of feet above, the beam shone on a crystal the size of a horse. The crystal refracted the beam, sending rays of light in a myriad of directions and lighting the temple interior.

The crew released a collective gasp.

The temple walls stood five hundred feet to either side of the group, and the length of the building was even greater than the width. The pedestal stood in the center of a landing located three stories above the temple floor. To either side of the landing and the staircase was a hundred-foot drop, the bottom blanketed in shadows. None of this compared to the grandeur of two features that dominated the temple interior.

Covering the vast temple floor was a labyrinth of twenty-foot-tall walls that shimmered in the light. Beyond the maze, far across the chamber, stood a giant statue that was decidedly female, her head and the upper portion of her bare torso both overlooking the labyrinth.

"Huh," Koji said. "I always imagined the Dark Lord was male."

"He is," Borgli confirmed.

Tor rubbed his jaw. "Something tells me that this temple does not belong to Urvadan."

Quell asked, "What is it, then?"

"I don't know. If it pays homage to a god…it would be a goddess instead."

Ekaji said, "I have never heard of a goddess."

"Neither have I. Regardless, we are here, and I intend to see this through."

"For my father's sake, so do I." Quell gave a firm, determined nod.

Borgli began down the stairs, stopped, and looked back at the rest of the party, still on the landing. "Why are you standing around? We have the statue of an oversized woman waiting for us."

Upon reaching the temple floor, Tor strode up to the labyrinth entrance and tentatively reached toward one of the walls. It felt cold and smooth to the touch. Light shone through the translucent material, but the milkiness made it difficult to see what lay on the other side. "It is crystal," he said aloud. He looked down at the floor – brown stone was visible beneath a few inches of crystal.

"Why make the walls of crystal?" Koji asked.

Quell added, "And the floor as well?"

Borgli grunted. "It might be to prevent someone like me from compromising the maze."

"What do you mean?"

"Stone shapers can manipulate anything found underground except crystal. It just won't...listen."

"Listen?" Quell arched a brow. "You make it sound like you sweet talk the stone."

"In a way, that's what I do. It hears me and bends to my will. Crystal, however, is quite pigheaded."

"Sounds like you two are a match, then."

He grinned. "Good one."

"I thought so as well."

Tor stepped into the maze opening and looked left and then right. A long corridor stretched in both directions. "It's too bad there is nothing in the journal to help with this."

"My father led us to this point, but the rest is up to us." Quell arched a brow in an obvious challenge. "I would expect the great Tor Ranseur to know what to do."

He closed his eyes for a beat and tried to recall the maze from when he stood above it. Relying on his intuition, he turned left. "We go this way. Whenever we reach an intersection, we turn left. It will ensure we don't miss a passage or get lost."

Tor headed down the corridor, the walls ten feet apart. Koji walked at his side while the others followed a stride behind them.

"Keep your eye out," Tor instructed. "Let me know if you see, sense, smell, or hear anything of note."

"Smell?" Ekaji asked.

"Yes. I would have added taste, but I think it unlikely that any of you will go around licking the walls or floor."

"Are you certain?" Quell asked. "What if I can convince Borgli that they taste like ale?"

"Then, I suspect he will go around licking everything in sight."

Quell, Koji, and even Borgli laughed.

In contrast, Ekaji frowned. "Do you always argue and prod at one another?"

"It keeps the mood light." Tor shrugged. "I don't mind so long as everyone does their job when the situation requires it."

They came to a ninety-degree turn, rounded it, and walked another fifty strides before reaching their first intersection, where they turned left.

~

Sharp turns occurred repeatedly. Sometimes Tor and his crew rounded the end of a wall and were forced to double back the way they came. They turned left at each junction, per Tor's plan. It was the only way to ensure that every path was checked and that they did not become lost. Thrice, they came to a dead end and had to walk all the way back to the prior intersection before advancing. From time to time, they walked beside walls along the outer edge of the maze, notable by the darkness lurking on the other side of the crystal.

As this painstaking process continued, Tor sensed the growing frustration among his crew. Yet, based on the position of the crystal in the temple ceiling, it was clear that they were progressing toward the temple's far end. When they turned a corner and followed an outer wall, the massive female statue finally became visible above the maze for the first time since entering it. The sculpture waited only a few hundred feet ahead, past a labyrinth wall where another turn waited.

The crew made for the statue and turned at the next corner, where Tor took a dozen strides before coming to a stop. Another turn waited two hundred feet away. Warm light came from around the turn, rekindling the hope that had slowly dwindled during the journey through the labyrinth. And while they had encountered no traps nor enemies during their exploration, exiting the maze might bring one or both.

Quell walked past him, heading for what appeared to be the labyrinth exit.

"What are you doing?" he asked.

She spun around, slowing but still waking backward. "The way out is just ahead."

"That is what concerns me. It could be a"— Quell's next step landed with an audible click, immediately followed by a rumble— "trap." Tor spun around to find a section of the wall break loose from the corner and move toward them.

Reflexively, everyone backed away from the advancing wall, which soon cut off access to the corridor around the turn. Tor spun around to find the wall at the far end of the corridor moving toward them as well.

"Run!"

Spurred by urgency, Tor sped past Quell, his gaze fixed on the maze exit as the opening narrowed. When it became clear he would not make it in time, he slowed to a stop in the middle of the corridor. His chin dropped to his chest, and he took a deep calming breath before turning around.

When his gaze met Quell's, she winced. "Sorry."

"There is nothing for it now." He spun around slowly, scrutinizing the shrinking corridor, the walls at both ends steadily coming toward him. "We need to find a way out."

The walls looked no different than the rest of the maze, each two stories high and made of unblemished smooth crystal. All the while, the rumbling continued as the end sections continued to advance.

"Tor," Koji said, "the walls aren't stopping. If this continues, we are about to become the filling of a very ugly sandwich."

"I know." Tor put his hand on the side wall with the warm light behind it. "The way out is on the other side of this wall. Maybe we can break through it."

Ekaji seemed doubtful. "That crystal is a foot thick."

Borgli pulled his war hammer off his back. "Perhaps the weapon of my forefathers can do it." The dwarf stepped up to Tor. "Stand aside."

As requested, Tor moved aside while Borgli held the hammer against his forehead with his eyes closed. A moment later, he opened his eyes, wound back, and swung. Tremor struck the crystal with a resounding boom. Tor felt the ensuing concussion in his chest. Borgli swung again, striking the same spot. This time, the impact emitted a thunderous echo. Nothing happened, yet the walls continued to close in. Undeterred, Borgli swung his hammer repeatedly. On the ninth blow, a crack formed. On the tenth, the crack spread. By then, the moving walls were only thirty feet apart.

"Again!" Tor urged the dwarf.

Borgli swung three more times, the cracks widening while pieces of crystal broke away.

"Step aside," Tor told Borgli.

The walls stood only fifteen feet apart, and Tor wound back, gripping Claw's shaft while eyeing the intersection of spidering cracks.

With all his might, he launched the ranseur at the damaged wall. It struck and crashed through the wall in a spray of glass-like shards, leaving an opening two feet in diameter.

"Borgli. You go first."

The dwarf nodded and climbed through the hole, followed by Quell and Ekaji.

The walls were only eight feet apart when Tor pointed toward the hole. "Your turn, Koji. I'll go last."

Koji nodded, ducked, stuck his upper body into the opening, and promptly became wedged. Desperate and running out of time, Tor planted his palms on the huge man's rather large arse and began to push. The walls were four feet apart when Koji suddenly fell forward, leaving the hole open. One wall, then the other, scraped against Tor's shoulders as he dove toward the hole. He fell through, landed on his hands, and rolled. A heavy thud resounded as the moving walls met, blocking the opening in the wall.

CHAPTER 28
THE WOMB

With his heart hammering in his chest, Tor climbed to his feet and pulled a shard of crystal from his forearm. "Ouch."

"That was close," Koji said.

"Yes. Thanks to Quell." Tor tossed the bloodied shard aside and squatted to retrieve his weapon.

"I think you'll forgive me." Quell stared off to the side and nodded in the same direction. "Look."

Tor turned to examine his surroundings.

They stood at the edge of a plaza, the nearest end bordered by the labyrinth with two openings in crystal walls. At the opposite end of the plaza, her back to a wall of rock, sat the largest statue Tor had ever seen. Her head was the size of a house, her breasts each larger than a rowboat. A particularly bright beam of light shone from the massive crystal in the temple ceiling to an opening in the statue's forehead.

The statue's legs were spread and stretched out with one foot looming over where Tor and his companions stood, the other at the opposite side of the plaza. His gaze followed the curves of her legs, noting diamond-shaped mirrors mounted to them fifteen feet above the floor. Where her legs met her body was a vertical opening with warm light coming from it.

"That is where we need to go," Tor gestured toward the light.

Quell snorted. "It figures. You men spend all your time trying to get in there."

A quip sped through Tor's head but was tossed aside as he focused on his task. In an even, distracted tone he said, "I'll admit that is a worthy quest, but ours is far more serious in nature…and far more deadly." He narrowed his eyes while staring toward the tunnel of warm light. "I am certain something dangerous still awaits us."

"What do you think it could be?" Quell asked.

"I don't know, but we need to advance with care. Now, be quiet while I think."

Tor stepped up to the edge of the plaza and noticed a silvery strip between the stone tiles. The strip ran the width of the plaza, from one statue foot to the other. Another strip just like it waited in the next seam, five strides away. He squatted beside the first seam and rubbed his jaw. It seemed to reflect the light coming from the crystal in the temple's upper reaches.

Deciding to test a theory, Tor backed up a stride and thrust his weapon forward. When Claw's shadow intersected the shimmering silver strip, he yanked it backward. A ringing sound arose, and beams of red energy shot out from the statue's eyes, straight for the diamond-shaped mirrors mounted to the legs. The light reflected off the diamonds and down to the strips between the floor tiles. A shimmering wall of crimson light shone above each strip, crackling with energy. A moment later, the statue eyes fell dormant, and the evil light faded.

Koji said, "That looks bad, Tor."

"Yes. I suspect anything that touches the light will be vaporized, as we witnessed in the plaza outside."

"How do we get past it?"

"We break the mirrors."

"But how will we reach them?"

Quell pulled her bow off her shoulder. "I can do it."

"There are sixteen mirrors, some of them two hundred feet away."

"I have sixteen arrows left, so we should be fine."

"Are you telling me you won't miss?"

She pressed her lips together, drew an arrow, raised her bow, and took aim. A beat later, the arrow darted across the plaza and shattered the mirror in the opposite leg.

Quell lowered her bow. "Shall I continue?"

"Impressive shooting." Tor pointed toward the nearest mirror. "Target this one for me."

She drew and loosed, destroying the mirror in one motion.

"Since the first pair of mirrors are shattered, let's try something before you use any more arrows."

Tor approached the nearest strip in the floor, readied himself, and quickly thrust Claw out. The moment the shadow passed over the strip, he yanked it back. Again, the statue's eyes came to life. Angry beams shot out and reflected off the mirrors, triggering the curtains of light. When the beams struck the spots missing mirrors, there was no reflection and no wall of light.

"Perfect." Tor stepped over the first strip and waved to the others. "We will walk down the middle and advance after Quell breaks each set of mirrors."

Quell stepped over the first strip, drew an arrow, and loosed, shattering another mirror. Again and again, she repeated the process as they slowly crossed the plaza. She did not miss once.

When the last mirror was destroyed and Tor crossed the final light strip, he nodded at her. "You are skilled."

"My father taught me well. In here, without wind to affect the arrow's flight, I could have destroyed them from twice the distance."

The warm light in the opening below the statue beckoned and images of treasure flashed in Tor's mind. He took a couple strides toward the opening and then spied words carved into the floor – in the old language.

Translating one word at a time, he said them aloud. "Enter...birth canal...unknown goddess...deadly guardian...awaits."

"Did you say birth canal?" Quell asked.

Koji nodded. "It does look like a birth canal."

"Did you say deadly guardian?" asked Borgli.

"I did, so we had best take care," Tor replied.

"Could it be darkspawn?"

"I don't think so." Tor was parched and needed a moment to think. "I need a drink, Koji." When the big man handed Tor a waterskin, he uncapped it and took a swig.

Koji tilted his head and narrowed eyes while staring into the opening. "Perhaps it is a queef."

Quell exclaimed, "A what?"

Unable to contain his reaction, Tor spluttered water out his mouth while the rest went down the wrong pipe, sending him into a coughing fit.

Straight faced, Koji turned to Quell. "You do not know?"

She gave him a flat stare. "I know what a queef is."

"Then, why do you ask?"

"Because that is the stupidest answer I have ever heard."

Tor continued to simultaneously laugh and cough.

Ekaji looked at Borgli. "What is this queef they speak of?"

"Perhaps it is some sort of monster?" the dwarf offered.

Ekaji drew her sword. "I will not fear this queef monster. If it attacks, it will feel the edge of my blade."

Borgli held Tremor up and clapped it with his other hand. "And the queef shall tremble at the thunder of my hammer."

Quell frowned at Tor as he attempted to recover. "This is ridiculous, and you are not making the situation any better."

Finally recovered enough to talk, Tor wiped the tears from his eyes. "I'm sorry. I just...I can't."

Ekaji frowned. "Why do you laugh so?"

Tor clapped a hand on her shoulder. "I would rather not explain." He forcefully calmed his laughter. "Let us just assume that Koji is incorrect and the enemy we face is something else."

"Very well."

Quell sighed. "Thank the gods that is over."

Tor grinned. "If we survive, this will become one of my favorite stories to regale over a round of ales."

She stared at him for a beat before chuckling and shaking her head. "I suspect it will leave others in tears."

Ekaji furrowed her brow. "I fear I missed something. I fail to see the sorrow in this conversation."

This time, Quell laughed along with Tor.

∽

Their laughter replaced by determined expressions and their weapons ready for a surprise attack, Tor and his crew approached the glowing tunnel. Tor carefully inspected his surroundings while leading the others at a measured pace.

The smooth tunnel walls shimmered with warm light, the source coming from somewhere around a gentle curve. The floor sloped upward, its surface unmarred like the walls and ceiling. As they rounded the bend, a chamber came into view. A dozen strides later, the tunnel opened into a circular cavern with a domed ceiling. The warm light emitted down from an opening in the ceiling and seemed to bounce off the smooth chamber interior, the brightest portion of the light shining upon a circular dais in the chamber's heart.

A stone altar stood upon the dais. On it rested a corpse wrapped in yellowed strips of cloth. A halberd lay across the corpse at an angle with its blade near the corpse's head. Two stone pedestals were positioned to either side of the dais. A small golden object rested upon each pedestal.

A short flight of descending stairs surrounded the room, giving it a dished appearance other than the raised dais in the center. Eight evenly spaced alcoves were recessed in the chamber walls. Inside each alcove were four coffins standing upright as they leaned against the alcove walls.

Quell said, "I thought we were entering a womb, not a tomb."

Borgli added, "And where is this guardian we are supposed to fear?"

Tor rubbed his jaw. "I am not sure. Worse, I see little of treasure or ancient relics...only those two artifacts resting on the pedestals on the dais."

Koji offered, "Perhaps additional items of value are hidden in the coffins."

"I certainly hope so. Remain here. I am going in."

Tor eyed the three steps before him, worried they might hide some sort of trigger. While it was possible to avoid treading on them, there was no way to avoid crossing the chamber floor, so he chose to minimize his risk. With a small jump, he bypassed the stairs and landed on the chamber floor with his knees bent and his weapon in both hands, ready for anything.

Nothing happened.

Soft steps took Tor across the room while he warily scanned the floor and his surroundings. He stopped before the dais to get a closer look at the pedestals. A circular, golden amulet marked by runes rested on an angled shelf atop the nearest pedestal. At the heart of an eight-pointed star on the amulet's face was a closed eye. When he shifted his position to peer around the altar, he found a similar amulet resting on the other pedestal. The only difference – the eye on that one was open.

He squatted and examined the staircase leading up to the dais. The stairs were made of stone tiles divided by narrow seams. *Any of them could be a trigger.* Standing, Tor backed up a few strides, took a running start, and leapt, lifting his knees as high as possible. He landed on the top of the dais, five stairs above the chamber floor.

Tor rose to his feet and glanced over at the altar beside him. The corpse lying upon it appeared centuries old and left him wondering why it was wrapped as it was. He turned from it and focused on the first pedestal. Made of pale stone, it stood nearly as tall as he did. It was roughly a foot wide, just as deep, and looked completely unremarkable other than the amulet resting on its slanted top surface. When he looped around the back, he noted that the cord attached to the amulet was looped around a nub sticking out from the pedestal.

With a prayer on his lips Tor reached for the cord, pinched it between his fingers, and gently pulled it off the knob. He then raised his arm, lifting the charm from its resting place. The amulet dangled from the cord and spun slowly as Tor brought it close. Enthralled by his prize, he examined it in the light.

Four inches in diameter, runes surrounding an eight-pointed star marked the face of the golden disk. In the heart of the star, an open eye stared back.

"Tor!" Koji cried out from across the room. "Look out!"

Spinning around in alarm, Tor dodged just as the corpse, which was now sitting on the altar, thrust the pointed halberd at him and narrowly missed. The creature growled, slid off the altar, and landed on its feet. It swung the blade around in a broad stroke, intending to remove Tor's head from his body. Desperate and still gripping the amulet with one hand, Tor raised Claw to block the deadly blow. The halberd bounced off the ranseur shaft with a clang, its trajectory altered just enough to pass over Tor's head.

Spurred by fear, urgency, and the need to defend himself, Tor leapt off the dais. He landed on the chamber floor, spun, and backed away while watching his undead foe turn toward him.

The creature opened its mouth in a wordless roar. To Tor's surprise, it leapt off the dais, moving far more nimbly than he would have guessed possible for a corpse. In midair, the monster raised the halberd high over its head and chopped down as it plummeted toward him.

Tor dove to the side and rolled as the halberd blade struck the stone floor, sending chunks of rock spraying about. He rose to his feet and realized he needed both hands to defend himself. While scrambling back from the monster, he slid the amulet cord over his head and gripped Claw with both hands. The creature came at him again, this time with a swing at his midriff. Tor spread his hands to the ends of Claw's shaft and held the weapon vertical to block the blow. He spun his weapon and countered the attack with a lunge. Claw's tines pierced the creature's chest and came out its back, the sound akin to the crackling of old paper. Tor yanked the weapon free, expecting the monster to fall. Instead, it attacked.

A flurry of swipes drove him backward while he desperately blocked blow after blow. No blood came from the holes in the monster's chest, nor did it seem affected by what should have been a mortal wound. Tor's heel struck the dais stairs. He fell back onto the steps, and the monster came in with a downward chop, prepared to split Tor in half.

Suddenly, Ekaji was behind the monster, her katana flashing as she slashed at it from behind, causing the creature to stagger. In rapid succession, she sliced at its back three times. The creature spun around with a roar, the halberd sweeping toward her midriff. Ekaji bent her knees and arched her back, dipping low enough for her hair to touch the ground. The halberd swept over her, leaving her unharmed.

Tor took advantage of the distraction and thrust his weapon into the monster's back. The tines emerged from its chest, causing the creature to stumble. Tor yanked his weapon free and backed away as the undead thing turned toward him.

Four holes in the wraps now marked the locations of its wounds, but no blood fell. The monster growled and came at him.

The monster swung high, so Tor ducked low and swung the claw end of his weapon at its ankles. The heavy iron claw struck hard, snapped the monster's bones, and sent it crashing to the ground. Ekaji darted in and chopped down. Her blade sliced through the monster's neck, severing the head from the body. The head rolled away and stopped at the foot of the dais. The monster fell still.

Tor wiped the sweat from his brow and nodded. "Thanks."

She nodded back. "As promised, the evil queef met the edge of my blade and has been defeated."

Despite the tense preceding moments, Tor chuckled and tucked the amulet around his neck and beneath his tunic. "This is going to make a spectacular story." He turned toward the dais. "Now, let us collect the other amulet."

With the guardian defeated and the threat addressed, he didn't bother avoiding the stairs. Once atop the dais, he removed the amulet in the same method as the first. He held his prize up as warm light glinted off the edges of the rotating disk. "I don't know what this is, but we have retrieved, it, so I think it is time to go."

A voice came from beyond Koji and the others.

"Well done, Ranseur." Grazal emerged from the chamber entrance, trailed by Heizer and his soldiers. "You will now hand over your prize, or you will die."

CHAPTER 29
THE STING OF TEARS

The Balmorian soldiers spread out in an arc behind Tor's crew. With weapons drawn and bows nocked, they stood ready while Grazal glared at Tor.

"I will take the amulet and anything else you have recovered," Grazal demanded.

Tor scowled back at the wizard. "You were to support our quest, not sabotage it."

"Any artifacts recovered here belong to my father, for the benefit of his people. I'll not ask again. Give it over now, or you will suffer for it."

Considering the archers ready to loose, the swords within striking distance of his crew, and a wizard to contend with, Tor could see no way to avoid giving in to Grazal's demand. Yet, the wizard was only aware of the amulet in his hand, not of the one beneath his tunic.

"Fine." Tor extended his hand while approaching Grazal. "Take it."

A longing filled the wizard's eyes. He descended the outer stairs, his gaze affixed on the object dangling from Tor's fist. The moment his foot met the second step, a brief hum ran through the room. The doors to the coffins standing in the eight alcoves flung open. Skeletons emerged, each armed with a shield strapped to an arm and a curved saber in the opposite hand. The creatures wore strange, black-tinted helms while spiked, black metal plates covered their shoulders.

"Look out!" Tor shouted.

The soldiers standing between the alcoves bracketing the chamber entrance, their backs to the attacking monsters, had no chance and were cut down in the span of a breath.

"Gather on the dais!" Tor waved toward the others while he retreated to the middle of the room.

Koji, Borgli, and Quell reacted, leaping down to the floor and racing toward Tor while the remaining soldiers fought off the nearest enemies.

The wizard, wide-eyed, held up his hands as four skeletons rushed toward him. A cone of flames burst from his hands and enveloped the charging monsters. Grazal backed away as the fire dissipated and the creatures emerged from it, their bones blackened but their bodies still very much animated.

Ekaji rushed in from the side and sliced with her katana. The blade cut right through a burnt skeleton spine, sending the separated torso into the others. One skeleton stumbled to the floor, but the other two sliced at Grazal, who unleashed another spell. The monsters suddenly flew across the room and smashed into the wall, sending a spray of bones in all directions.

By the time Tor and his crew reached the dais, a dozen monsters were converging on them while the others focused on Heizer and his men across the room.

"Spread out," Tor said. "Don't let any of them on top of the dais."

∼

Borgli ascended the dais and stopped three stairs up, where he turned to face the animated skeletons. Among his people, there were stories of an ancient dark magic that was thwarted long ago – a magic that could raise the dead. He had always considered those tales to be myth, but he could not deny what he saw before him.

From the alcove nearest to him came a wave of monsters, their white bones yellowed in some areas and tinted green in others. When the lead skeleton drew near, Borgli wound back and swung. His war hammer crashed into the creature's side. A pulsing thump echoed in the chamber as the enchantment in the magical weapon released added power to the blow. The skeleton shattered in a spray of bones.

Swept up by the thrill of battle, Borgli roared with a backswing. His hammer connected with the next creature's helm, the tremendous impact separating its head from its body and launching the skull across the room.

∼

Koji deflected a sword attack with his machete, reached out with his gauntlet, and grabbed the attacking skeleton by the neck. He lifted the creature and bellowed as he flung it at a pair of charging monsters. In a terrible collision of bones and metal plates, pieces broke off the three creatures and sent broken bone shards spraying in all directions.

Another skeleton rushed in from the side and thrust, forcing Koji to fall back onto the stairs. The monster raised its blade overhead, preparing for a downward chop, but it crashed to its back when Koji lashed out with a kick, sweeping the monster's legs out. The creature rolled and tried to climb to its feet, but Koji found his footing first and jumped down the last few stairs while slamming his gauntlet down. His fist pounded into the skeleton's back and broke its spine in two.

∼

Out of arrows and finding no use for her hunting knife, Quell stood back and watched the others fight. When a cluster of skeletons charged and attacked Tor, she noted their position and saw an opening. She pressed her shoulder and hands against the nearest pedestal and pushed. The heavy object tipped up and rocked back down. Straining, she thrust into it as a skeleton wound back to strike Tor's exposed side.

∼

A trio of skeletons began up the stairs near Tor, and he swung Claw around in a broad arc. The claw end of the weapon struck a skeleton skull with frightening force, cracking it and sending the monster tumbling. Another monster came at Tor with a swipe of its saber. He spun his ranseur and blocked the strike with a mighty clang. Tor attacked with a thrust of the forked end of the weapon. The two tines slid to either side of the skeleton's neck bones. Tor lifted and twisted hard, snapping the skull right off the skeleton. The body collapsed, bones breaking free as the headless skeleton tumbled down the steps and clattered across the floor.

The third monster wound back, ready to swing its sword at Tor's exposed side, too soon for him to react.

A stone column crashed down the staircase, bowled through the monster's bony legs, and flipped it over. The skeleton crashed down headfirst and shattered into a pile of bones.

Tor spun around to find Quell standing where the pedestal had been.

"I thought you could use some help," she said.

"Thanks." He nodded to her, climbed up the last few stairs, and took stock of the situation.

To one side, Koji backed away from a skeleton torso. Its lower body was gone but it still clawed its way across the floor. Koji jumped forward and chopped down, his machete slicing through the neck bones, decapitating the monster. The skeleton fell still.

Across the dais, Borgli swung his hammer in a broad arc, the heavy weapon blasting through the humerus and ribs of an attacking monster, sending the remains to join the heap of bones at the bottom of the stairs before him.

Below the dais, Ekaji and Grazal fought back-to-back. Her katana blocked and returned attacks from a pair of skeletons while the wizard used spells to lift monsters off the ground and fling them into the cavern wall. Across the room, Balmorian soldiers fought against a trio of skeletons. Bones and fallen warriors littered the chamber entrance.

The last skeleton fell to Borgli's hammer, and the fight suddenly ended.

Of the soldiers, only Heizer and one other swordsman remained standing. The others lay on the stairs and near the entrance. Blood pooled around the bodies, most unmoving although two groaned in pain before falling still. They had been sandwiched between the two alcoves, their backs to the monsters when the attack began, and half of the soldiers had died before they had a chance to defend themselves.

Tor lowered his weapon. The fight, fast and furious, left him panting for air despite its brief nature. "This is over. We are leaving."

Grazal turned toward him. "Not with the relic...not until you hand them over."

"You lost your advantage, Grazal." As he spoke, Tor shifted Claw to his left hand and unhooked his bola from his belt. "We now outnumber you, and if you try to fight us, you will die like the others."

The wizard grimaced and extended a hand toward Tor. Anticipating the magical attack, Tor spun his bola one quick rotation, and loosed. At the same time, he tossed Claw into the air and dove away from the ranseur. A bolt of lightning shot out and struck the iron weapon.

Grazal raised his hand to block the incoming bola, the other still outstretched toward Tor, but the bola cord struck Grazal's forearm. The weighted disks whipped around his arm in opposite directions, wrapping tightly. When the cords shortened and the disks slapped against his arm, he stiffened and collapsed.

Tor climbed to his feet and retrieved Claw as he descended the dais stairs. He then approached the fallen wizard, who twitched from the stasis spell.

"You wizards think yourselves superior to the Ungifted. This causes you to forget the frailty of the human body." Tor squatted beside the man. "If I wanted to, I could end your life right now, and you would be helpless to stop me." The wizard's eyes flicked wildly while his body remained in the throes of convulsions, the only sound in the chamber the rustling of his robes as involuntary jerks racked his body. Tor began to unravel the bola from the incapacitated wizard's arm. "Betrayal is among the most bitter of dishes, difficult to swallow. It also leaves a distaste most find impossible to forget. Despite this, I am willing to let you live. Should you or your men turn on me again, I will not be so kind." Tor hoped the wizard and the remaining soldiers feared the coldness in his voice despite concerns he kept masked from view.

"What did you do to him?" Heizer asked.

"He is caught in a spell and will remain that way for a while." Tor stood and hooked the bola back on his belt. He then removed his knife and cut a strip off the wizard's sash. "It is time for us to leave. But remember, if any of you turn on me again, you will die."

Heizer sheathed his sword with a grimace. "What of the fallen soldiers? It isn't right to just leave them like this."

"This tomb is as good as any. If you wish to give them a different burial, that is up to you." Tor tied the cloth around the wizard's head, blindfolding him before tying it tightly. "As I said, we are leaving. The day is waning. It will take a while to return to the entrance, and we need to get out of this canyon before darkness falls or we may all need a burial. If you wish to travel with me, you will obey my every order."

The lieutenant considered the situation before sighing deeply. "We agree to your terms."

"Good. We will help you deal with the dead, but first, you need to shackle Grazal, so his hands are behind his back. I'll not risk sabotage by way of his magic when he recovers."

Heizer nodded. "It will be done."

∽

STILL BITTER ABOUT Grazal's attempt to betray him, Tor crossed the plaza below the statue of the unknown goddess. Koji walked at his side, Quell at his other side. She had refilled her quiver with arrows from the quivers of dead soldiers. Borgli and Ekaji followed, each still gripping their weapons and appearing ready for a fight. Finally, Heizer and Bravacci, the other surviving soldier, each held one of the blindfolded wizard's arms as they guided him, his hands shackled behind his back like a common prisoner. The corpses of Heizer's men remained in the tomb, or womb, depending on your point of view. While the lieutenant seemed less than pleased at leaving them behind, he had come to accept that the situation required it. Tor's compromise to ease the man's concerns was to place their bodies in the empty caskets and close them, giving the dead soldiers a modicum of peace in their final resting place.

As they neared the far end of the plaza, passing the small opening Borgli had made, Tor spied a much larger hole in the crystal wall straight ahead, while the normal maze exits still waited to the left and right.

"What happened there?" Tor asked.

Heizer replied, "Grazal did that with his magic."

"So, he cheated to get through the labyrinth faster?"

The lieutenant shrugged.

Tor did not mind using the wizard's actions to his own advantage. "Well, we will use it. Besides, mazes are always easier when passing through them in reverse." He headed toward the opening, stepped through, and continued down the corridor toward the temple entrance.

∼

AFTER A DAY FILLED with activity and stressful moments, Tor climbed the long staircase leading to the pedestal, the beam of bright light still streaming up from it. At the landing, he paused and looked up at the entrance, a hundred stairs above where he stood. He circled the pedestal and yanked the cross free. When it disengaged from the pedestal, the light winked out. Darkness crashed in, thick and unrelenting.

"Koji?" Tor spoke into the gloom.

"I am on it." The rustle of Koji digging through his pack came from nearby. A moment later, the light rod bloomed to life. "Here you go."

Tor accepted the light rod. "All right. Let's finish this climb." Holding the light in his hand as a beacon for the others, he continued the ascent and soon came upon the corpse of Quell's father. He paused to consider Quell's feelings. "Koji. Would you mind carrying Joaquin up?"

"What will we do with him?"

"This is no place for his body to rest. We will give him to the magic in the plaza out front."

Quell said, "You wish to vaporize him?"

"It's just his body, Quell. His soul moved on weeks ago."

A quiet beat followed before she nodded. "Very well."

Koji squatted, picked up the man's body, and cradled him in his arms.

Tor's breath came in gasps by the time he reached the entrance hall, where he approached the hole Borgli had made in the door. He peered through it and found the skies still illuminated although shadows covered the valley floor.

"Come on. We have little time." He scooped up his pack and climbed through the opening. "Koji, hand Joaquin to me."

The dead man's upper body was passed through the opening. Tor gripped him under his arms and dragged him from the hole before laying him down beside the plaza border.

The others climbed out with Heizer helping Grazal, who remained shackled and blindfolded. When everyone was out, Tor turned to Quell. "Do you want to say any last words?"

She nodded but remained silent for a long moment before speaking. "Thank you, Father, for raising me. I know it was difficult after Mother died, and I know I often made things harder than they needed to be, but you prepared me for life the best you could." Tears tracked down her cheeks, her voice tightening as her sorrow welled up. "I am who I am because of you and the sacrifices you made. I only wish we had more time together." Sniffling, she turned away.

Tor felt her sadness, but not as much as Koji did. The big man reached out, wrapped his thick arms around her, and hugged her to his chest. Amazingly, she did not resist, instead giving in to sobs. While Tor did not wish to disrupt her moment of grief, the pink clouds in the sky above spoke of the sunset and the approaching night. With darkness came dangers he desperately wished to avoid.

Again, he squatted and picked up Joaquin beneath his arms, lifting until the dead man leaned against him. Tor then moved the corpse to the edge of the nearest tile. "May you find joy in the afterlife." He pushed the man away from him and stepped back. Joaquin's body fell to the tile. The red gem in the plaza center bloomed with crimson light, striking the mirrored panels on the surrounding pillars and reflecting in dozens of different directions. A beam struck the corpse, vaporizing it before the light faded from view.

"Alright." Tor scooped up his pack and turned toward the plaza. "Let's cross this thing and get out of this valley before it is too late."

CHAPTER 30
RACING THE DARKNESS

Driven by a sense of urgency tempered with caution, Tor led the crew across the plaza, retracing the path they had taken to safely reach the temple. Still blindfolded, the wizard had to be hauled across. Despite Grazal being a grown man approaching two hundred pounds, Koji carried the wizard over his shoulder with ease. It was another reminder of how much of an asset the man's strength was to Tor's crew.

Once they were beyond the plaza, Tor led the party northwest toward the tunnel they had taken to reach the hidden valley, but the skies were darkening. They only made it to the hillside above the lakeshore before hoots and howls arose from the narrow canyon leading east.

Urgency turned to alarm. "Darkspawn are coming. We need to run," Tor said.

Heizer asked, "How can we do that with Grazal blindfolded?"

Tor stood before the wizard. "We are going to release you. Cause any trouble, and you will regret it. You might have your magic, but as I have proven, you are as susceptible to physical attacks as any of us."

The wizard nodded. "I will obey your orders. Just get us out of here."

Reaching out, Tor yanked the blindfold off Grazal's head. "Undo his shackles, Heizer. We need to run." Spinning around, Tor took off at an easy run down a path parallel to the lake below.

The shadows in the forest thickened as they jogged across the canyon floor. By the time they reached the incline leading to the tunnel entrance, the color had faded from the clouds and stars had begun to emerge from the darkening sky.

Already winded, Tor and his crew climbed a steep hillside covered in scrub and rock. There was no true trail to follow, so Tor picked his route as he ascended, oftentimes forced at an angle parallel to the hillside before climbing upward again. He stopped to wait for the others while scanning the rocky cliff above him, searching for the entrance. The shadows made it difficult to discern boulders from recesses.

A cacophony of hoots and howls caused Tor to turn around as dozens of goblins emerged from the forest.

"They've seen us," Tor yelled. "Keep climbing. We have little time."

He scrambled up the hillside, rounded a boulder, and then looked up to find the tunnel entrance twenty strides above him. Tor dug into his pack, pulled out the light rod, and handed it to Koji. "Take this. Activate it once you reach the tunnel."

"What about," Koji panted, "you?"

"Quell, Grazal, and I are going to slow the monsters down while the rest of you catch your breath."

Grazal stopped below Tor and bent over with his hands on his knees while gasping for air. "When...do...I...get...to...catch...my...breath?"

"It'll have to wait. I need your magic and Quell's bow. If we don't deal with these goblins, you won't be breathing much longer anyway."

"Magic...requires energy. Mine...is waning."

"Do what you can." Tor pulled Claw off his back. "The rest of you, get into the tunnel. Now."

Quell drew her bow. "Let's see how Balmorian arrows fly."

"Where do you normally get your arrows?"

"My father studied with a fletcher when he was younger. He taught me how to make my own."

"Impressive. Now, if you will excuse me. I have work to do." Tor started along the hillside.

"What do you want me to do?"

"When you know you won't miss, start killing goblins."

Grazal asked, "And me?"

Stopping, Tor turned back. "You are the wizard. You figure it out."

Tor turned to resume across the steep hillside, but his foot slipped, and he rammed the claw end of his weapon into the ground to catch himself. He then climbed up a rock face, positioning himself behind a boulder that stood as tall as his waist. He squatted, found a gap beneath one side, and wedged the claw end of his weapon beneath it. Pulling hard, he caused the boulder to lift slightly, but kept it in place, as goblins scrambled up the slope, their eyes bulging with bloodlust.

Standing twenty strides to Tor's side, Grazal raised his arms high and slammed them downward. A mighty gust of wind blasted forth and flowed down the hillside. Goblins toppled and tumbled, many bowling over one another, cries and shrieks arising from them. However, the wind had only affected a third of the charging monsters.

Quell, positioned between Grazal and Tor, began to loose arrow after arrow. Goblin shrieks came from below as monsters stumbled, staggered, and collapsed with arrow shafts sticking from their bodies.

Tor tried again to move the boulder, but his weight proved insufficient.

"Grazal!" he called. "Get over here."

The wizard scrambled past Quell while Tor wedged Claw deeper into the crevice beneath the boulder. Although Quell repeatedly dropped monsters with her arrows, the horde continued to rush toward them. By the time Grazal reached Tor, the monsters in front were less than a dozen strides away.

"Grab ahold of the other tine," Tor said. "Now pull down on three. One. Two. Three."

Tor put all his weight into it. When joined by Grazal, the boulder tipped up. The rock, likely weighing a thousand pounds, tipped forward and rolled down the hillside. The boulder bounced, and smashed into the lead goblin, rolling over it as if it were nothing but a bug. It crashed over half a dozen others, while those near its path shrieked and dove aside in fear. The falling boulder shook smaller rocks loose, causing them to rain down on other goblins, pelting them and adding to the chaos.

Tor turned to Grazal. "Do you have enough energy left for another attack?"

"Perhaps…but it cannot be a draining spell."

"What about light?"

He shook his head. "Illusion is difficult for men."

Quell warned, "I am running low on arrows."

Out of ideas, Tor shouted, "Let's go!"

He climbed along the hillside at an angle, heading toward the tunnel entrance. When he reached it, he looked back to find Quell and Grazal hastily following. The goblins, shockingly, were no longer in pursuit. His brow furrowed in confusion until he spied a small fire at the base of the hill. Just beyond it, a pair of goblins with bone necklaces danced while facing the flames. The fire suddenly bloomed twenty feet up and formed a fireball the size of a carriage, the image like a sun come alive in the failing daylight. The ball of flames began to spin, rotating faster and faster.

Quell and Grazal reached Tor, stopped, and turned toward the warm light of the fireball.

"What the blazes is that?" Quell asked.

"Shaman magic," Tor said. "Inside, now!" He pushed her into the tunnel.

The fireball burst forth and arced toward the tunnel entrance. Quell, Tor, and Grazal rushed in toward the light rod held by Koji, who was twenty strides ahead.

"Koji, run!" Tor bellowed

The big man's eyes widened as he turned and bolted.

The fireball struck the tunnel opening and burst into smaller pieces, dozens of which splashed into the tunnel, filling the entrance with bright firelight. Flames struck Grazal, who trailed the others, igniting his robes. He cried out, stumbled, and caught Tor by the ankle. Tor fell, taking Quell with him.

Grazal screamed and frantically rolled while flames licked his body. Tor removed his pack and pressed it against the flames, snuffing them until the tunnel fell dark. The wizard's whimpers and groans echoed in the narrow confines.

"Koji," Tor said, "bring the light."

As Koji drew near, light shone on Grazal to reveal the extent of the damage.

The wizard's robes were in tatters, the fringes still smoldering. The skin on his back was covered in blisters that were red, black, and raw. Similar burns scarred the back of his exposed calves.

Tor dug a waterskin from his pack, uncapped it, and dribbled water on the wizard's burns.

Still lying on the tunnel floor, Grazal spoke between clenched teeth. "How bad is it?"

Tor could not lie. "The burns are bad and will be life threatening if we can't get you to a healer soon."

Ekaji, who stood beside Koji, said, "The healers in our village are skilled wizardesses."

Hoots and howls came from outside.

The darkspawn are coming. "Can you walk?" Tor asked.

Grazal crawled to his hands and knees, groaning as he stumbled to his feet. "Let's go."

Tor took the light rod from Koji. "We need to get out of these tunnels fast. Can you carry Grazal for a bit?"

"Of course."

"What if we can bury the tunnel entrance?" Quell asked.

"No good." Tor shook his head. "There may be other darkspawn already in here. If we do that, we would be trapped with them. No, we will see about sealing the tunnel when we are out of the other side. I just hope we don't get lost."

"I know the way," Borgli said. "Follow me."

∾

Borgli, whose eyes excelled in darkness, led the way with the others trailing amid the bloom of Tor's light. As a dwarf, navigating tunnels was instinctive, as integral a part of him as his ability to shape stone. Despite this, he felt anything but comfort, for the calls of pursuing goblins haunted him and demanded that he hurry. Thus, the return flight through the tunnels passed much faster than their initial foray. Ten frantic minutes after the fireball, they emerged in the adjacent valley. Beneath the light of the moon, the party gathered outside the entrance with Koji stumbling out last. The man continued a dozen strides to the side, knelt, and set Grazal gently on the ground, where the wizard lay motionless with his eyes closed. A groan came from Grazal, informing Borgli that the man was still alive.

The sounds of the pursuing goblins echoed in the tunnel, slowly drawing closer.

"The darkspawn use this route to reach Zialis," Ekaji said. "We must seal this tunnel, even if it costs us our lives."

Heizer nodded. "Agreed. It must be done, but how?"

Tor turned to Borgli. "Can you do it?"

Borgli knew exactly what was required. He set his pack down and pulled the hammer off his back. "It will be done."

Scrambling up the hillside, Borgli followed the curve in the rocky face. Once above the tunnel entrance, he knelt with his palm against the rock and closed his eyes. Hoots came from the dark tunnel below him, but he ignored them as he extended his will deep into the rock.

∼

Tor knelt beside Grazal and patted his cheek but got no response. "He's unconscious."

"They draw near." Ekaji drew her blade and positioned herself between the tunnel opening and a boulder resting a few strides from it. "I will hold them at bay."

Tor stood, drew his weapon, and moved toward the tunnel mouth. "I can help."

"No!" She held her katana in front of her. "I do this alone. Anyone else would only be in the way."

The thumps of bare feet on stone came from the tunnel. A gray-skinned, wiry-built creature burst into the moonlight. It raised a rusty sword as it charged at Ekaji. She lunged and sliced high, lopping the sword arm off before the attack could land. The goblin's shriek was cut short when her following slice tore its throat open.

Another monster appeared and died with the thrust of her katana. A third fell with an eviscerating slice. A fourth leapt over the fallen goblins and drove a spear toward Ekaji, who spun to the side, her blade trailing in a broad slash across the creature's exposed ribs. The goblin screeched and fell. Tor darted in and thrust the forked end of his weapon into the creature's back. It convulsed and fell still.

A deep roar came from inside the tunnel.

"Oh, no," Tor groaned.

"What was that?" Quell asked.

"Ogre." Tor urged his companion, "Hurry, Borgli!"

The dwarf, still kneeling on the rock hillside with his eyes closed called back. "Almost ready."

Heavy thumps came from the dark maw, steadily drawing closer. A creature taller than Koji and twice as broad stepped into the moonlight. With gray-green skin and thickly muscled limbs, ogres were known to be even stronger than they appeared. Worse, their hide was tougher than leather, making them notoriously difficult to kill.

Ekaji met the monster with a sweeping stroke that raked across its torso but drew no blood. She followed with a series of quick slashes, the razor-sharp katana bouncing off its flesh without affect. The monster bellowed a tremendous roar and lashed out with a giant paw, catching Ekaji by the shoulder and tossing her a dozen strides before she hit the slope and tumbled down the hillside.

Tor, desperate to keep the monster at bay, rushed in and drove the forked end of Claw toward the creature. When the tips of the tines dug into the monster's stomach, the ogre took a step back, releasing a mighty roar.

Borgli, positioned on the rocky shelf above the tunnel's mouth stood and raised his hammer high. The dwarf slammed the hammer down into the rock. A thump echoed in the night, and as he had before, Tor felt the concussion in his chest. The rock split down the middle. The crack divided and spread down to the cavern entrance. And then the entire rock shelf collapsed.

Tor scrambled to the side as massive chunks of stone crashed down. The ogre spun toward the sound as a boulder the size of a horse fell on it. Rocks, large and small, poured down from above; the landslide spread and branched while Tor raced to escape it. After running a few dozen strides, he stopped and turned back to see what had become of the monster.

Thousands of pounds of rock covered the tunnel mouth and piled against the boulder that had once masked the entrance. Nothing could be seen of the ogre other than a single, massive hand protruding from the rubble. To the far side of the landslide stood Tor's companions, other than Borgli, who was still on the hillside above the collapse, and Ekaji, who lay a half dozen strides below Tor. Concerned for her, he climbed down and rolled her over.

The Zialan warrior groaned and held a hand to her shoulder. "Is it over?"

"Yes. The tunnel is buried. The ogre as well. How are you?"

She sat up with a grimace. "Sore but alive." Rolling to her hands and knees, she gasped and rose with a wince while cradling her left arm. "I think I broke my collarbone."

"I am not surprised. That ogre threw you a good fifteen feet."

Ekaji stumbled a few steps, bent, and picked up her sword. "We are taught that ogres are best fought from behind and by more than one warrior. Now I know why."

Tor chuckled. "They are dangerous beasts, difficult to kill and stronger than just about anything. Thank the gods they are only about as smart as a box of rocks." He turned his gaze toward the landslide. "Now that this one rests beneath a few wagonloads of rocks, we need to find a place to make camp. We've a long day ahead of us tomorrow, and Grazal is likely to slow us down."

CHAPTER 31
THE STRONGHOLD

After a night of little sleep, often disturbed by distant hoots and howls, Tor and his party set out across the long valley leading back to the Zialan Stronghold. As he feared, Grazal slowed their progress. The wizard could walk no more than a mile at a time before he had to rest. At various points throughout the day, Koji carried the wizard, but even he could not do so for very long. All the while, the sun traveled across the sky, and by the time it fell behind the peaks to the west, they were only approaching the slope that led to the saddle where the Zialan Stronghold was located.

Beneath the darkening sky, Tor led them along switchbacks that climbed the steep rise. To one side of the slope was a rockslide, to the other, a cascading waterfall. The top of the rise waited hundreds of feet above, looming like a challenge after a day-long hike.

Grazal, who grimaced in obvious pain, staggered along the path as if any footstep might be his last. They were no more than halfway up when the stars emerged from the sky and the calls of darkspawn arose from the valley floor. Knowing that time was short, Tor pressed on. More than once, he considered abandoning Grazal, knowing it would be a fitting punishment for his betrayal, but concern about the reaction of the wizard's father squashed such musings. No more than two hundred feet below the crest where the slope leveled, he stopped and looked back to monitor his party's progress.

Quell hiked up the hill with determination, proving once again that out of their group she was best equipped to keep up with Tor. Koji followed her, his shoulders slumped from exhaustion after the journey and the added weight of carrying Grazal for sizable portions of the day. Behind him, Borgli climbed at a steady pace. For all his grumblings, he had demonstrated impressive stamina. Tor wondered if the dwarf would tire if they continued throughout the night. Ekaji came next, her arm in a sling crafted from a cloak, its ends tied behind her neck. And last were Heizer and Bravacci, his one remaining soldier, both with an arm around Grazal as they helped the wizard up the hillside.

Movement at the bottom of the slope caught Tor's eye. Goblins poured into the moonlight, and when they spied the humans, hoots and howls of excitement rose above the rush of the waterfall. The sound drew the attention of Tor's companions, who turned back to find the monsters scrambling up the slope, paying little attention to the zigzagging trail. Then, a massive creature, easily eight times the size of the scrawny goblins, emerged from the forest. The ogre thumped its chest and released a roar.

"Hurry." Tor continued up the slope. "We have little time."

They crested the rise and began the trek along the floor of a narrow canyon bordered by steep cliffs. There, Tor stopped and contemplated the speed of the monsters compared to his own party. The monsters likely slept the entire day and were well rested while Tor and his companions fought weariness that slowed their progress, even without Grazal's obvious malady.

When Heizer, Grazal, and Bravacci finally reached the top, Tor stepped in. "Quell"—he chose her since she had the most remaining energy— "you and I are going to help Grazal for a while. The rest of you, we need to keep a good pace, or we won't reach the tunnel beneath the waterfall in time."

The two soldiers surrendered Grazal to Tor, who pulled one of the wizard's arms over his shoulder while Quell took the other side. The three of them hurried after the others – as much as they could hurry with Grazal's feet often dragging on the ground.

Time seemed to slow, and while the dark outline of the Stronghold was visible in the moonlight, the distance between it and them closed far too slowly for Tor's liking. When they were halfway to the Stronghold, hoots and howls came from behind them. He glanced over his shoulder to find goblins racing toward them.

Tor shouted, "Here they come! Head for the tunnel!"

Ekaji stopped. "No! We are too late and cannot expose the passage to our village."

The others stopped, everyone looking at her first and then turning toward Tor.

He said, "We are outnumbered and exhausted. What else can we do?"

"We make for the Stronghold."

"What about the traps?"

"I know them well. Follow me closely and do as I say." Ekaji ran off toward the shadowy pillars of rock.

"You heard her. Go!" Tor and Quell carried the now unconscious wizard while the others ran toward the dark structure.

Ekaji slowed as she entered a gap between two monolithic boulders. Five strides in, she stopped. Thirty feet ahead, moonlight shone down on a stairwell that descended into darkness.

"Go no farther."

Heizer pointed toward the stairwell. "Can't we hide down there?"

"Yes, but you must follow my footsteps." She turned sharply and walked with her shoulder against the boulder beside her.

"Koji," Tor said, "it's your turn."

The massive warrior bent over, wrapped an arm around Grazal's waist, and lifted him over his shoulder.

"Go," Tor told Borgli, who mimicked Ekaji and followed her.

The charging goblins were now only fifty strides away. The hulking silhouette of the ogre trailed them.

Heizer drew his sword. "We will slow them."

Quell pulled an arrow from her quiver, nocked it, and took aim. "That is my job."

She loosed. The arrow struck the lead goblin, felling it. Two trailing monsters tripped, their arms flailing.

"Go," Tor said. "She and I will come last."

"You don't have to stay." She took aim and released another arrow, causing another pileup.

"I am the leader. It is my job." Tor held his weapon, hoping he would not need to use it.

Quell loosed seven more times and then lowered her bow. "I am out of arrows."

"In that case, GO!"

The monsters were no more than twenty strides away when Tor spun around to find Ekaji standing at the top of the stairs.

"Hurry," she waved. "I will draw them."

He darted into the shadow of the rock, pressed his back against it, and shuffled along, following Quell. Once past it, she ducked low and scrambled across an open space, toward another gap. He copied her actions, and when he reached the gap, she again turned and followed Heizer through a narrow arch despite a much larger one standing beside it.

Suddenly, Ekaji was again visible, still standing in the doorway leading to the stairwell. Despite her arm in a sling, she stood resolute and weaponless while waving her healthy arm.

"Here. Come get me, you blazing darkspawn!"

Tor stopped beside Ekaji and turned toward the charging darkspawn.

The lead goblins rushed in, and when they passed the first row of pillars, one tripped on a wire. A dozen short, metal spears thrust up from beneath the sand, rotated forward, and launched in the direction of the monsters. Goblins shrieked, fell, and died while those trailing tumbled over the fallen monsters.

Ekaji spun around. "Go down. Do not step on the tenth stair. The others are waiting."

Tor headed into the stairwell and darkness enveloped him. He counted each step and after he reached nine, took care to squat low and extend his leg. When he found the eleventh step, he continued down while digging his light rod from his pack. He activated it to reveal Koji, Borgli, and the others standing at the bottom, a dozen stairs below.

As he, Quell, and Ekaji drew near, the Zialan warrior said, "Go left. At the first intersection, turn left again. Then, go right twice. Wait in that chamber."

Hoots, howls, and wild shrieks came from above, the sounds drawing closer. With Koji in the lead, Grazal still on his shoulder, they followed Ekaji's directions. After a dozen strides, Tor turned at the second left, and amber light flashed in the tunnels, followed by a burst of heat. Wails of anguish came from behind them.

Ekaji chuckled, her voice echoing in the narrow corridor. "One of them found the tenth step."

They continued, taking two consecutive rights with a long corridor in between each turn, which brought them to a chamber ten strides across and half as deep. There were two ways out of the chamber – the corridor from whence they came and one on the opposite corner.

"Now what?" Tor asked.

"We wait." Ekaji responded. "Prepare to defend both entrances in case some monster gets lucky.

They settled in and waited, gripping weapons, sweating, and gasping for air, partly from the exertion and partly from the rising tension. Death stalked the night. Would it claim the darkspawn, or would it come for Tor and his crew?

~

Hoots, howls, booms, thuds, shrieks, and wails echoed in the stronghold, but no monster reached the chamber where Tor and his crew huddled. Something between ten minutes and two hours – it was difficult to gauge beneath the weight of their anxiety – passed before all fell silent. Tor found himself holding his breath, his ears straining for any audible warning that monsters still lurked somewhere nearby.

Ekaji said, "Follow me. We will leave using a different route." She headed out the opposite door.

Tor said to Koji, "Can you carry Grazal again?"

Although his shoulders were slumped with weariness, Koji bent and scooped up the unconscious wizard.

Holding his light rod up, Tor followed Ekaji while the others trailed behind him. After two turns, they came to an intersection and paused. Ten strides ahead lay a cluster of three dead goblins, their heads removed from their bodies. Turning there, Ekaji led them to a stairwell. Just beyond it was a pile of goblin corpses riddled with tiny, dart-like shafts of wood.

The party climbed two dozen stairs and emerged on the moonlit field of boulders. A massive shape lay between two pillars across from the stairwell opening. A thousand-pound stone block leaned against the creature's bloodied skull.

"The ogre," Ekaji said. "Hajako will be pleased that we killed another one."

She turned left as Tor stored his light rod in his pack. They stayed close to the boulders until they were beyond the second row of pillars.

There, they turned and followed a route perpendicular from the Stronghold. A hole in the ground came into view, three strides across and twice as long. The pit was riddled with goblin corpses skewered by sharp stakes jutting up from the bottom. Once past the pit, Ekaji turned again, circled a boulder, and led them out of the death zone.

They circled the pool and approached the tunnel entrance beneath the waterfall. Tor passed through the swirling mist, which dampened his hair, face, and clothing, and then entered the tunnel.

"Hold," a voice came from the dark.

"It is me, Ivaak."

"Ekaji?"

"Yes."

Light flared in the darkness as a torch was ignited to reveal a trio of Zialan warriors, two males and a female. While none appeared older than thirty, one wore black beads in his braids while the others wore gray like Ekaji.

"What happened to you?" one of the men asked, his voice marking him as Ivaak.

"I was injured fighting an ogre."

"We saw one enter the Stronghold."

"That one is dead, as is the one I fought."

"Two? We have not seen any in a year and now two at one time...it is troubling."

Tor, anxious to rest, said, "We seek shelter in the village."

The speaker nodded. "I will escort you."

Ekaji turned toward Koji, who still held the wizard over his shoulder. "The wizard, Grazal, is in need of a healer."

Ivaak waved to the others. "Ryvia, Korren, go fetch the litter."

The two warriors ran off into the dark tunnel and turned at the first intersection. Moments later, they returned with two wooden poles held together by a sheet of cloth.

Ivaak said, "Place the wizard on the litter. It will make transporting him easier. When we reach the village, I will find a healer while the rest of you retire to the common house." He then turned to Ekaji. "You must face Hajako for disobeying his orders."

Ekaji's chin dropped to her chest, her shoulders slumping. With the wizard on the litter and Heizer and Bravacci each holding one end of the poles, they all headed down the tunnel and began the climb to the village.

CHAPTER 32
THE RETURN

After a long day in the saddle, the wall dividing the wizardoms from the Wilds came into view. Daylight lingered beyond the sunset, but torches already illuminated the top of the wall and the soldiers manning it. Tor, riding at a trot, led the party until they drew near the wall and another horse rode past his.

"Let me deal with the guards," Grazal said in a loud voice, his gaze affixed on the closed gate.

When his horse was twenty feet from the wall, Grazal pulled the reins. The white stallion raised its head and whinnied as it stopped and turned with shuffling hooves.

"I am Wizard Grazal, son of Z'Kawl, High Wizard of Zialis!" The wizard announced boldly. "My party has returned from our quest, and we seek shelter in the city."

A guard on the wall called down, and the portcullis began to rise.

Beneath darkening skies, Tor's original party and the two guards followed Grazal down the corridor to the inner gate. The second portcullis opened, and they entered the lonely city streets.

While Tor longed to ride off and leave the city behind, Grazal had convinced him otherwise. To return and not visit the keep would invite the high wizard's rage. Still, Tor remained concerned about Z'Kawl's motives after Grazal's attempt to confiscate one amulet. Neither Grazal nor Heizer knew about the second talisman, still hidden beneath Tor's tunic.

They crossed the drawbridge, rode into the keep, and dismounted in the stable yard.

Grazal said, "Heizer. Take our horses. I will escort Tor and the others to my father for a full report."

"Yes, sir."

"Come along. Let's get this over with." There was as distinct ring of resignation in Grazal's voice.

Tor reached out and caught the wizard by the arm. "You promised…"

"And I intend to keep that promise."

Narrowing his eyes, Tor asked, "Were you acting on your own or following orders?"

"The latter."

"Then, what will your father say?"

"Let me worry about him." The wizard turned and swept past the guards manning the door.

Tor cast a worried glance toward Koji, who returned the doubtful look, mirroring the unease churning in Tor's gut. Despite this, he forced himself to follow the wizard inside.

The journey through the castle was brisk, and Grazal's pace deliberate. When he happened upon a pair of guards, he asked them where his father could be found. The response altered his path and led them to a portion of the keep Tor had yet to visit. They entered a hall with tapestry-covered walls and other connecting corridors. At the far end of the hall, guards in gray and yellow bracketed a pair of closed doors.

Grazal approached the guards and stopped two strides from the door. "I have come to report to my father and was told he is inside."

"Yes, Wizard Grazal," one guard said. "He is meeting with Chancellor Fosston and requested privacy."

"This cannot wait." Grazal's tone left no room for negotiation.

The wizard pushed a door open, glanced back, and motioned for Tor and the others to follow.

An aisle up the center divided a room occupied by benches. At the fore, a wooden throne stood upon a dais. An enchanted lantern rested on a desk in the far corner of the room, to one side of the dais. Z'Kawl sat at the desk, writing something in flowing script while Chancellor Fosston stood before him with his hands clasped behind his back. At the interruption, Z'Kawl looked up and Fosston turned toward the entrance, the latter scowling immediately.

Grazal strode down the center aisle with Tor, Koji, Borgli, and Quell close behind.

"Grazal. You have returned." The high wizard stood, circled the desk, and stood before it. "What are you wearing?"

Grazal stopped and glanced down at the loose black robes he had been given before leaving the Zialan village. "This is a gift from Hajako."

"What happened to your own robes?"

"Burned by a shaman fireball."

Z'Kawl's eyes reflected concern. "Thank Bal that you are well." He turned his gaze on Tor, his mouth turning down in a frown. "What prize did you bring back with you?"

Grazal shook his head. "There will be no prize. The temple we found was not Urvadan's, but rather built to honor some long-forgotten goddess."

The high wizard shared a glance with his chancellor, who grimaced. "And there was nothing of worth? No items of power?"

Grazal glanced at Tor, as if considering his reply. "The items recovered there were promised to Tor Ranseur."

Z'Kawl clenched his fist, his lips tightening. "I gave you clear orders..."

"You sent twenty men with me and only two survived!" Grazal snapped. "Like them, I would be dead if not for Tor. At risk of his entire party, he kept me alive through a desperate flight and multiple battles against darkspawn. The Zialan healer, a skilled wizardess, told me I would have died had I arrived in the village mere hours later." He raised a hand to his forehead and closed his eyes. When he spoke again, the fire in his voice had been snuffed out. "I was in such pain...I wanted to...to end it." He dropped his hand and lifted his gaze to meet his father's. "When the darkspawn were upon us, I found myself welcoming the death they would deliver, but Tor would not have it."

The high wizard grimaced. "You would have me give up the potential to help our people, so you can avoid feeling guilty for it?"

With his hand held out in supplication, Grazal stepped closer to his father. "Tor has already helped our people. Not only did his party kill dozens of goblins and a pair of ogres, but he sealed a path the darkspawn were using to reach our border."

"The darkspawn threat has ended?"

"I...I can't say that for sure. I only know that one path they used to reach our valley is now impassable. That only occurred because Tor located that hidden route and destroyed it."

Z'Kawl stared at his son for a long, silent beat before sighing. "Very well. Whatever the cost, at least my son is returned to me safe."

Fosston exclaimed, "What? You cannot allow this filthy grave robber to walk off with wealth and power that is yours by right."

Z'Kawl spun on the other wizard. "You are not high wizard, Fosston." He stepped closer to his chancellor, power crackling from his clenched fist. "Unless you wish to challenge my right to rule."

Fosston blinked and backed a step. "I...misspoke, Your Grace."

Z'Kawl glowered at the other wizard for another beat before

pointing toward the exit. "Out. Now, before I forget myself and rid my district of your conniving ways."

The chancellor gave a quick bow before slipping past Tor. The room remained silent as he strode down the center aisle and passed through the door.

The high wizard's posture relaxing visibly as he turned his attention to Tor. "I wish to thank you for my son's safe return."

"My conscience would allow nothing less." Tor did not speak of Grazal's betrayal.

"Well, now that is behind us, I would like a full report."

Grazal said, "And you will have it…once Tor and his companions are safely away."

Although the high wizard's grimace spoke of his disapproval, he acquiesced. "Very well. Devotion begins soon. You and I will dine alone afterward, and you can explain in detail what happened." Z'Kawl turned to Tor. "You are free to go."

Relieved, Tor said, "Rule well, Z'Kawl. Your subjects rely on your wisdom and honor."

While the high wizard remained silent, his frown said all Tor needed to know. His point had been made. Anything more would test the man's temper, and that was not something Tor was willing to pursue.

He turned, waved for the others to follow, and left the two wizards to themselves.

∽

WITH THE RISING sun just above the eastern horizon, Tor stepped onto the front porch of Quell's cabin. He remained hungry, since she had no food, and intended to make a brief stop in Zialis for breakfast and trail rations before heading west. Their horses stood beside a trough, still tied up while Koji saddled them with Borgli's poor assistance. The dwarf had improved tremendously as a rider, but he remained ignorant to the practical aspects of horsemanship.

Quell's voice came from behind him. "This place was always lonely when my father was away. Now..."

He turned to find her standing in the doorway. While he lacked Koji's depth of compassion, Tor did feel sorry for her. "You have my condolences for your father's passing. I am sure you miss him."

"Here is where I miss him the most." She looked back at the cabin interior. "This building now feels like an empty shell, like his spirit has abandoned it as it had his body when we found him."

"You could go elsewhere."

She turned back to him. "Where would I go? I am no more than a cursory friend to a few people in Zialis. In the entire world beyond that...I don't know a soul...except you three."

Tor looked down at his feet, his heart and mind reaching a decision before he raised his head and met her gaze. "You could join us."

Quell's eyes flared slightly. "Join you?"

"While my crew has always been three in the past, we do lack someone with bow skills." He shrugged. "Of course, that would mean you would have to deal with three vulgar, smelly males..."

"I accept." A grin spread across her face.

Tor glanced back at Koji, who stood frozen with a saddle in his arms. Beside him, Borgli grinned broadly. "Do you two have any objections?"

The dwarf chortled. "She is a wench after my own heart. I am happy to have her join the team."

Koji tossed the saddle to the ground and approached the porch, his face dark and stoic. Suddenly, his arms spread, and he lunged for Quell. She tried to shy away but was too late. Lifting her up, Koji spun in a circle. "I am so happy to have a little sister join our team!" In his excitement, he tossed her up, causing her to bang her head on the porch roof.

"Ouch!" She ducked and winced.

Abashed, Koji set her down. "I am sorry. Are you alright?"

She peered up at him, her lips twisted as she rubbed her head. "You big oaf…"

When Koji's chin dropped to his chest, she sighed and hugged him.

His arms wrapped around her. "You are hugging me," he noted.

She stepped back and looked up at him. "Don't expect it to become a habit."

Tor cleared his throat. "We need to get going."

Quell stepped back and nodded toward the open cabin door. "Give me a few minutes to gather some things and lock up."

"What about the cabin?"

"It'll be here when…if I ever come back." She stepped inside and began shuffling around the small interior.

Tor turned toward Koji to find the big man grinning at him. "What?"

"You are turning soft in your old age, Tor."

"I am not. I merely…" Tor struggled to find a suitable response. "It just seemed like the right thing to do. Now, let's get these horses saddled. We've a long journey ahead of us."

CHAPTER 33
FAMILY

The return trip to Lamor was far more relaxing than the expedition to Zialis and beyond. Rather than press, Tor chose to ride at an easy pace, rest often, and make camp early during their journey back to Fralyn. When given the choice between riding and sailing, Borgli voted to go by land, as did Quell. Again, not feeling rushed and enjoying the pleasant weather, Tor agreed. Thus, by the time they rode into Lamor, three weeks had passed since their original departure.

With the sun licking the sea in the distant west, they rode up to the city gate and slowed when met by the soldiers on duty. In a refreshing change, the city guards did not give Tor a hard time. Their questioning ended upon Tor explaining that his quest had been to find Quell's father and that while he had been found, it had been too late. Thus, the young men focused on Quell, who appeared dutifully filled with remorse while toying with her hair...and their hearts. Even Tor had to admit that she could be adorable...so long as she kept her sharp tongue caged.

Beneath clouds of pink, they rode into the city and followed a street just inside the city wall. While it was not the most direct route to Vanda's manor, it was the best choice to reach it on horseback and the only way to get there when pulling a wagon or a carriage. Just shy of the manor, Tor led the others down a narrow gravel road that ran alongside the manor wall, past the cellar entrance, and to a courtyard in the rear, nestled between the manor and the steep hillside. There, they unsaddled their horses and stowed the saddles in the stables. The horses, with a trough of water and a stack of hay, were then left behind before Tor and his team returned to the street and entered the manor through the front door, but not until he warned them to try another route would be a fatal mistake.

When he opened the front door, he jerked in surprise, for a man in black robes stood in the otherwise dark entrance hall.

"Vanda," Tor's heart thumped like thunder in his chest. "You nearly gave me a heart attack."

The sorcerer said, "While there are other hearts I might chose to stop, I would not do so without reason. Yours, I happen to find far too useful to bring to an untimely end."

The dark and strange comment was unsurprising. Tor had come to expect such statements from the man, even if the context was bewildering.

Vanda extended a hand, and the orbs in the wall came to life with violet light. His gray eyes examined each person as he or she entered – towering Koji, squat Borgli, lithe Quell.

"I see your team is finally complete."

Tor blinked. "You knew I would return with Quell?"

"I suspected. Her temperament and skills ideally complement the crew you had already assembled. In many ways, she and Borgli together replace what you lost when Navarre died, and at the same time, each adds valuable skills Navarre could never equal." The man waved and turned. "Come. Dinner is waiting for us."

As the sorcerer faded down the dark corridor, Tor glanced toward the others.

Koji nodded knowingly.

Borgli shrugged.

Quell furrowed her brow. "How did he know we were coming?"

Tor snorted. "I stopped asking questions years ago. He knows things. Just get used to it."

They passed by the parlor, entered the dark corridor, rounded a corner, and emerged in the dining hall illuminated by the warm light of a candelabra resting on the dining table. Five goblets surrounded the candelabra, designating the end of the table where they were to sit.

Vanda was already seated at the head of the table, so Tor claimed his usual chair between Koji and the sorcerer. Quell and Borgli sat across from them. As soon as everyone was seated, Ivanka and Goren swept into the room, one carrying bowls and spoons, the other with a steaming black pot. Ivanka left the bowls in two stacks and rushed out of the room. Goren set the pot on the far end of the table and used a ladle to fill the bowls with the contents of the pot.

"What is that smell?" Quell squished her nose.

"Spiced chicken soup," Goren said. "Do not worry. It tastes far better than it smells."

Ivanka returned with a basket of fresh bread. The smell caused Tor's mouth to water. In her other hand was a carafe filled with red liquid.

"Wine?" Koji asked, his expression hopeful.

The filled bowls were placed in front of each of them.

"Farrowen red," Vanda said. "From six years ago."

"A wonderful year." The Kyranni warrior reached for the carafe, poured himself a full goblet, and swished it around while sniffing it. "This is a most welcome surprise. What is the occasion?"

The sorcerer shared a rare smile. "We are here to celebrate your return and the assembly of a team that is destined for unparalleled success."

Tor asked, "What of our quest?"

"What of it?"

"Aren't you curious about the artifacts we discovered?"

Vanda chuckled. "A major event recently occurred, bringing life to prophecies long dormant."

Tor frowned. "What does that have to do with us?"

"Tell me, did you recover an amulet?"

"Two, actually."

"And when did that happen?"

Tor counted the days back to when they discovered the temple. "Twelve days ago."

Vanda leaned back with a knowing smile. "Which is exactly when the prophecies I speak of came into being."

"I don't understand."

"That is because prophecy is beyond your understanding." The sorcerer held out his hand. "Give me the amulet, please."

Tor reached into his tunic, pulled out the amulet hidden there, and lifted the cord up, over his head. He placed it in Vanda's palm.

The sorcerer gasped and dropped the amulet as if bitten. The disk-shaped artifact bounced on the table and twirled once before settling. The eye in the center stared up toward the ceiling.

"Where did you get this?" Vanda exclaimed, aghast.

Tor frowned at the strange reaction. "It was in the temple we discovered – a temple dedicated to some unknown goddess."

Vanda jerked again. "Goddess?" He rubbed his jaw. "This is most troubling. I thought we had erased her from this world."

"You thought..." The statement confused Tor, causing him to shake his head. "This temple is thousands of years old and likely has been dormant for many centuries."

The sorcerer stared down at the amulet with a grimace. "This is not the amulet I expected."

"As I said, we found two of them."

"The other. Where is it?"

Tor looked across the table. "Quell is wearing it."

She reached into her tunic and pulled out an artifact that was nearly identical to the first, the only difference being that the eye engraved in its face was closed. When she removed it, Vanda accepted it with greed in his eyes.

"This is it!" the wizard declared in a giddy tone.

Tor had never seen the man like this – a man who was often cold, aloof, and always mysterious. For him to act like a boy with a new toy... well it was disconcerting.

Vanda stood. "I must do some research and some thinking as I consider what we shall do with it."

Koji asked, "What about dinner and the wine?"

"Enjoy yourselves." Vanda's gaze remained fixed on the amulet dangling from his fist. "My hunger and thirst are sated."

Tor asked, "What about the other amulet?"

Vanda blinked and looked down at it. "Oh. Yes." He carefully lifted the amulet by the cord. "I must store this someplace safe, someplace where others cannot find it."

With an amulet swinging from each hand, Vanda headed out the door, leaving Tor, Koji, Borgli, and Quell alone.

"You are right," Borgli said. "That man is odd."

Quell poured herself a glass of wine. "I'd say the oddest I have ever met."

"Yet"—Tor filled his glass— "he funds our quests, gives us a place to live, and feeds us well." He lifted the glass. "Raise those goblets, for it is time we toast Quell and Borgli." Their goblets clinked when tapped together. "You both acquitted yourself brilliantly. Koji and I are thrilled to have you as part of the family."

"Family?" Borgli asked. "I never really had a family."

"Yes." Tor nodded, serious and heartfelt. "Like family, we must trust and support each other. Often, our lives depend on it."

Quell wiped a tear from her cheek. "I can't believe I found a family."

"Do you need a hug?" Koji asked.

"Only if you want me to poke you with my hunting knife." She held her glass to her lips. "Let's drink instead."

And Tor took a long drink, allowing the wine to warm his tongue and throat as it slid down.

They proceeded to eat followed by an evening of chatting and laughter and camaraderie. All along, in the back of Tor's head, he wondered where his next quest might lead him…until Vanda burst back in.

Tor sat forward at the interruption. "What is it?"

The sorcerer arched a brow as he strode into the room. "Have you ever heard of Shadowmar Castle?"

Rubbing his chin, Tor nodded. "Yes. I believe it is a castle of legend, located somewhere in the Ghealdan Mountains."

Vanda held an amulet from his fist, the gold disk swinging like a pendulum as the closed eye in the center held Tor's attention. "A castle of legend it is, and you four are heading there straightaway. You have a quest to fulfill, one unlike any other you have undertaken thus far."

The adventure continues in
Castles of Legend

Note from the Author

I hope you enjoyed the first adventure featuring Tor and his misfit crew. More novels featuring them are coming soon. In the meantime, I have crafted an EXCLUSIVE short story outlining Tor's very first adventure as a relic hunter, where he earns his enchanted weapons and Koji gains his unique gauntlet.

To read about this unique tale and to discover why Borgli was exiled from Kelmar, join my author newsletter at www.JeffreyLKohanek.com.

Best Wishes,
Jeff

Follow me on:
Amazon
Bookbub
Facebook

ALSO BY JEFFREY L. KOHANEK

Fate of Wizardoms

Eye of Obscurance

Balance of Magic

Temple of the Oracle

Objects of Power

Rise of a Wizard Queen

A Contest of Gods

* * *

Fate of Wizardoms Boxed Set: Books 1-3

Fate of Wizardoms Box Set: Books 4-6

Fall of Wizardoms

God King Rising

Legend of the Sky Sword

Curse of the Elf Queen

Shadow of a Dragon Priest

Advent of the Drow

A Sundered Realm

Fall of Wizardoms Boxed Set: Books 1-3

Fall of Wizardoms Box Set: Books 4-6

Wizardom Legends

The Outrageous Exploits of Jerrell Landish

Thief for Hire

Trickster for Hire

Charlatan for Hire

Tor the Dungeon Crawler

Temple of the Unknown

Castles of Legend

Shrine of the Undead

Runes of Issalia

The Buried Symbol

The Emblem Throne

An Empire in Runes

* * *

Runes of Issalia Bonus Box

Wardens of Issalia

A Warden's Purpose

The Arcane Ward:

An Imperial Gambit

A Kingdom Under Siege

* * *

Wardens of Issalia Boxed Set

Printed in Great Britain
by Amazon